T0067591

I Wish I Could Hate You

I Wish I Could Hate You

SUJATHA KANNAN

PARTRIDGE

ISBN: Softcover 978-1-4828-5982-9
eBook 978-1-4828-5981-2

All characters appearing in this work are fictitious. Any resemblance to real persons, living or dead, is purely coincidental.

Because of the dynamic nature of the Internet, any web addresses or links contained in this book may have changed since publication and may no longer be valid. The views expressed in this work are solely those of the author and do not necessarily reflect the views of the publisher, and the publisher hereby disclaims any responsibility for them.

Print information available on the last page.

To order additional copies of this book, contact
Partridge India
000 800 10062 62
orders.india@partridgepublishing.com

www.partridgepublishing.com/india

Contents

Author's Note

Greetings to everyone who are reading this book right now. I am very happy to meet you as an author of this novel. This first literary work of mine is very close to my heart not because this is my first work but due to several other reasons.

Life is like a train journey. Not all the people we meet in our life are meant to be with us forever and that is the reason we mention them as 'Train Friends' or 'Passing Clouds'. During our course of journey, we accidentally meet someone with whom we wish to spend our rest of our life. There is no specific reason why we wish only that particular person to stay with us. We can dream thousand moments of our life with them but the reality is that not everyone is lucky enough to retain the loved one of their life. There will come a day where our destiny and their destiny will branch out in different directions and we will have to bid goodbye to them forever.

Writing was my hobby during my childhood. Whenever I read a National Best Seller novel, I would dream of becoming an author one day and publish my own book. However I never took writing seriously until I became the one of those unfortunate soul who failed to retain the desired person of my life.

I don't know if I will succeed as an author in this vast literary world. Fortunately, with the blessing of God and support and encouragement of readers like you, if I am fortunate enough to establish myself as a writer, no matter how many books I write in future, this book will have a special place in my heart. Though the characters and the incidents in the novel are not completely real, it is the collection of several inspirations from my life and from lives of the people whom I have met who failed to retain their loved ones.

I would like to mention few words about Infosys Technologies, the company where I worked during the making of this novel. Like this book, it is another important thing which has special place in my heart. Though I don't work there anymore, it remains and will remain the closest company of my life.

Hope to meet you all again in my next work and I wish you all a pleasant reading experience.

Sujatha Kannan

Acknowledgements

Let me begin thanking the Supreme Almighty for giving me a passion and the power to pursue. Without the patience, faith and most importantly the gift of creativity and writing which you had given me, I could have not been in the place where I am right now.

Next I would like to express my gratitude to my parents Shri. Kannan Krishnamoorthy and Smt. Radha Kannan for tolerating all nuisances which I created during the making of this book. Only because of the support received from the family, a creator is able turn the impossible to possible.

Next I would like to thank my colleagues Ashok Kumar and Dinesh for allowing me to use their few mannerisms as an inspiration to the characters I have created in this story.

I would like to acknowledge and thank like to acknowledge all my school friends, college mates and colleagues who were the source of inspiration for several characters which I created in this story.

Last but not the least I would like to thank all the readers who are right now reading this page and this book encouraging my first step in this literary passage. I would like express my gratefulness for purchasing this book and supporting me in my writing journey.

This book is my special dedication to all the people I mentioned above.

Sujatha Kannan

Prologue

Eight years back

'Girls, please come soon. Aradhana is in critical state' said my classmate anxiously

Every one of us left our food in the middle and looked at her with shock.

'Critical state?' I asked her

She breathed heavily and said 'I assume she attempted suicide'

'What non-sense?' I screamed 'Where is she now?'

'At the open air theater. She is lying unconscious. Come on. Let us not waste time.'

We did not waste even single second then. All of us rushed there as fast as our legs could carry us. The scene at open air theater left everyone shocked. The girl in front of us was lying unresponsive and few tablets were scattered around her. My heart started to beat so fast.

Everyone surrounded her and some of them sprinkled water on her face.

'Aara, come on. Open your eyes' I tried to bring her back to sense.

She did not open her eyes. All of us tried their level best to wake her up but nothing worked.

'Suma, it is useless. She has consumed lot of tablets. We have to take her to hospital immediately' said one of the girls

'Yes. The more we delay the more danger is for her.' said another girl.

'Let us take her to first aid center now. Some of us can stay with her while one of you please inform our Mam.' I said to some girls.

Remaining few of us took her to the medical center in the college campus. Luckily doctor was available at that time. We admitted her and waited outside anxiously.

'Did she fight with her boyfriend once again?' I fumed 'What the hell has happened? Why is she doing like this'

No one answered. Few minutes later doctor came outside worried.

'I don't understand how she got these many sleeping tablets.' he said 'She has to be admitted to hospital immediately'

'Is she fine?' I asked him

'She has to be taken to hospital as soon as possible. This is a police case. She will not be admitted easily. Now time is the important factor than everything. The main question will be the availability of the tablets. How did she get?'

No one was able to answer. Meanwhile some of the girls brought our class lecturer Mam and Head of the department. Both of their faces were horrified.

'What is going on here?' asked our HOD anxiously.

'Sir, Aradhana consumed lot of sleeping tablets and attempted suicide' I told him.

'Sleeping tablets?' asked our HOD.

Our HOD's face showed utmost dismay. He went inside to look at her. Our class lecturer Mam came to us angrily.

'You people will not let us live in peace even for a second?' she said angrily.

We all looked at each other's face.

'For the past few days I was watching her. She did not focus in studies properly. I thought of calling her parents to our college to report about their daughter's behavior. What is wrong with her?' she asked us

We were not sure if we are supposed to open her secret to our Mam. But if we don't reveal the truth even now, no one can help her. We might lose her.

'Mam, she is in terrible depression.' I said 'due to love problem'

'Love problem?' she exclaimed with shock.

All of us stood silent. She looked at us disgustingly.

'Love problem for an 18 year old?' asked our Mam with shock. 'Rubbish! Do your parents pay fees for you to study or fall in love? How come you people can be so irresponsible? This girl has consumed tablets due to love problem. Her parents will be here at any moment. What you people expect us to do with them? It is their daughter who did the stupid thing but we are answerable to them. If she decide to end her life why can't she do it in her home? We are losing half of our life to manage you all inside the classroom and you are sucking our other half of life in this way' she burst like a cracker.

Now we looked at her disgustingly. She is so concerned about getting into trouble rather than thinking about saving her life. But she is right. Aradhana did a horrible mistake of her life.

'What kind of love problem?' asked our Mam

'Mam, her lover is getting married to another girl in few days.' said the girl who informed us about Aradhana first.

We all others got shocked. Our mam's face turned pale and worried. Our HOD came out and his face showed tension.

'She has to be admitted in hospital as soon as possible. I will make arrangements for that. Has her parents been informed?' asked our HOD

'Yes Sir.' replied our Mam

Our HOD turned towards us and said 'Students, I am very disappointed with you all. You are her classmates and friends. You all let it happen. Had any one of you informed us or her parents about her weird actions may be this could have been avoided. Now we have to handle all kinds of headaches.' said our HOD angrily.

We all looked worried. Aradhana, why? You could have chosen some other option before attempting this extreme step.

'You all now get back to your classes. We will take care of her.' said our HOD.

We did not want to leave her and stood there hesitantly but the hard face of HOD did not allow us to speak another word. One of the girl who is her hostel roommate was alone allowed to stay there. Rest of us came out of that place.

'Who told you that her boyfriend is getting married?' I asked the girl who answered our Mam.

'I rushed to her when I saw her lying down. I saw the tablets and a wedding invitation around her I understood everything.' she said

'This is ridiculous. How can she make such a cruel decision? She wanted to take away her life just because she cannot have the person whom she loved. She did not think of her parents. How can be so selfish?' I burst

All remained silent

'Is Love so precious than life?' I yelled again.

No one was happy with the way she reacted to her boyfriend's marriage.

'We have to think how much pain she has gone through. She is not able tolerate the reality of losing her loved' said Shradhdha

'Don't support her. Whatsoever may be, this is not a right decision. We don't have any right to take away our life. Every being born in this world has to die one day. We have to live the fullest of our life and fight each and every moment. Taking away the life for a silly reason like love failure, I just cannot imagine how stupid it can be.'

'Suma, don't be too judgmental.' said Shradhdha' I am not supporting her. What she has done is absolute non-sense. But we have to understand each and every pain of her. Being her friends, none of us have not taken her sorrow seriously. I have many times seen her trying to share her grief to us but no one cared to listen to her.' she said.

I got shocked

'What do you expect us do?' I yelled at her 'She always lamented about how her boyfriend ignored and insulted her etc. etc. Etc. How many times she can expect us to hear it?' I said.

'She is correct. You cannot blame us completely' said another girl 'She always used to cry about her boyfriend and every one of us tried to console her'

'Few days back she was so worried. Do you remember what happened on that day in our classroom?' asked Shradhdha

I remember. It was one day in our classroom when our lecturer was going on, Mam suddenly threw the chalk piece at her. She got terrified and also us who were sat behind her bench. Mam came to our place with full anger and grabbed the mobile phone from her hand.

'What is this?' She asked her angrily

Aradhana got tensed.

'Do you think I am jobless here? How dare you operate mobile inside the class! Don't you know that mobile phones are not allowed inside the campus and you dared enough to use it during the class hours' yelled our Mam

'Mam…' stammered Aradhana

'Get out of my sight.' she screamed 'don't ever think of getting it back. You bring your parents to meet the HOD and only then you will enter inside my class for this semester.'

Aradhana stood like a statue.

'Did not you hear what I said? Leave this place before I grab you by your neck and push you out of the class.'

Our mam screamed like anything. Tears rolled down from her eyes and she left the class. Mam turned to us and started to shout.

'Why do you want to come to college? To chat with your girl friends or boyfriends? You can choose some lover's park or beach and sit there how much time you want and do whatever nonsense you want. One or two of them will want to attain success in their life. They are more than enough for me to take class. I am strictly warning you all that you will have to accompany her if you don't conduct yourself properly in my classes.' said our Mam.

Aradhana's behavior inside the class made others playing with their mobiles to keep them inside their bags. No one will dare to use it at least for next two to three days. After the class got over we all went to the dormitory to console her.

'Aara, what is this? What you have done? Even the most patient lecturer will get angry on what you did today' I told her

She started to sob deeply.

'Today he spoke very badly about me. I was not able to tolerate. I was in a rage to retaliate and that is why I did not notice anything around me'

'You both started to fight again?' I asked

'He says I don't deserve to be his girlfriend.' she said and her sob increased

I got furious.

'Why do you want to stick with him then ever after this much of humiliation? Just get rid of him' I said to her

'I cannot do that. I love him a lot'

'Don't you have any self-respect? You are chasing a guy who does not love you. What is the point in sticking to something without any meaning?'

'He is mine. I cannot have any other girl to have him. The very thought of imaging him to be some other girl's husband makes me crazy. No matter what happens I will not allow him to get rid of me easily. I cannot imagine my life without him. I wish I could die instead of accepting the truth that he is not mine. I wanted him to understand how much I love him and no girl can make him happy except me' she vowed firmly

'It is not his opinion. He thinks any other woman other than you can make him happy.' said Shradhdha 'Aara, don't spoil your life. Forget everything and move-on. You have a great life ahead.'

'Please don't say like that. I need all of your help to get him back in my life.' she pleaded us

'What you expect us to do?' I asked with surprise

'Please help me in some way to convince him'

Everyone looked at her with pity.

'There is no use in talking with you. You are sinking yourself in your sorrow. Now that your parents have to strain themselves to get you back in your classroom' I said angrily

'Girls, let us leave her alone' I said to everyone 'Thank God your mobile phone was taken away by our Mam. You will not chat with him and waste your time in crying.'

We left the place leaving her alone. I recalled the incident and felt guilty.

'We should have not left her like that' I told them 'Now what is that we can do?'

'Can we meet her boyfriend and explain him?'asked one girl

'Rubbish!' I yelled 'Don't you have any common sense. Did not you hear that he is getting married? What is the point in talking to him? He already made up his mind to throw her out of his life.'

'We have to stay with her and bring her out of this. We have to make her understand this is just an ending of one chapter and not the end of the story. She has lot of things to do in her life.' said one girl

'For that she should come back to life' said other girl sadly

I cannot stop myself getting angry on this stupid girl. What nonsense feeling is this? I have heard 'Love is blind' and for the first time I have seen it with my own eyes. She lost her focus, lost marks in her exams, lost her self-respect, lost her happiness and now she is losing her life slowly. Are the people who fall in this groove are destined to become like this?

Five years back

'The movie was so awesome. I wanted to watch it once again' said Shradhdha

I did not answer immediately. The whole movie ran once again in my mind.

'What is there to watch it again?' I asked

'Don't you see?' she asked surprised 'The movie was so romantic. I felt my heart was going to burst.' she said

'I don't think the movie was so nice to watch more than once' I said to her

'I get it.' she teased me. 'You always want lovers to unite in the end. You are not fond of anti-climax'

'Yes. See both of them fell in love very deeply but they were not able to unite finally. The love was separated in the name of religion. This is not fair.'

'This is not first of its kind. There were several movies which made out of this genre. Hero and heroine are from different religious backgrounds or caste backgrounds. Parents do not accept them and finally couple elope and thereafter they shall live happily ever after. But before that happy ending hero will speak pages of dialogues to explain how divine is love and how parents are totally against it in the name of caste, religion etc. etc.'

'That is true. How funny it is! Earlier the education was not prevalent and awareness is also very less. Elders were so adamant of their marrying off their children to someone who belong to their caste. Now how the current world is changing and still parents are not ready to change their mentality. I don't understand why. Look at this movie. It was shown that the heroine's father is very stubborn and persistent of not marrying off his daughter to some guy who do not belong to his religion. He was shown as highly educated man. This is not something imaginary. Even many parents are persistent about this in real life too' I said

'Of course. The reason is only known to them. Aradhana faced love failure because of that. He left her because his parents did not accept his relationship'

'Please don't remind that.' I said 'I lose all the respect for the love the moment when I get reminded of her. She has made me allergic to love feelings. Not only me whoever hears her love story will sure never think of falling in love in their life. She is one main reason why I am not fond of relationships before marriage.'

'No pain, No gain' teased Shradhdha

'I don't want the end gain of this pain. I am seeing many girls who are in relationship and I feel so sorry for them.'

Shradhaa smiled

'It need not be. If we right partner our life will so bright and colorful. No other happiness can match in front of the feeling of being loved.'

I did not say anything.

'But for that we will need a truly loving guy like the one who played hero character in this movie.' she said

I sarcastically smiled.

'Yes I accept. Getting such a partner is not so easy. Real life love is not as fun as in the movies.'

'This movie is fine for me in every aspect except one point' I said

'What?'

'How it is possible for a girl to fall in love with a guy who is younger to her? The heroine fell in love with him even she knew that she is younger to him. That sounds weird.'

'Why do you say that? Should not an elder girl fall in love with younger guy? Is there any hard and fast rule about this age?'

'Come on' I said 'Our ancestors are not fools to formulate such a rule. There are quite a lot of reasons they have mentioned that husband should be elder than wife. I don't feel this kind of union is right.'

'It may not be right but it is not wrong either.' Shradhdha argued.

'I am not sure. I seriously don't encourage these kinds of things'

Shradhdha smiled

'It is not correct according to me. When I come to know a guy is younger than me, immediately I start to see him like a child. Even if he is one year younger to me. I cannot imagine such a thing in my life. I don't understand how these people have minus age differences like two years, six years etc.'

'It all depends upon the people. True love has no such barriers. It all depends upon our individual thinking'

'I am happy with the ending of the movie. Our society is not used to these kinds on unusual things.'

'Hey! Nowadays a boy is romancing a boy and girl is romancing a girl. Still this is better than falling in love with younger guy or elder girl'

'Exceptions cannot be rules' I said firmly

'You keep your opinions with yourself' she yelled at me

I smiled at her.

'One is loved because one is loved. No reason is needed for loving' – Paulo Coelho

Dedicated to all those who have truly fallen in the abyss of 'Love' and got lost in that bottomless pit.

Today

'I just cannot understand what your problem is. Everything is crystal clear and now it is your time to make a good decision. What is stopping you and confusing you?' asked my mother.

I held my head with my hands to heal from the headache.

'Suma, I don't think there could be any other best option for you right now. You have no reasons to deny it. Had anyone else in your place they would have typed their resignation letter by this time.'

I looked at my mother. She wanted to convince me at any cost.

'What else you want? You are getting promoted to higher designation, hike in salary and this company is one of the big giants. Isn't it?' asked my mother to my father

'Second biggest company in India' said my father.

I looked at him helplessly. The number of favorable points are increasing. I really cannot find a reason to decline this job offer.

'I am saying a thing for sure. If you don't join this company, sure you will regret later. It is a real surprise for me on looking at your dilemma. I still remember the day you were so upset when you missed the opportunity in your campus interview for this company. Now you got offer from the same organization and you should have jumped with joy on this occasion. You are acting in reverse' said my mother in an irritated voice.

'You just hold' said my father to my mother. He came to me and said 'We are not compelling you but before making any decision you should analyze all the pros and cons of staying in your current job and switching to your new job. Unfortunately you have only less time within which you have come to a conclusion. Now let us know what your problem in accepting this offer is?'

'Appa, I still cannot figure out why I am hesitating. Like Amma said, I should have jumped with joy the moment I saw this offer letter but I am scared of something. I am feeling like joining in this company is not good for me.'

'Now let me put it in this way. Are you afraid of the new job responsibility as this is higher post than you are now? Are you scared of work load?'

'No, I am never afraid of workloads'

'Are you afraid of work timings?'

I hesitantly nodded like 'yes'

'I have heard from one of my colleague that this company is strict in working hours. If I don't maintain my working hours my leave or salary will be deducted.' I said to my father

'I don't see it as a negative point. When you got a job and responsibility to fulfill you don't have to worry about your timings. Next?

I thought for a while. Sure something is eating my brain about this job offer. What would be that? Yes I got it.

I said to my father 'Appa, you forgot about the distance?' and looked at him.

'Appa, my current office is just 10 kilometers away from home but this one is around 50 kilometers. How can I travel to such a long distance? I reach office here in half-an-hour but there I just cannot imagine the time.'

'The girl in our neighborhood who works in the same company travels that much distance for past three years. Isn't she a human being?' asked my mother

What can I say for this?

My mother continued 'You are forgetting one thing. You are working in night shift for many months in your current job. You come home at mid nights. Your sleep cycle got affected and this is affecting your health. I feel this is a good reason for you to switch to new job'

I don't have any other option other than keeping quiet. Every point which my parents are listing are valid and reasonable. Great company, once upon a time my dream company too. Higher designation, salary hike. No one other than a stupid will decline the job offer.

'Suma. Again I am saying the same thing. We are not compelling you to take up this offer. If you decide to decline this offer what we need is a valid reason. We respect your decision provided if it is reasonable. We don't want to affect your career by your silly attachments which you have in your atmosphere' said my father to me.

Perhaps he is right. I am finding reasons to decline this offer because I don't want to leave my current company.

'We are always very comfortable with what we have but to achieve great things we have to come out of our comfortable zone and take up things which are hard to digest. One day or other you will get used to it.' said my father

'Appa, the distance and travel time was so long. I even once got trapped in a very heavy traffic for five hours. From that day I am scared to traveling long distance.'

'Your suffering on that day was purely your lack of planning. You starved because you did not eat properly on time even after I instructed you several times. Anyway those days you traveled by bus on road. Chances of getting stuck in traffic for hours are high. Here you are going to commute by train. You will not suffer any traffic' said my mother

Finished. Now I have no reasons to decline the job offer.

'But such a long distance and time….' I said hesitantly 'It looks like I will come home only for taking my supper and sleeping. I cannot spend time with you all at evenings. The time which I am at home will decrease.'

'Well, what makes you to rush home when you don't even assist me in daily household works.' mocked my mother.

I gave an angry look at her.

'If you are scared for the distance and time we will figure a way to tackle it' said my father.

The conversation ended in that manner that day. I saw the printout of the offer letter in my hand. The salary package is very attractive for a three and half year experienced candidate along with next designation.

It was during one day in a week I had to work continuously for 18 hours. I reached office at 11 am previous day and left home the early next morning at 5 am. Not a big deal. There are people who work continuously for 24 hours, 36 hours etc. It is their capacity but my capability is not this much. My mother got angry on this and she insisted me to switch to new job.

Everything happened so swiftly. The posting of updated resume, interview call from the giant company, interview schedule etc. etc. etc. I don't understand why I felt like my whole world got destroyed when I saw the offer letter delivered to my mail box three days later. Had it been someone else they would screamed equal to thunder. What is pulling me from here? Why my destiny wants me to move me from this place so quickly? What is waiting for me in the new path which is opened for me to travel?

My father at any cost wanted me to accept the new job and so he took as much efforts to convince me. He took me to the company where he wants me to work and persuaded me that commuting is not going to be much difficult as I think. He wondered at the vast area and huge building which the company possessed. The building does looks amazing. The company size is so huge than I expected' said my father

I too felt the same. The auto rickshaw traveled towards the entrance of the building which was far away from the place which I admired. There were many buses entering inside the campus carrying the employees.

'You should also take this shuttle bus to commute from station. There are no other modes to reach the office from there' said my father.

I smiled at him. He almost came to a conclusion that I am ready to accept the offer.

My father said 'I want you to think wisely before you make a decision.'

I was not aware that I will myself will be compelled to detach my bond with my current company and move-on.

'Have you accepted the offer?' asked my colleague Simran.

Deepak also turned towards me waiting for the answer.

'I am still confused. Not sure' I said

'This is ridiculous. What is there to think about? Just accept it' said Simi.

Deepak looked at me and conveyed the same message through his eyes. Everyone who knew about my offer were asking the same question. I am fed up hearing it again and again.

'The company is a big company. You should not miss this opportunity' she said.

What is she saying? I did not get it at first.

'Suma' called my team leader.

I did not like the commanding way he called me.

'Suma, you want me to remind you for each and every time about the tasks. You have not updated the status for the bug you are working.' he yelled.

'I am working on it' I said controlling my anger.

'You were saying this for long time. When can you complete?' he asked

'I will complete is soon'

'You want to work in this simple bug for two days? For your experience you should have completed in two hours.' he said

I started to lose my temper.

'What am I supposed to answer in the status call tonight?' he asked

I looked at him furiously. I think he has promised someone to make me angry.

'Already Sanjay told not to involve you in this bug. I made a mistake. I should have assigned Simran for this task. She would have completed it far before than you. Even last time she fixed the bug finally when you struggled to with it.'

I was so shocked by this statement. What the hell is blabbering? He compares my performance with my junior. Simran fixed the bug last time not only because of her effort but also my assistance. We both together solved the issue. Even at that time he was complimenting only her when we both worked together despite Simran repeatedly told she did with my help. What happiness does he get in overshadowing my performance?

'I will fix it before the tonight call' I said angrily.

'You were not able to solve for two days. How the hell you can solve in few hours?' she mocked me.

'That is my head-ache. You don't have to worry about it.' I yelled.

This guy has a terrible psychological problem.

I was literally so upset by whatever happening there. I worked very hard trying to keep my word of completing the fix of bug before the tonight status call. The bug is not co-operating with me. I got fed up. We all our team members went to cafeteria to have our dinner.

You have not treated us for your birthday still' asked one of the testing team member Abdul

It was very hard for me to control my irritation.

'You want treat from me?' I asked 'You never bothered to celebrate my birthday. You people never cared to wish me on that day. Each time you collect money from team for any team member's birthday for cake-cutting ceremony but it looks like you people never bothered to spend for me'

'Oh! Come on' said Abdul 'What is there in cake-cutting when you have our tons and tons of love for you' he teased.

'Oh really! Then you can also have tons and tons of love as my treat for my birthday. Finished' I said to them.

Everyone laughed at this include Abdul except one guy around. My team member named Prashant, another replica of my team lead.

'Suma' he said 'Please don't mistake me. I cannot stop myself from saying this. It looks so awkward when you ask us for celebration for your birthday. If team wants to celebrate your birthday, we will do it by ourselves. Why do you ask for it? You are an educated woman. It should be done voluntarily out of affection. When team is not taking efforts for celebration you should not demand it. It looks so weird'

What the hell he means? Is he saying that I am compelling my team to celebrate my birthday? I am demanding birthday gifts? How dare he would say like that?

'What do you mean by I am demanding?' I asked angrily 'He asked me treat for my birthday and I replied him back. What is there to feel weird about?'

'Don't demand anything from anyone. You have to be matured.' he said.

'What is wrong in demanding?' I asked

'When you people demand contribution for other team member's birthday celebration, I have offered money several time. My birthday was over seven days back and yet no one initiated any cake-cutting. How can you expect me to treat you?'

'May be we can return your money' he said.

'You are insulting me' I said angrily.

'We are not compelling anyone to contribute. We had deadline pressure and everyone were busy. We thought of celebrating sometime this week. Now it won't look good.'

I felt very angry on his angry.

'Suma, please take this advice from me. Please stop this behavior in future. It is so similar to begging' he teased me.

Everyone laughed at me as if they have heard some funny joke. How he has turned a simple funny conversation to some public insult. He mentions me as a beggar in front of my team members.

'This is my sincere advice to you all. Asking for a treat to someone who is not willing is more similar to begging than what I said. I think you people should stop this behavior first before advising others' I said and left the place.

My mood was turning as bad as it could. I was not able to focus on my work out of anger. Another incident added fuel to the fire of my fury.

My manager passed by our cubicle and went to the white board placed there. It displayed the names of the team members and some stars against their names. I saw him drawing some stars against each of the team members' name. He drew four stars against Sushant, one of the youngest team member, three stars against the name of my lead, two against the irritating guy's name, and three stars to other three of them including Simran and Deepak. He did not draw any star against my name. When he was about to leave the place he saw me seeing him and went to the board again and drew one star against my name.

Only one star for working several hours and meeting the deadline and that too out of guilt and shame he drew it on the table. One guy is irritating me by comparing me with my junior, other is insulting me as if I am a beggar and now my manager gives me a star reluctantly. I cannot stop myself from rewinding the incident of how my team lead got the credit and appreciation certificate from the clients for the solution which I have provided.

It looks like I am holding attachment on a stupid company and team. I decided what should be done next.

It has been two months since I resigned my job. My manager did made some attempts to make me to drop my decision but after all what he did with the feedback from my cunning lead, I was stubborn to quit Days rolled so fast when I served my two month notice period.

During my notice period, I enjoyed my every minute with my friends. I did not give any respect to my lead after my resignation. I did not talk to the guy after that insulting incident. I behaved as if he did not exist.

The lead guy showed his evil nature to others in the team especially more to that Prashant. Both had horrible fights very frequently. I enjoyed watching the ugly fight of two most dreadful enemies of mine. I wished this to continue forever.

It is not a good thing to have bonding on someone or something or someplace. I heard a saying by Dr.A.P.J.Abdul Kalam 'Love your job but don't love your company because you never know when you company stops loving you'. I finally got relieved from there detaching all bonds which I had. I decided not to have any attachment with anyone or anything in my life thereafter. Now I am in new company with new job.

Today is my first day in new company. I commuted in train in first class coach. The first class season ticket fare is double than second class fare. I am not in a position to mind about it. I entered inside the vast campus with dreams of new goals, achievements, etc. etc. etc. This company is famous for one important thing. The company's employees just like that travel on-site. I imagined myself boarding the flight like them one day. I was told to report to building number three ground floor.

Where am I going to find building number three in this ocean? Luckily I took help one of the newcomers and we both went together to the place. It was a hot April month beginning of the summer. Morning 9 am had some tolerable heat. I entered inside the hall and saw there many several new joiners seated already. Within few minutes some HR people entered the training hall along with some documents which I assume to be joining documents.

For the next few minutes everyone became busy with the joining formalities as instructed by the HR lady. After our joining formalities were done, orientation program started post lunch.

There were different presentations shown about the company launch, growth, success, awards, achievements etc. The HR lady presented the sessions so proudly and she tried to instill the pride within us. Following the presentations, the next set of presentations started which conveyed about the policies of company with employees.

'The timings policy as you all know you have to maintain the working hours as specified' said the lady to us.

I got irritated on this. This is not fair. Why a company does compel its employees like this? When we have work we would work extra and when we don't have to can't we start early and go home.

'The average is a yearly average. At the end of the year your average should be maintained so that you don't face any deductions in your leave or salary. So ensure you maintain it as required'

My face turned bright on hearing this. This is a good deal. We work for extra hours one day means we can leave when we don't have much work on another day.

'Earlier it was monthly average. Every employee should maintain the average every month but very few years back it was changed to yearly. So you can give a sigh of breath' said the lady.

Whosoever had brought that rule, I really have to thank him or her thousand times. The next thing which that lady told wiped my entire anger.

'For the past two years, people were given waive-off for the lagging hours. However I am not sure if you will be given waive-off. Hence I suggest you to maintain as expected and don't blame me'

The calculation and waive-off process will take place only at the end of next March. Now it is just April. There are twelve months of time. I don't have to worry about these unnecessary things.

Next presentation started which explained policy about Anti-Sexual harassment and strict company policies against such behaviors.

'Folks, please listen to this presentation carefully. Anti-sexual harassment is very strict policy here and no unwanted acts are encouraged directly or indirectly. Behaviors which are considered as sexual-harassment are like making unwanted sexual gestures, usage of words which your colleagues are not comfortable, giving unwanted gestures, unnecessary touching of your colleagues, showing of obscene scenes/ videos in media, messaging etc. Hence if you are charged with such complaints, the decision authorities will first take the action and only then you will be given chance to explain your side. Hence try to maintain your professionalism as much as possible'

It is really valid thing on one side but on other side innocent employees may also be charged wrongly or for any revengeful purpose.

'Anti-sexual harassment policy is not biased by gender. Male or female, everyone is equal in front of this policy. There are some occasions where even women give tortures to men. This is also not encouraging thing. Those women will not be spared at any cost. Sexual harassment by same sex is also not spared. If man sexually abuses a man or a woman sexually abuses a woman, even then it sexual harassment. Same kind of punishment is awarded' said the lady in a firm tone.

Everyone in the hall smiled at the last statement as this state is still not much exposed to homosexual culture like many other states.

'Are any action taken for sexual harassment incidents done outside the campus?' asked one guy from the back.

'Yes. Employees misbehaving with other employees outside the campus are also not spared from severe actions if any complaint is lodged. It is better you maintain the discipline, decorum and professionalism with co-employees where ever you are.'

'Moreover I would like to highlight on one part. Though this behavior is not directly covering under sexual-harassment still it is not acceptable behavior'

Everyone looked at her to continue

'Romance in office. This is an organization and you are paid to work here and not for romancing. There may be instances where you will find someone among your colleagues as attractive and impressive you may go and propose them. You are fine to do that however outside the campus not here. We expect you to maintain strict discipline and professionalism until you are inside campus.' said the lady with smile but in a firm tone.

I did not care much about this part because this policy is not for me.

'We once had to charge a couple who were married for some weeks. They did not give much importance to the professionalism. They did not conduct themselves properly. Many employees saw them doing some unwanted things which they consider it as romance. We had to warn them severely. We got a reason from them that, theirs is a joint family and they don't get sufficient time to spend with each other at their home and that is why they behaved like this. Folks, this is also not a good. You and your partner/spouse working in same area does not mean you can do things which your colleagues are not comfortable with.'

Everyone smiled at her statement.

The lady continued 'Another important is that you may find someone in your workplace whom you wish to be with you forever. Falling in love is natural but forcing the other person to fall in love with you is something idiotic behavior. If the person does not wish to have any kind of relationship with you, we expect you to keep away from them and maintain only professional relationship. Insisting to accept you directly or indirectly is also a harassment for which you will be charged with sever action same as anti-sexual harassment.'

This is definitely a valid point. No one is supposed to be compelled to accept a relationship. It is their life and they have full rights to make their choice.

'We once had a complaint from one of our female employees where a male employee kept torturing her to accept him. When we asked him, he was lamenting that why she is not accepting him. What was lagging with him? Why she is not thinking that he is right match for her? He told that he will marry and make her life colorful and asked us to recommend to her for him and make her understand how much he loves her. That guy repeatedly persisted and compelled her to accept his love. Does not it look non-sense?

Why she is not accepting my love is a stupid question. She is not accepting. It is her wish and choice. It should be respected. We really had a tough time with that employee and only after severe warning he consented to stay away from her' said the lady to us.

This was really a new concept for me. I have never heard about this kind of tortures and harassment inside a working place. Can people really do such things with their colleagues? How can one develop love relationship with their co-workers? How it is possible for anyone to fall in love in workplace? I remember reading in one book which states that having relation with a colleague is one of the blunders one can ever do. That should be avoided. I will never fall in love or marry my colleague at any cost.

I still cannot come to a conclusion whether staying as bench resource is a boon or bane. You will not be contributing to the company's growth anyway yet company pays you every month. You don't have to rush to work on time to attend calls, no delivery pressure, no work, you can have fun inside the office with your co-bench friends and you get paid for it. Bane, you will never evolve as a productive product and one day you will become useless to work in this industry.

From the day two onwards, I joined the list of bench resources in that company waiting for someone to pick me up and accommodate me with them. I was all alone. All of them who joined with me scattered at different directions. I did not know many of them and few whom I spoke with on the day one got assigned to the project the very next day and started their contribution for the organization. I was waiting for my turn to come. All I did in those days were commuting to office, wandering in the entire campus alone not knowing where to go and sit, not knowing anyone there. According to me, bench is a punishment period in any company.

Luckily God did not let me down for long time. Not that I got assigned to a project rather I met a woman who was wandering like me not knowing what to do. Sometimes I got random systems which can be occupied by anyone. I checked my in box one day and I got my first good news in that company. I got assigned to one unit named Finance and banking Services and I was told to submit documents for background check. For many weeks after my submission of documents, I did not hear anything from them.

Days, weeks and months passed. It has been two months since I joined in that company and living as bench resource. The lady with whom I used to wander also got assigned to a project few back and I was left alone after that. A heavy cloud of loneliness occupied my mind and started to haunt me.

'Oh God! Why are you doing this to me? Did I ask for a job like this? Why you are making my life so miserable? Why did you bring me here? What is the purpose of my entry in this company? What you kept for me here? If you don't answer me, sure I am moving away from here' I scolded the God angrily.

God has no time to care about me and my feelings. According to him, if I stay or leave this job it is not his concern.

'Appa, I cannot stay here anymore. I feel like I am getting insane day by day.' I screamed at my home.

'I wish I could get a job like yours. Not doing any work but getting paid for that. May be you should come and work in my office. Only then you will understand how much you are blessed' said my mother.

I stared at her angrily.

'I am ready for this exchange but sure you will never talk like this once you go through my situation. The most impossible thing to do in this world is doing nothing. I am doing that nothing right now.'

'You can utilize your time for learning something. You can go to library, read some books' said my mother

'Mrs.Intelligent! I am staying here hale and hearty only because I am doing all those things which you said now. But I cannot live a life like this for more number of days. I am going to quit' I said to my parents

'Fantastic. Very well you can feel proud of your daughter' said my mother to my father.

'Suma, I don't think you have to quit your job for silly reasons like this. Never a company lets it employees enjoy long time without working for them and getting salary alone.' said my father

'Appa, there are resources who were not assigned to projects for more than nine months. What if it happens to me? I am not having a place to sit and I wander like a nomad begging for machine to access my mailbox. Except food court and library I cannot enter anywhere as those are restricted ODCs' I said to my father

'Restricted ODCs?' asked my father

'ODC is Off-shore Development Center place where people work for their project. Each building has several floors and each floor will have one or more ODCs. Restricted ODC means only employees working for the project alone are authorized to enter in it. If I go without authorization I will be asked several explanations as if I am a terrorist trying to enter parliament' I said angrily

'Why would they restrict their own employees like this?' asked my mother

'It is because they think they are protecting their client's secrets.'

'Alright. Is there no single ODC you can enter without such restrictions?' asked my mother

'No'

My parents looked at each other and then at me.

'So you have decided to quit?' asked my mother

'Yes. I cannot continue like this?'

'I feel you can give some days of chance. Always trust God. He will do good things to you. You have never expected to get job offer in your dream company. Everything happened suddenly. I personally feel God wants you to be here for some specific purpose. The speed in which your job switching took place implies me that something God wishes to give you and so he brought you here. Patiently wait and watch what happens. Follow your heart' said my mother

'Amma, I am not any divine angel to fulfill any divine task. You are too much philosophical. What can God give to me inside an organization other than work? He gave me job but he is not doing anything to give me work. What is the point of having a job without any work? My career will get spoiled. I don't see any purpose of my visit here.'

'Please explain to her' said my mother to my father 'I don't think she is taking a wise decision. It is not easy to get new job right now. She is too emotional and making mistake.' asked my mother angrily to him

I looked at my father. 'Suma, I suggest you to give chance of few more days' he said to me.

I looked at him helplessly. He completed the chapter so firmly. Now I can do nothing else other than to abide it. I looked at the God's photo in front of me hanging on the wall.

'I don't know what have you kept for me. What the hell is that?' I stared angrily at Him.

It was first week of the month and I got my salary two days back for doing no work. So I was not angry for that. As my mother said only people working in software companies are blessed to get free money like this. The happiness did not last long as the same thought of forth coming days started to haunt me. A slight improvement in my idle life came when I was informed to collect a security token. I don't know what was it and where it should be used. That secure token was sufficient to hold me in this organization for few more days. However every starting has an ending. There came the day which made me to feel why I did not enjoy my days in bench and craved for getting assigned to project.

Evening when I was about to leave for the day my mobile ranged.

'Am I speaking to Sumana Krishnan?' asked a male voice from opposite.

'Yeah, Sumana speaking'

'Hey, this is Ashwin. I saw your profile for one of opening in our project. I would like to discuss about it further'

Thousands of butterflies fluttered colorfully around me within few seconds. I was just waiting for this day.

'Yeah sure' I said to him.

'I wanted to know few things about you. What is your experience?' he asked me

'Four years'

'Do you have experience working in Struts framework?'

Oh No! I have not worked in Struts framework. I have worked only in a framework built on top of Struts. If I say this sure he will not pick me. I have to do something.

'Yeah. I have worked in Struts' I said to him. God please save me and make this guy pick me for the project.

'Your experience in J2EE, Servlets and EJB?' asked the guy

I have worked in those areas very long time back.I was wondered. What the hell I was doing for these many days?

'Yes. I have experience in that too.' I said to him with full trust that God will help me.

After a pause 'Can you come and meet me now?'

'Yeah sure. Where?'

'Please come to building number eight ground floor. But I have a call right now? When can we meet?' he asked

Time was 5.15 pm. General business closing time.

'Can I come tomorrow?' I asked him

'No. Today we have to meet. Please come to building number eight ground floor at 5.30 pm. I will meet you there' said the guy

I will surely say that I got irritated. I was just planning to leave for the day but if I miss this chance I cannot get any work. What kind of campus is this? I am always getting lost here and cannot find where I am and what is the number of each building. After some struggle locating the building number eight after a long walk I finally reached. It has been two months in this company and yet I am not able to identify which building with its number. I waited at the reception area for the person to come.

I saw some people coming outside from elevators and some people coming down from stairs. Each and every time I mistake someone to be Ashwin but he won't be. Once I saw a man who was so fat and dark coming from the elevator. I don't know why did I pray to God that he should not be Ashwin? What bothers me if he is the one? Does my mind expect Ashwin to be a handsome young chap? I cannot stop myself to feel a sigh of relief that he was not Ashwin.

My mobile ranged. It was Ashwin calling.

'Hello Sumana, where are you?' he asked

'I am at building number eight ground floor reception' I told him.

I saw a man speaking in mobile coming from elevator. A normal man with height little shorter than average height for male species. There is no appealing figure fair enough to attract any woman. On my God! If he knows what I am thinking about him sure he will kill me or feel bad about me

'I think I saw you' he said. I saw some one waving hands at me hesitantly.

The man with mobile came to me 'Sumana?'

'Yeah'

'Hi! I am Ashwin' he extended his hand for a warm handshake. 'My manager referred your profile for our project.'

I gave a formal smile.

He continued,

'This project team is scattered in different places. Have you ever worked in such environments before?'

'No' I said 'In the projects I have worked, mostly all of us were in the same place.'

He smiled. 'Then this is going to be new experience for you. You have to mainly involve in co-ordination of people working from different locations. We have some kids in our project who will work in development part. You have co-ordinate them, technically guide them etc etc etc. you will have to speak a lot. Are you getting it?'

I was not able to get the picture of what he is saying but I was in a position to say yes alone to whatever he says.

'My expectation is give your fullest performance and work in an environment without any internal or external politics' he said finally.

‘It is not a problem to me. Even I am not interested in any kind of politics’ I said to him I had enough of politics in my previous company. If he really means what he says then sure I am in a right place. I wish no one should be like the people whom I was working in my last company. I believe God will not let me down this time.

‘OK then. Right now we need to get access to the ODC. I will drop a mail to our ODC anchor and get temporary access to you. Once you get in ensure you get permanent access. Until you to come to the ODC occupy a temporary place in this building and finish the entry formalities’ he said to me

I nodded like ‘OK’. What is that ODC anchor? I don’t want to think too much as I was already too tired.

‘OK. See you then. Call me tomorrow once you got temporary machine’ he said and left the place.

My goodness! After two months of struggle and frustration I finally landed into some place in this vast campus. No more idle days hereafter. My previous company released me from the project during my two months of notice period. Here I have been idle for two months. So after four idle months I have to work.

I have to accept one thing here. I cannot avoid myself to long for those bench days.

Next day I occupied a temporary machine in the same building ground floor. My actual place is supposed to be at seventh floor of this same building. At first I got confused with building numbers and then one building had more than one wing. It took me many days to identify building and wing. I am going to work from Building number Eight C wing. This is a very good achievement according to me. Sure it will take some decades to identify other buildings and their wings in this campus. Right now I don't have to care about other latitude and longitude of the other locations here.

That day passed as usual except that I am seated in front of some system. I called Ashwin and informed about my arrival as he told. After that for a long time I did not get any instruction from him and I started to rewind my days in this company from day one no much before that right from the day I got a sudden call from HR team to attend the interview. I also reminded of the words of my mother

'God has kept something to give it to you and that is why he has brought you there'

I have to sure accept that fact. I am supposed to be in this place this very minute for some reason which I don't know. When people struggle hard to get into a reasonable and descent job how did I manage to get one such without much efforts. All I did was just posted my resume in a job portal, got interview call, attended interview and got offer. I was so mean that I hesitated to accept the offer which is a day dream for many engineering graduates. Just because I am getting things very easily I don't value it. I don't know how to value things and yet I am getting.

For every man/woman there will be next step to move forward. I got good education, got good marks, descent degree, and good job with super salary package yet I am still standing in same place. Most of the friends from my school and college got married. I am still single but not ready to mingle as I am not able to find a guy with some high status, highly educated, good looking handsome young man.

I can proudly say that I rejected almost ten grooms till now for many reasons. I know how my mother was angry for rejecting a guy whom they felt was potential in many aspects. I did not accept a proposal as I did not like his tooth arrangement. My father out of the affection on me did not say anything but felt so bad for rejecting a guy for which I told the reason as he is so dull. Whatever may be the case, my parents have to find me a suitable guy as I expect and get me married to him.

I did not make any attempt to find a guy of my own choice. One main reason is I did not want to cry each and every single minute and waste my life on some worthless guy. Moreover no man in this world is impressive enough to attract me. Only God knows if any such man, making me fall in love with him madly, deeply and truly has born in this world or not. If such a man exist in this world, then I would get an instinct that he is my man. God will give me a signal to help me to identify him. I am waiting for such a signal.

The instant messenger suddenly flashed with a message from someone. It said '*hi*'

The name of the sender was written as Ganesh Shankar at the top IM window. Who is he?

I replied '*hi*'

Few seconds later the next message flashed

Ganesh Shankar: Ashwin told me to assist you in getting access to the ODC and machine
Sumana Krishnan: Ok
Ganesh Shankar: Can you tell me your full name and employee number?
Sumana Krishnan: Sumana Krishnan and employee number is 659793
Ganesh Shankar: You need to get a machine allocated to you but before that you need to get a cubicle allocation in ODC. We will drop a mail for your access and then for the space in ODC. You can take printout of that mail, hand it over to security and get inside the ODC
Sumana Krishnan: Ok.Fine

Someone from the team is helping me to get inside. I looked at the photo of the guy Ganesh in the small IM window. I did not like the face at all. He looks like a roadside rogue. Why God is not merciful enough to give me good looking colleagues? It is wrong to interact with people based on their looks. Why should I care about the look of the person with whom I am going to work? He is helping me to get inside the ODC but I am analyzing his looks and start to dislike him. Nowadays I have become more prejudiced. I should change my attitude. He is my colleague and I don't have to care about how he looks. I have come here to work, give my fullest co-operation and contribution for the project along with others. I am so worried about his looks as if I am going to marry him. How funny!

A little later, I got a mail which read that it approves for my temporary access in the ODC. Few seconds later IM flashed from the person Ganesh Shankar

Ganesh Shankar: You got the mail isn't it?

Sumana Krishnan: Yes

Ganesh Shankar: You can take printout of the mail and can come inside. But still machine is not allocated for you. I am right now working with IT support team to get you a system. I will inform once you got cubicle and machine.

Sumana Krishnan: Thank you so much for your help.

Ganesh Shankar: You are too formal. It is not required. :-)

Sumana Krishnan: Formal means?

Ganesh Shankar: No formalities required.

Sumana Krishnan: Ok Baba

Ganesh Shankar: Baba? What is that?

Sumana Krishnan: It is my way of calling someone very friendly

Ganesh Shankar: Oh. The only Baba which I know is our superstar's movie

Sumana Krishnan: How is the project and work? Is it heavy or normal?

Ganesh Shankar: Daily I and Ashwin leave only at 8 pm

Sumana Krishnan: Are you a Technology Analyst?

Ganesh Shankar: No. I am software engineer. You are the TA and apart from you one more TA is here.

Software engineer designation is the junior position in this company.

Sumana Krishnan: Which year passed out you are?

Ganesh Shankar: 2012, you?

Sumana Krishnan: 2009

For the first two weeks I had nothing to do in that project as I had to get sufficient access to work in the project environment. I got all sufficient login credentials one day and started to work only to find out my part of work is not going to help me in growth of my career. I was even more disappointed when I heard there is no on-site opportunity the main reason why I wanted to join here.

On that first day of the project, Ganesh helped me to get temporary access to enter inside the ODC. I felt so thankful to him for taking efforts for me but within very minutes he himself erased the gratefulness which I had for him. I hardly ask for help from someone fearing of refusal. I had the same hesitation when I interacted with this guy but his friendly approach gave some courage to ask for help. But I hate at times for being right about asking help from others.

Sumana Krishnan: I am not having printer configured in the system here. Can you get me a print out of the mail copy and take me inside the ODC?

Ganesh Shankar: I cannot do it. I got an important call.

I did not expect this rude reply. I wish he could have been little gentle in refusing the help. What he is going to lose had he included a phrase 'I am Sorry' in front of the sentence he wrote? Has this company ever trained its fresh employees on office etiquette and how to interact with senior colleagues or has his parents ever taught him to be polite to others? I wish I could break the fingers which types replies like this. I was really angry on him even before meeting him. I again hated the look in the photo which he posted as display picture. Earlier I was thinking that I am going to work with some rogue but it looks like I am going to be work with an arrogant rogue. Sure I am going to have tough time working with the guy.

I somehow managed to take help from IT admin for the printout and finally entered inside the one of the most secured and protected ODC of the world. The ODC was no so large but sure I will get lost for few days.

I was so angry about the guy Ganesh. I did not want to meet him at all. I never allowed anyone to reply me so rudely. How dare he would!

'Hi Sumana, finally you are in' said Ashwin

'He is Mr.Ganesh.' said Ashwin pointing to guy seated at one corner of the cubicle.

'Hi' he said with smile

I was just not able to believe that this cute looking guy in front of me is the one who refused harshly to help get inside the ODC few minutes back. Neither he looked like the rogue as in the display picture nor was his reception so arrogant when he spoke to me. He was tall and stout. He worn spectacles and was wearing a formal shirt so casually. I liked the way of his dressing. Somehow something attracted me with the guy. I have to surely say that I got happy that I am going to work with some smart looking. Wait a minute! Why I am thinking he is cute and smart looking?

Somehow I got know who are all other members scattered in different locations. It was definitely a new experience to me. My days in the project rolled in a reasonable speed for next six months till November. On the other hand my days rolled in another different way in my personal life spoiling my peace of mind.

'Suma, we have got three potential horoscope matches. We are arranging a meeting with one groom this week' said my mother

I looked at my parents helplessly not knowing what reason to say to escape from these non-sense meetings. Got educated, got settled with a good job and most important my age which according to my parents already crossed average wedding age of a girl was sufficient for my parents to vigorously search for a potential groom and get me settled. Does Indian penal code punish the women who are not married after 26 years?

'You are always giving some reasons and delaying your marriage. Look at your friends and other colleagues. Even the boys of your batch started to get married. When have you planned to settle down or you wanted to stay all alone life long? What is your expectation from a groom? You are dreaming some of handsome prince to come to you and marry like a fairy tale story?' asked no burst my mother.

'I have never said like that. But none of the grooms you choose are attracting me'

'If you expect Ajith Kumar, Hrithik Roshan or Tom Cruise in every boy sure you no one can impress you. Don't get carried away by appearance. It is not going to last long. We choose a groom on seeing his background, his education and salary. Is it not sufficient for you to marry him? You always find fault in everyone' said my mother in vexed tone.

I did not say anything.

'You rejected a guy because he was so dark and so fat. As far as the another boy whom we met at temple six months back, I don't see any reason to reject him. The fault you found in him was totally absurd. You did not like him because he has no interest in going outings, traveling like you do. You rejected another guy because he did not talk with you properly during the meeting. You are not ready to listen that he was sick.'

I got angry on hearing this.

'Not once or twice. You have rejected almost ten guys for hundred reasons You have to understand that somehow you have to tolerate some imperfections and get ready to marry someone. This is real life not any movie that you wait for a Prince to come in an horse and marry you. You are not sure of what you want and you are getting confused.' said my mother

'I am not waiting for any Ajith Kumar or Hrithik Roshan or any prince on a horse. As a normal woman I expect a normal guy with education more than mine, salary greater than mine, with a house owned by him. Don't I deserve a guy like him? Look at my friend. She is living the life which I dreamed. Should not I expect my marital life higher than hers? Her husband is an IIM graduate. He owns two houses in city. He owns a car and he is a very good designation and most important he is very handsome. I wanted to surpass all of her husband's qualifications'

'You are doing a biggest mistake. Happy life is more important than anything. Your friend got such a groom and it is her destiny. Don't compare your life with hers. Why you want to compete with her and that too in this sensitive issue?'

'Amma. He is so social and he has got a great sense of humor. He has ability to make people happy around him. He is so mischievous and makes people laugh. I want such a person to come to my life'

'Why do you think the grooms you meet won't be like that? No man in this world exposes his full behavior on meeting a girl first time. You will get to know someone only in subsequent meetings. He may be of guy more than your expectation. You have to give someone a chance. You have to consent to some guy for further meeting only then you will know what type of person he is.' argued my mother

'You want me to consent to a marriage with a guy in just a meeting of less than one hour?'

'I met your father only once and just for half-an-hour before I consented to marry him'

'Your time period was different. Moreover Appa was more educated than and more earning than you. You are a science graduate and you married an engineer. You married someone in better position than you. Should not a five digit salary earning professional deserve someone better than her? This is an arranged marriage. So I want my expectations to be fulfilled.'

I turned to my father and asked 'What was your case? You agreed to marry Amma within the same half-an-hour time?'

My father smiled and said 'No. I did not decide in half-an-hour like your mother.'

He gave a pause and said 'Just five minutes.'

My eyes were not winking for few seconds.

'Five minutes' I exclaimed 'What made you decide in that few minutes?'

He smiled.

'I have a read in a book. The groom consents to marry the bride in less than five seconds. In later part of story he states that was the reason that lady was his wife in his previous birth. I think you consented for similar reason' I teased him

Both of them smiled.

'Have not you met any other women in this world or you have met more woman to come to this conclusion? Have not you fallen in love with any woman?'

'In those days the word 'love' is a bad word not supposed to be pronounced by us. I had commitments to fulfill so I had no time to fall in love. As a matter of fact no woman impressed me to fall in love'

'Did somebody fall in love with you?' I asked him

'Not one or two. I just don't remember the count.' said my father with pride.

I smiled at him and said 'Appa, this is too much. You mean to say you were a dream-boy of women of those days. Each and every woman proposed you and you rejected them. What was your score?'

'Not really. But somehow I managed to attract women at that time. I still remember one of the fathers of a girl was chasing me to fix alliance for his daughter. You cannot imagine how much I struggled to get rid of him. In another case, without my consent my marriage was about to get fixed. I got very angry on this behavior. When I was in Delhi, I heard women talking about myself that I am a very descent and charming guy but unfit to stay for a longer time.'

'When we were newly married, we visited you father's boss home. The wife of boss asked me how you are surviving with such an unromantic guy in this world' said my mother

'Well, it looks like no woman proposed you and still you consider this as a great pride?'

'As I said, the word 'love' was not prevalent in those days. Had the culture was like now at that time, women would have proposed me'

'You would have married any one of them?' I asked

'Not at all. Some people are not meant to do some things. Love is not something meant for me. I would have surely rejected them had they proposed'

'No woman managed to attract you. What made you to decide Amma will be good choice for you? What was that which impressed you with Amma?'

'I felt those women were not meant for me or I am not the person for them. When I met your mother I thought she will be correct partner for me and I can manage my life with her. I got an instinct that we will be compatible and chose her. In our case it proved to be correct. Moreover arranged marriage is safe compared to love marriage. We will get support of elders when we get into trouble in the marriage. If we do a love marriage society will not respect us and elders won't allow the family to run smooth'

I did not the like the last statement. Every man in this world wishes only this. I got reminded of Aradhana once. How her love was broken by the same policy her boyfriend had! Men seem to be strong physically but they are mentally cowards.

'How can you marry someone whom you don't know?' I asked with surprise

'I consented to marry your father because I trusted my parents. They showed suitable match for me and out of blind trust on them I agreed. It worked.'

'In arranged marriage, this instinct will help us a lot and most of the time it will be correct.' said my father.

I have seen them living for each other from my childhood. Arranged marriage may be good but love marriage is not something meant for coward Indian men. It will be utter foolish to fall in love with an Indian guy. At the same time it is not possible for me to marry some stranger. I got into a great dilemma whether love marriage or arranged marriage will better suit me.

'You should also trust your parents. We will not marry-off you to any roadside passer-by or a beggar the immediate next day. There are lot many things to do after we fix an alliance. But you are not giving us those chances. You are not letting us to proceed to next level. What is your idea?' Her voice gradually increased as she spoke to me.

'Until I meet a guy who attracts me, I am not getting married. This is final.'

'Then sure possibilities of your marriage in this birth is less. We are not able to answer the people around us, my colleagues and especially our relatives. Do you know how much torture we face because of delay in your marriage? Just think of our position'

This time my mother's voice started to beg,

I really had to feel bad on her frustrated tone but this is my life. I cannot marry someone force the sake of my mother who is not able to face the society

'I am sorry. That is not my headache' I said indifferently

'What do you expect from the groom to attract you? Every one of them are human beings.

'It is very simple. The moment I look at them I should feel he is my man.'

My mother frowned. I continued

'Dressing with shirt, t-shirt, jeans, trousers alone does not make a person a man. The moment I look at him I should get an impression that he is capable of living his life by himself.

His eyes should shine with confidence. If the confidence is below limit he will not be capable to live his life on his own. He will depend upon his parents to make even simple life decisions. If the confidence limit exceeds, he will be an arrogant guy. He makes all decision by himself and will not respect people around him. No woman can live with such a guy. All the grooms whom you have shown fall in two categories. No one is matching that exact confidence level I ask for.

Amma, I want manliness from my husband. Why don't you get my vision?'

'How you will know about this on first meeting?' asked my mother

'I can find in few minutes' I said 'He should be bold enough to face anything. He should not be a coward. He should respect elders but if he has to make any critical decision of his life he should be bold enough to make it by himself even if elders don't support him. He should know when to follow brain and when to follow heart. He should love to travel as I do and explore new things. He should be mischievous making people around him happy. The mere presence of him should make atmosphere so lively. Everyone should miss him and feel unhappy when he is not around.'

'It looks like you have bench-marked some guy in your mind and you are searching a groom like him or are you in love with someone?'

I did not like this question.

'I would have not agreed to meet those guys you showed had it was case' I replied with anger

'You are expecting too much from a guy. I don't think you will find such a guy in your life.You find someone.' she spoke to me anger mixed mocking tone.

'There is no way I fall in love with a guy. I don't have to put my hands in fire to find out if it burns or not when I already am seeing people burning their hands. No man in this world can break my stone heart and get inside it. I am a strong woman and that is the reason you are not able to find a suitable match for me' I said.

My father smiled at me with the same pride. He was silent spectator during the whole conversation.

'Suma, you are our only child. You are very good girl and you have always made us proud and happy. Right from your birth all we worry about is your happiness. As your mother told you have to trust us. We cannot see you suffering in pain at any cost. Nothing is more important to us than your happy life. However do not postpone things so long. Nothing against your wish will happen in this house. You have full freedom to choose your life. I trust you that you will utilize your freedom properly' said my father to me.

I happily looked at my father and felt sorry for my mother too. All I can do was to pray to God so that they could find the person as I wish so soon.

I have to surely say a lot of things happened in my office. First of all Ashwin Kumar. He is my team lead. The thing which surprised me a lot was his in-depth knowledge in subject. I have to sure admire him for that. A good thing to mention about him was he was not doing politics as my previous company lead. I have to appreciate him for that. At the same time I have scold him with all the bad words in this world for his irritating behavior. I am not sure if he is aware that his way of people management had earned him lot of discontent among the team members. Why all the team leads are irritating people in one way or other?

He used to speak some standard dialogues which can provoke a most silent person into a psycho killer. Had not it been for law, I would have stabbed knife in his mouth.

'Sumana, The tasks needs to be closed today. How it is progressing?'

'I cannot complete it by today. I will need at least one more day. I was working in that design document and did not get time to complete this.' I told him.

'Today the document needs to be submitted. I told you isn't it? You should have managed your time efficiently'

'But those design documents are to be delivered to clients. You told they are priority tasks and I worked in that. It is already 6.30 pm. I cannot complete it half-an-hour'

'That is not my concern' he said indifferently. 'Is there any hard and fast rule that you should leave by 7.00 pm? Why can't you stay late and complete the work?'

I wanted to push him from that seventh floor.

'The document is not going to be delivered isn't it? This is for internal reference purpose. Can't it wait? I can complete it by tomorrow' I asked him controlling my anger

'You can stay late night and complete the work today. You have cab facility. Why do you always focus to start at 7.00 pm? You don't bother to complete the work. That girl is leaving the company in few days and you have to get the knowledge transfer from her before that and prepare handover document. But it seems you never care about that. You juniors are working hard till late night and completing the work. You are senior to them and you have more responsibility. You have to own your tasks. Look at me yesterday I stayed late night till 10 pm because one task was not completed. I am owning the task which I work. I am expecting that from you.'

That is not fair. Even the company management insists employees to leave on time. He orders me to stay late and work.

'I have seen you several times browsing some websites which are not part of work. This is something I cannot encourage.'

Who are you to encourage? Yes, I agree. I browsed some online magazines sometimes when I get bored with work. How can a person keep working without any diversion?

'Many times I have seen you with bugging Facebook. I am often seeing your head bent towards your mobile than on the monitor' he added fuel to fire

What bothers you if I browse Facebook in my mobile? This complaint of 'always' is applicable only to the guy seated beside me and not me. Whenever I see him, he is operating his mobile phone and the screen is either in blue color (Facebook) or green color (WhatsApp). If you use the word 'always' for me what word will you use for him?

I was so adamant on that day that I did not agree to stay late night and complete the work. It created a tiff between him and me. How cruel it is to hear the phrase 'That is not my concern'

Another incident added fuel to the rage I had on him.

'Sumana, have you completed the fix of the issue which you reported? What is the progress?'

No Suma. This is the time for you to hold your patience. Stay calm and answer him politely.

'I am trying to fix the issue. I am not able to find the solution' I said to him.

'You have to find the solution more fast for your experience. You lack speed. I am so disappointed'

Do you think I am magician with a magic wand which can fix issues in seconds?

'Yeah I am looking at it. Actually I am not able to figure why this issue is coming. The error log is also not displayed with details. I am not able to figure what is the issue first.' I said to him

'That is not my concern' he said 'or you expect me to do?'

You! You! You! Did I ask you anything? It is you who asked the progress of the task and reported the status. Why God is creating creatures like this?

'Do you expect me to come and do the work for you?' he asked me in mocking tone.

I have never been this much calm in my life before.

'You asked for the status and I answered your question.' I tried my best maintain the polite tone. It was not so easy.

'You are leaving only after fixing the issue' he said with commanding voice.

That is it. I would have surely tried to fix the issue. Now there is no way I am doing what he says. Time was 7.30 pm. Last shuttle bus to railway station is at 8 pm. I have to catch the next available shuttle.

'I will fix it tomorrow' I said to him and started to pack my bags

'What is this?' he asked me angrily. 'Did not I tell you finish the work and leave?'

'I am having severe head ache. I cannot work today anymore' I said

'You are not taking responsibility of the tasks assigned to you. You should own the tasks and complete it on time. Your attitude should change. You always want to rush home early than finishing your work.' He spoke coldly

What a pathetic situation I am in right now? I have to give explanations to leave for the day at 7.30 pm being a lady staff who has to travel 50 km to reach home. Whatever may be the case, I am not obeying him and staying late night. I firmly left for the day.

Ganesh, you have not fixed many of the review defects and some of the defects which you fixed are also not correct' I said to him with utmost frustration.

In the last few months I had a tough time with this guy. I never knew doing a review of the deliverable prepared by fresher would be this much difficult task. Especially reviewing a deliverable prepared by this guy has become a nightmare for me.

'I will fix it' he said casually.

'You have to fix it correctly' I said 'Time is running out and we have to deliver this today'. God! Please give me patience so that I will not strangle his neck.

'Don't worry. I will fix it before time. I told you isn't it? I will never let down anyone who trusts me' he said casually again.

I was not able to hold the anger on him after that. No matter how much I am angry on him it is not lasting if speak with him for two minutes. I was able to see bright spark which blown with right velocity can glow into a bright star. I have seen him working hard and he never bothers to stay late night to finish the work. I can surely say he is a hard worker but surely not a smart and efficient worker. He stays late night because he is not planning his work properly. I have several times noticed something unusual with him. At times he never seems to be fine. Though his lips smile it does not reach his eyes. I was not sure of it.

'Had you been clear in what is wanted you don't have to stay late night and work. Have you heard a saying? Do not just do what is said rather do what is required. Always remember this. You are just doing what is said. You can still work on the presentation part without waiting for reviewer to come and point out. Every document looks bad in presentation'

'Excuse me. Don't accuse us unnecessarily. We are struggling hard and giving our best to meet the deadlines. Don't speak as if you don't make any mistakes at all. I have seen you getting scolding from Ashwin often. You don't have to speak like as if you are so perfect' he mocked at me.

Technically I should get angry on him for speaking like this rather my anger turned towards Ashwin only. He pointed out my mistakes in front of this stupid and now I am not able to advise him about perfection.

'When anyone advise you something good learn the habit of listening to it. You people have to thank me in one or other way because I am filtering your mistakes at my level and that is why Ashwin is not scolding you people much. If I don't pin point your mistakes you have face him directly. It is fine for me if you want to face the lion in own cave. Who cares?' I tried to speak indifferently. But it did not create any impact in him.

'It is not a big deal. You are the one who is struggling to handle him. It is not as difficult you think.'

'How?'

'There is technique.'

'Teach me also'

'It cannot be taught. It should be a natural one'

'Oh hello! There is nothing in this world you cannot teach to anyone and there is nothing in this world that you cannot learn. It all depends upon the attitude. I have attitude to learn new things but people like you do not wish to transfer the knowledge you gain.' I said with irritation.

'Then can you please give me an example which you cannot teach.'

'I cannot accept this fact. If so can you please give me an example which you cannot teach.'

'Very sorry. I cannot speak about that further. I feel so shy.' his eyes sparkled mischievously and he smile had some naughtiness. I was not able to understand what he meant.

I observed one thing about Ashwin and Ganesh. Though have some arguments and fights regarding the work, they are very much close with each other off-work. I have seen many occasions where Ashwin mocks and pulls legs of Ganesh with so much fun. They share a high level of comfort with each other. Ashwin often pulls Ganesh in one center point.

'Boss, I need some help to fix the issue here.' said Ganesh

'What issue? Let me see' I said

'It points to some files not available. I have referred all the files.'

I saw the issue he shown me.

'This is very simple and basic thing. You are breaking your head for this and asking for help.You have to refer to this system file and only then this error will get cleared off. You are saying you don't know about it?'

'You are senior and you know to handle. I am just a fresher' he said

'Yes, but when it comes to delegating your work to others you are far senior to all of us. We should learn that skill from you. Even then we cannot master in that like you' teased Ashwin

Ganesh smiled and so did I.

'Boss, how many times I did like that? I remember only once I did'

'But I remember not even single instance of you working without delegating. Sumana, stay away from him else you will have to do his work too. He is somewhat dangerous' said Ashwin

'Boss, I have....' he interrupted in the middle and started to wave hands at someone

I and Ashwin looked at the direction. A girl was passing by waved hands at him with a smile

'Look, is this how I am respected here. I am talking seriously but he is very busy to wave hands at a girl.' said Ashwin

'Boss, she is my friend.' he said

'Boss, all are my batch mates. We are all from same training batch. And moreover whenever you are with me girls friends are alone waving my hands. All my bad luck' he said with fake frustration

'Outer lips says bad luck but inner lips murmurs as good luck. I hardly see any guy waving hands at you.'

'Boss. Don't talk wrongly. They are my good friends.'

'Good friends or girl-friends?'

'Oh my God! if I have all of them as my girl-friends I will have to get rid of this material world and take up Sanyas'

'I feel like you are Krishna surrounded by Gopikas. You are naughty playboy' I joined with Ashwin

'No. Please don't use that word. It will damage my good boy image'

I pretended to search here and there.

'What?' asked Ganesh

'Where is the good boy?' I asked 'Very funny' he said

While we were talking another girl waved a 'Hi' to him. Ashwin and I started to laugh at it. Ganesh felt very awkward.

'Boss, that girl is like my younger sister'

'Oh' exclaimed Ashwin mockingly. 'All women in this world are your sisters then?'

'No. She is the only one girl.'

'Then what about other girls?' I asked him

'Only that girl. Not all women are my sisters. She is getting married shortly. So don't talk bad'

One thing was sure. Ganesh not only looks cute to my eyes but also for many other women. Except those few instances where I saw some cloud occupying his eyes, I always saw him doing harmless mischief with the people around him. The cloud could be my imagination also. I have observed a sudden silence many times for no reason. I got used to the behavior of both of them in last few months especially Ashwin. I was able to see a lot of change in his behavior while dealing with the team. His harshness reduced drastically. I somehow heard unofficially that one of the team member complained to our manager regarding his harsh behavior. I assume it could also be a reason of his change. Whatever may be the case, I can start to feel a good change in my working environment. I have many times felt frustrated and cursed the sun for rising daily. But now I started to expect the Sunrise so eagerly.

The change in the behavior of Ashwin paved way for a good professional friendship among us. We started to go for evening coffee breaks to cafeteria and we started to travel in train together. As usual some girl will wave hands towards Ganesh and Ashwin will start to make fun of his relation with his girls' friends.

When one such girl waved hands at him, Ashwin asked 'She is also your sister?'

'Boss. Not at all. She is my close friend'

'Oh Friend! Sister-friend?'

I laughed at this comment. As far as Ganesh is concerned, our new meaning for the word 'sister' is 'girlfriend'

'Boss, don't spoil a purity of the word'

'OK. I see a lot of sisters of you. You are whole universal brother of all women in this world.'

'Boss, I already told isn't it? I have only one sister friend. I cannot accept all women as my sisters. They are my friends'

'Friends. You have then lot of benefits for having many girls as friends. Friends with Benefits' said Ashwin

'Oh My God! Boss. Thank God you did not mention this word in front of my girlfriends. Had they heard this, my whole reputation would have got spoiled'

Both I and Ashwin wondered as his reaction.

'Hey, I just heard about this movie somewhere and I mentioned casually. Why this much reaction?'

'Boss, seriously you don't know anything about this movie?'

'Friends with Benefits? I have never heard such a name' I said

'Super. He does not know what the movie is all about and you don't know the name of the movie. Now I understood I am working with grannies and grandpas'

'Hey, just tell me why you reacted so much for this movie. What is it all about?' I asked him

'How to say? It is a kind of adult movie.' he said

'That is why I was not aware of it. I am a girl from descent family. How am I supposed to have knowledge about adult movies like few people?'

'Oh hello. Don't speak like good girl. I know about you watching movies like 'Original Sin', 'Killer Joe' etc. Do descent girls watch those movies?' he teased me.

I have to blame myself. I should have not told him about these movies. I smiled at his comment.

'Hey, When I watched I did not know about it.' I said with fake anger

'I don't care. You are also watching 'that' kind of movies.' said Ganesh 'Friends with Benefits is adult movie not a porn movie. There are lot of adult contents. It is a story of two friends who have some blah blah blah things between them'

'Friends having blah blah things? How it is possible?' I asked

'That how do he know?' asked Ashwin in kidding tone. This is another trademark dialogue of Ashwin.

'Thanks Boss. I am just telling the content of the story. See we can take three points. Love, Friendship and Sex. We can join like this 1) Love with sex, 2) Love without Sex 3) Friendship without Love 4) Friendship with love 5) Friendship with love and sex 6) Friendship without love but with sex. This movie falls under the last category. There are two people who does not love each other but have physical relationship. This movie is all about.'

'Ashwin, look at him. How in detail he explains the concept. We have to understand we are interacting with what kind of guy. He is very much aware of these concepts.' I pulled his leg.

'Madam, I have not watched that movie till now. Just heard of it'

'You are able to explain this much without watching the movie?'

'What is wrong in watching those movies? After all we are all youth. We can very well watch any kind of movies.'

'Friends with Benefits' is not the phrase I heard for the first time. Few days back a movie got released in our state which critics from film industry reviewed it as an inspiration from this movie.

I don't know why I downloaded the movie FWB and copied it to my mobile. I don't know how he will react when he finds out that I watched that movie.

'Do you have any interesting movies in your mobile?' Ganesh asked me while we were traveling train to our homes. He did not wait for me answer rather he grabbed my device from me and started to check. He started to be so friendly with me and moves very casually. Normal case I will not allow any one to behave with like that. Somehow I have to accept I like the way he moves with me. I felt bit awkward as I have that FWB in it.

'If you won't get me wrong I want to tell one thing' I said to him

'I will never take you wrong. Tell me'

'I have that FWB in my device' I said to him with little shame. What will he think about me? Already he teased me for watching 'Original Sin'. What he is going to say for this?

'What?' he exclaimed 'What kind of a girl you are? I did not expect this from you. How can you be like this? Unbelievable' he asked me angrily

I looked at him with shock.

'Why you have not told me this before? You have wasted my time. You should have transferred it as soon as you downloaded it. You are too bad. I am very angry on you' his eyes sparkled

Both of us laughed at each other.

'Oh My God. Why you have linked me with these dirty fellows?' Ashwin pulled our legs.

'I never knew you would watch these kinds of films' said Ganesh

'Hey, don't take in other sense. I never watch these kinds of movies. I heard that one of our regional movie is an inspired by this. Just wanted to watch what is in it.'

'Then what about 'Killer Joe'? Any other regional inspired it?' he asked

'Hey, shut up. I told you already isn't it that I did not know. It was 'that' kind of movie.' I said.

'But once you came to know you should have stopped watching it right. But you watched full movie. I have heard somewhere that we should never trust silent women' he teased me.

I smiled with shame.

'Your key-chain looks cool' I said to Ganesh

'Thanks'

'Where did you get this?'

'It was gifted by my friend. When she went to Darjeeling she made it for me' he said

Friend is a 'she'. His 'She' friends are showering more affection to him than his 'He' friends. I cannot why but whenever he mentions about any of his 'She' friends I don't get any good feeling. I cannot explain what it is but some negativity is occupying my mind.

I looked at his key chain. His name 'GANESH' was engraved in it. I liked it very much.

Andy: Hi Sumi

The instant messenger popped in my system with message from one of the testing team member.

'Hi Sumi' Ashwin made fun of me on seeing the IM.

I got irritated on seeing this.

'Ashwin, please stop.' I said to him angrily.

'It is too bad. Andy always cares only about you. How many long days professional bonding I have with him yet he never called me with affectionate nick name like this.' Ashwin once again made fun of me.

My irritation increased further

'How can your name be shortened? May be he can call you as Ash' I mocked at him.

'Why? You can even shorten as 'win'. I am a winner' said Ashwin

Andy dropped several messages and once in three messages he addressed me as Sumi

'See, he is so fond of calling you as Sumi'

'Ashwin, now I will turn you into ash' I said angrily

Andy: Why still you are staying? You have not left for the day?

'Excuse me, if you please finish your conversation we can continue with our work' Ashwin said with a mixture of fun and seriousness in his tone.

Sumana Krishnan: Got some priority work. I have to complete it. Else my lead with kill me

Andy: Don't get scared Sumi. Just run away without his knowledge.

'Bloody non-sense, this guy is spoiling my resource' said Ashwin on looking at the IM

Sumana Krishnan: Yeah. Sure

Andy: Ok bye.

'Hi Sumi' said Ganesh

I got angry.

'Please stop it. I don't like anyone to call me with this name' I said to them

'You are letting him alone to call you Sumi' teased both of them

'I don't know how to stop him from calling me like that'

'Why are you getting angry?'

'If someone calls me like that I feel very awkward. I feel like the person is taking advantage and rights over me. I can allow anyone to call me as Sumana or Suma but definitely not Sumi. This is a special rights which I want to give my future husband. Only he can call me Sumi and no one else.'

'If you don't like him calling like that, why don't you say this to him?' asked Ashwin

'He may feel bad. I don't want to hurt anyone knowingly'

'Then there is no other way you can stop him.' he said

How am I supposed to hurt someone who calls me without any bad intentions? I am not comfortable with that intimacy.

Andy: Sumi

Another another day IM popped in my monitor. Oh No! Not again. I looked at Ashwin who was seated beside for reviewing my deliverable document. Why the guy always messaging me when Ashwin is around? The smile in Ashwin's face made me embarrassed.

'Please go ahead. Let me know when we can continue.' Ashwin said in kidding tone.

'No need. Let us continue' I said angrily.

Andy: Today also lot of work? Why are you still staying? Run away.

I hated the smile in Ashwin's face.

'I knew this guy for more than six months. Never ever he called me with nick name like this. Within short span of time some people managed to make them call so affectionately. See how caring he is?'

I gave a proud expression to them

'It is a magical power gifted by God. I have ability to make people care about me and think only about me just like that.' I said to them.

'Excuse me Madam! You don't have to develop too many feelings for him. He is just caring for you in friendly manner. There is nothing to feel proud.' said the stupid behind me.

I gave an angry glare and started to attack him. No one in this world was able to save him from me for the next two minutes.

'Help! Help! Help! Boss, what is this? You are watching as if you are watching a comedy show. Please rescue me from this bandit queen'

When I tried to give a thrash on his head he held my hand and said 'Don't touch my head. I don't like when someone touches or thrashes my head.' his voice was not casual and soft.

'Why? What will you do if I do? I won't get scared for this' I said

'Don't means don't touch. I mean it. If you do, you will be sorry then.' he said in a different voice which I never heard before.

The modulation was bit cold. I thought it would be better if I abide to it. In this past few months, I have not heard such a cold accent from him. I have seen him speaking to me in a very friendly tone. His voice, his action towards me was so soft and I have seen him only smiling when he was talking to me. However that day turned out to be something which I did not expect from him.

I have to admit that tone had shaken me a lot. I was not able to feel normal then. I never meant to hit him or harm him or insult him but why did he speak in that manner. Somehow it triggered an anger in me towards him. He very well knew I did not mean to harm him. It was an ordinary playful attack on someone with whom we share good comfort level. When everything was going casual and playful why would he turn it to something serious? I cannot understand people why they want create trouble and turn the atmosphere to serious? I did not like when a tear drop peeped out in my eyes. This is not my character at all.

I did not feel like speaking to him afterwards.

'What do you think of this girl? Does not she look cute?' he asked me.

I don't want to look at him nor reply him but what can I do when a cute looking guy comes close to me and talks to me casually.

'Look here' he flashed the photograph of the girl in front of me. 'What do you think about her appearance?'

The girl looked good. As usual I got some negative feeling on his mere mentioning of the girl. I have to attend this as soon as possible..

'You seemed to be so concerned about this girl. Is she so special for you?' I tried to hide my irritation.

'Yes. She is my best friend. Very close friend'

I did not like that way I felt. Why should I feel bad if that girl is his friend?

'Now look at this photo. What do you say about this?'

I looked at the fat girl photo he showed and then looked at him.

'Can you identify this girl?'

'No'

'She is the same cute girl which I showed you just now. Look at her transformation. How she was before and how she is now?'

It was sure a surprise for me. The transformation of that girl was incredible. Had she not been his friend I would have surely appreciated the girl.

'This photograph was taken during her marriage reception. She looked so cute and I was not able to believe at first if it was her'

Again I did not like the way I felt. What was it? Happiness? What is there which makes me happy and relieved? For what I am feeling happy?

'She is also my close friend.' He said and showed me many photographs of some women.

'You don't have male friends at all, huh?' I asked with irritation once again.

'I have lot of male friends right from school days. These girls are my batch mates in training. I am special to every girl. You know one girl got her wedding fixed. I told her playfully that she could have loved and got married to me. She laughed at me and asked why did not I propose her so that she could have said 'yes'. She also said that even now it is not too late.'

He said and laughed as if he cracked a joke.He expects me to laugh with him. I gave a fake smile.

'I told you on that day that you are like a Krishna surrounded by Gopikas, remember? You said that I am damaging your image but whatever you say coincides with my statement. You are definitely a playboy'

'Playboy is a serious damage term. I just flirt with my girlfriends but I don't cross my limit. Can you show me a single playboy who is descent with the woman he hangs around with? I am a very good boy'

'So flirting is descent according to you? I did not know that good boys flirt with women. Thanks for the information. From now on, I will term everyone flirters as Lord Ram. You also change your name from Ganesh to Ramachandramoorthy' I said with irritation.

'I will not accept your statement. Nowadays boys who just flirt alone can be considered as good boys.'

'Why do you want to flirt with every girl?' I asked

'If we don't flirt you girls won't accept us as men.'

What a logic! I have never heard of anything like this before

'Who said?' I asked 'Women like men who don't flirt'

'You women expose false impressions like that. Truth is, women like flirters more than the non-flirters. Inside deep in your heart you want men to flirt with you. If he does not do it, you are not considering them as unfit to be man' he said

'You are teaching me women psychology to a woman?'

'I wonder that a woman does not know the actual woman psychology. Now twll me will not you feel happy when an handsome guy flirts with you?' he asked.

'No man will ever think of flirting with me.' I said.

'That is not my question. If a man flirts with you, will you feel happy or not?'

I was not able to answer the question. Will I be happy or not? No man flirted with me before. I angrily glared at him.

'Perhaps you may be right in this point. One more truth you have to know. Girls may get attracted to flirting guys but when it comes to marriage a woman will choose a non-flirty over a flirty. Flirting men make women feel insecure every moment.'

'We may flirt with thousand women but ultimately only one girl will be our soul mate. A man will do anything for her. I will do anything for the girl who I love the most. It is my duty to be honest and sincere to her and I will abide to it.' he said

I smiled. All the anger I had for him vanished in a minute. At that time, I reminded my mother's words

> *'You have bench-marked a guy and you are searching a groom like him'*

I did not set any guy till then. But I felt what is I set him as the bench-mark?

I am not able to understand why things are not going in the way as we think. I am meeting this girl nearly after a span of eight years and why my fate is making me to meet her in such a horrible condition.

'What is going on here? Did I come here long way just to see you in this condition?' I yelled at her angrily.

She did not answer me. Tears started to roll down the cheeks a frustrating smile in her lips. Her eyes turned red in color and her hand carried a bottle of booze. The whole room was untidy with papers, bottles, tables, chairs and many others things scattered and broken in every corner. When I went inside the house she was lying down drunk.

'Do you know how happy I was when I heard you have returned India? I rushed to come to see you to recreate our old memories. I seriously did not expect this from you. What is wrong with you?'

I did not get answer even now. She turned her head aside to prevent me from seeing her tears.

'Do you really think that you deserve this pain? I am not able to see you suffering like this. Your mother spoke to me some minutes back. She told me be with you as much as I can and help you in getting out of the sorrow you go through right now.'

'I don't think I can come out of this sorrow for rest of my life' she opened her mouth finally

I got angry on this statement.

'Why can't you?' I yelled at her 'I don't think you are only one in this world who has fallen in love or facing a break-up. Nowadays I am seeing the love and breakups as hot trends. It has become a fashion. The same has happened to you too.'

She looked at me angrily and tears started to roll fast into her cheeks

'From your perspective, it is easy to say. People who go through the real pain know the actual impact.' she said to me.

'It may not be as easy as I think but at the same time it will be not as difficult as you think. Do you remember one girl in our class? She had relationships with two guys in a span of six months. She even did not concentrate on her studies properly, got arrears in her exams, she lost her respect among our lecturers in our departments. You now? She got married within an year after our college. She was able to move on. You can take her as inspiration.'

'Probably she did not love either of them deep from her heart. It was an infatuation' she said

I don't know what to say for this. She is correct. She did not love them deep from her heart. This girl thinks that she loved her boyfriend truly.

'Do you remember Aradhana? How she madly and deeply loved her boyfriend? She even took extreme step of taking away her life. Mine is that kind of love' she said.

'Why do you want to do the same mistake as she did?' I taunted her 'Don't you remember how we all scolded her for taking an extreme step. Now you have turned yourself into such pathetic state. Don't do the same mistake as she did. I am begging you. Forget everything. Accept the truth and move-on' I said

'How can I accept?' she screamed 'I loved him so deeply and truly. How he is supposed to dump me like that? What wrong I did other than loving him?' she bemoaned.

She burst for tenth time in last one hour. How am I going to console this girl and bring her out of this? I hated all the men in the world at that very minute.

'It is ok, baby. If he does not want to continue the relationship, what is the point of you alone struggling to save it? Let it go'

I advised her desperately. Which person in this world will listen to advice of others in love and relationship? I was worried.

'I cannot let it go. I want him to be in my life forever. I cannot live my life even a single moment without him. I need him. I love him. God please do something and get him back in my life.' Shradhdha cried heavily

I saw her helplessly not knowing how to relive her out of the pain she faces. I am hearing the same dialogues once again in eight years. I let her cry until she herself stopped it. I took nearly one hour to bring her tears to control. It was not successful completely. Tears secreted continuously in her eyes and she slept in my laps.

I felt so sorry for the girl and her sufferings. I can still remember how she was happy and delighted until before two months before her relationship split. She posted the photographs of hers with her boyfriend in Facebook very frequently. Whenever I opened my Facebook, I saw her status to be 'feeling loved', 'feeling delighted', 'feeling happy' and some of the statuses saying 'I am the lucky person in the world'.

Suddenly things started to change. Her statuses turned from 'feeling delighted' to 'feeling sad', 'feeling frustrated', 'feeling furious' etc.

'I don't know what happened suddenly with him. He started to distance himself from me. He was not picking my phone calls, responding to my messages. He gave me reasons to avoid the outings which I planned. He told he is busy with his critical official issues. Once he told me that he is at office and planned to work in weekends and he cannot spend time with me that week. I fought with him for that but he disconnected my call in the middle. I was so angry that I waited for a week for him to come and apologize to me. But he did not come even after two weeks. I myself called him and he said nothing but the cruelest sentence which I can hear in my life'

'He told that'it could never work between us. It is over. At first I was thinking he was kidding me but he was serious and he meant it. You cannot imagine how I felt when I heard this. I felt like I should end my life that very minute. How could it be possible? How can things end between us? I was not able to believe it. Even now I am not able to believe that everything is over between us. I cannot accept it.'

'Why he felt like that?'

'He told me that he is not happy in our relationship. How can he say like that? Only I and God know how much I did strive hard to keep him happy. I was always available whenever he called or messaged me. I have not slept for several nights so as to spent time with him in the instant messenger. I did everything he wanted. I changed myself in many things according to his likes. I have stopped doing many things just because he did not like them. What else he expected me to do?'

I could do nothing but to pity her. At the same time I got angry on her too. She changed herself for the sake of her boyfriend. How could she do this? Is not a true love supposed to accept the things as it is? That so called stupid guy turned her completely and made her like a puppet. He used her for his benefit.

'How was your relationship romantically?' I asked her. This is supposed to be a personal one but I had no other go but to know it. I am not any relationship expert but I believed speaking among us can help us in finding out what went wrong.

She did not answer me immediately. I had to persuade her to open up.

'He was not romantic at all. It was me who used to do all romantic stuffs like gifting, surprising etc. He never surprised me on my birthdays also but I would organize a surprise party at the midnight. Earlier even though he would not surprise me he will wish me without being reminded. This year he did not wish me at all. His friends wished me but he didn't. I failed to sense that that was beginning of our split up. I got angry on him for forgetting my birthday but he did not seem to care about it. He said a simple sorry and closed the topic.'

What else she expected him to do? Perhaps she would have thought that he may bend his knees and apologies her. Poor girl

'On the day of our second love anniversary, we were talking about moving our relationship further.'

'You mean getting married? What did he say?'

'He neither said yes not said no. He told that he has to speak to his family and he is waiting for right time.'

'Did he speak to them?'

'We had a horrible fight when I opened that topic. He yelled at me harshly that he cannot move things as per my wish. His parents may get mad on him if he tells them he loves a girl.'

'Did not he think about it when he was in relationship with you?'

'He got furious when I asked the same question? He did not talk to me for next three to four days. I struggled very hard to convince him and accept my apologies. From then on I was scared about talking about marriage.'

'Do his parents know about your relationship? Have you met them at least once?'

'Everything was over before. He told me that his parents will not accept the girl of his choice. They are strongly against love marriage and they will surely want him to marry girl of their choice. According to them, love marriages are dishonor to one family.'

'When he knew it already why he was with you for two years? You answer this question. Did you guys cross your limits at any time?'

She did not answer this question. My heart started to beat heavily on her facial expression. I am sure she would have not done something which she can regret for rest of her life.

'You were conducting yourself, is it not?'

'We did cross the limits sometimes.'

Shock is a very simple word to explain how I felt on hearing her answer. I cannot find or even coin a new word to express my feelings. What did she say? Sometimes. So it is not one time. More than one time. I got very angry and disgusted on what she said

'I told you already is it not? I was offering myself fully to him.'

'Aren't you ashamed for saying this and you are shameless for allowing him to do everything before marriage? Now I understand why he left you. What is left in you for him to explore when you yourself made you available completely. How disgusting it is to hear this from you?'

'What else I can do? I was deeply in love with him and I was not able to refuse. I thought what is wrong in doing when I am going be his wife in future.'

'How can you so shameless? Are not you supposed to control your feelings? Does failing in love mean losing your self-respect? Did not you think about your parents? When they come to know that their daughter has gone to this extent how they will feel?'

'Please, stop. I don't want hear anything' she screamed

'You have brought dishonor to your family. If you have crossed your limit means are you pregnant?'

I felt so awkward when asking this question and hated to look at her.

'We followed all safety instructions'

'I have heard girls crossing limits before marriage only in story books and newspapers. First time in my life I have met a girl who did it.' I said angrily to her

'I did not think about it at that time. My heart was filled with love and affection for him.'

'When you were sure of marrying then why should you rush up for these things in pre-marital stage? Do you think you are living in America or Australia where these things are common? You are living in India. We have culture and tradition which the whole world salutes. Even people in West have started to follow our footsteps but our country is forgetting its culture and goes worst day-by-day.'

She kept silent.

'See he has exploited you as per his wish and now it is you who is suffering. He has no regrets. He left you forever. Yours is not pure love rather it is blind love.'

'Just stop it' she screamed at me. 'You don't have any rights to talk about us like this. What do you know about love? Have you ever come across this kind of situations in your life? Have you ever experienced true love? Even you would have done the same thing if you were in my place'

I got angry.

'Definitely not. Why would I do this? Even after seeing two women in my life suffering out of pain like this I will not do this mistake.' I said firmly. 'Even if I fall in love, I will not be blind enough to offer myself completely as you did. I don't believe in true love. There are two ways to learn lessons in life. One is learning from others' mistakes and other by learning from our mistakes. Moreover there is not man in this world who can impress me and that is the reason I am still single'

She smiled amidst her tears rolling down the cheeks

'What?' I asked her angrily

'I wish you don't do mistake in your life. I don't want you to suffer like how I am suffering now.'

'Sure. I will never fall in love. I don't want to suffer like this.'

'You cannot decide that sweetheart' she said 'Love is not something you can ask for or deny. You will never know when and where you will find your man. You may meet him anywhere far away or he may be next to you. When you find him no one in this world including you will stop you from offering everything he needs. There is nothing correct or wrong in a true love. There is no meaning for the word self-respect in a true relationship'

I clapped my hands

'Superb dialogue. If I become a film maker one day sure I will hire you for dialogue writing' I said in mocking tone.

She smiled and kept smiling.

'If it is the case, I don't need that non-sense in my life. No man in this world can make me to dance for his music. I have the habit to controlling men and never ever I will let a man to rule my life. Even if he is my husband' I said

'When you are bitten by love bug, your eyes, your ears and your entire brain is automatically taken control by the person who you love. From then on, you are no more a human being but just a robot. The person may be your boyfriend or husband. It is the fact. Once you are in love your brain stops to function and heart will take over the tasks of brain. You will follow only what your heart says.'

'Do you know one thing? No man in this world can fall in love with me and there is no single man in this world can make me to fall in love with him. I have seen men who hesitate to sit beside me. Men are scared of me. Though I never meant to scare them men are keeping me away from them. So chances of me falling in love and blinding myself are very less. I wish such things should not happen in my life'

This is not the problem of hers alone but of entire world. Relationships are very complicated and men are more complicated. I cannot understand what made her boyfriend dump her. She is smart, beautiful, well-educated from good family. Her parents are well settled upper class people. Her parents are so loving and caring for their daughter. They will accept her choice of her husband and marry of her to her boyfriend. She loves her boyfriend so much. What else that stupid guy wants from a girl. Had he loved her truly, is it not his duty to convince his parents for their marriage

Men are so heartless. Their entire body is made up of stone. They never realize how much they are hurting the souls which truly loves them.

'Women are so heartless. They don't have any emotions. They are so selfish and they never care about the men who love them truly.'

I heard an angry sound from beside.

What is wrong if I push this stupid from the 10th floor of this building? I looked at him angrily. It has become his daily routine to start some controversial topic and waste time in arguments. Today he chose women and emotions. I will have to shut his mouth at any cost.

'What?' He stared at me 'I am not scared of you. Why should I get scared to express the truth?'

'What truth you are talking about?'

'The one which I said about women.'

'If you think it is truth, probably you are mistaken or probably you are have lost your ability to think and analyze. Precisely saying you have become mentally retarded. I can suggest some good doctors for you.' I said

'You are wrong. I would say that it is you who need some psych artist to check your mental illness. You are not ready to see and hear what is the truth and you argue for everything. You women take men for granted. You women play with our emotions as if we are your toys.'

A psycho calls me a psycho. Bullshit!

'Even I can say like that. Men also take women for granted and play with their feelings'

'So you accept that men also make mistakes'

'Yes. I accept. Men are making mistake by falling in love with women.' he said angrily.

'Yeah. Women are making mistakes by falling in love with you species. You are all cheaters' I replied angrily

'Women are cheaters' he said firmly.

'So you say men never cheat on women?'

'But the ratio of women to men is so high' he replied.

'Sometime back you said all women are cheaters. In both the community there are people who cheat and there are people who are sincere and honest to their partners' I asked angrily

'I did not talk about honesty here. All I am talking about is how women behave when taking the relationship to next level. They love to be in relationship with some guy, enjoy all the romantic pleasures, financial gains from the boy. Once their family doesn't accept the boy they love, they immediately nod their heads to the groom of their parents' choice. They never care how heart-breaking it would be for the guy whom they have loved'

A voice heard in my head

> *'He told me that his parents will not accept the girl of his choice. They are strongly against love marriage and they will surely want him to marry girl of their choice.'*

I gave an angry glare at him.

'What else you expect the girl to do? She was given birth by her parents, raised by them, educated by them and they shower their love and affection on her. You all guys expect a girl to throw away her family for someone whom they knew for few weeks or months in few seconds?'

'Why don't they think about them when they are in love? For enjoying material pleasure they need a lover but to bring honor to their family they need another man.'

'Don't talk as if only women are doing these mistakes. Even you men are hiding behind your parents when it comes to take relationship to marriage. If your parents don't accept the girl you, will you throw your parents for the girl or girl for the parents?'

'Why should we throw one for other? Parents are important people at the same time our partners are also important. We have to convince the parents and make them accept for the marriage. We have to convince them that our happiness lies only in their presence in our life. For that we have to be strong in our love. Even if boys are ready to face any consequences, girls are not willing to. They want to settle safely with full security. We are not needed to them.'

I wish I could stab him with a knife. What a baseless blame it is!

'I have a friend who is deeply in love with a girl. Even parents from both sides accepted. But my friend has an elder brother who is yet to be married. The girl's parents were in hurry to finish their marriage and started to pressurize my friend's family. The elder brother's wedding got canceled and because of which my friend's marriage was about to get delayed. Do you know what the girl's parents did? They fixed her marriage with some other guy. She did not resist to that and my friend was left heart-broken. The girl played with the feelings of my friend. Had she was true in her love she would have stopped her wedding.'

'Even I have a story to tell. My friend fell in love with a guy and was in relationship for two years. When she asked him to marry her he backed off saying that his parents won't accept the girl as they consider love marriage is a dishonor to a family. He did not even open up about his relationship to his parents and he dumped her. She is left heartbroken and that guy played with her emotions. What you have to say on this?'

He did not reply

'I can say all men are heartless and stones. Even men are so feeling so safe to marry girl of their parents' choice. What is there to blame women alone? When it comes to breaking a heart either of them over take others. Remember there are women who fall in love a guy more than their life. So stop blaming us alone' I replied angrily

He kept silent

'You guys will never throw your parents for your girlfriend but you expect your girlfriend to throw away her parents for you. This is not fair.'

'I did not say like that' his replied in a low voice.

'Both men and women equally do this injustice and both sides there are people who are honest and sincere.'

'I cannot accept your facts completely. There are men who dump girls but the dumping ratio is the difference I am talking.'

'Parents have to change. Nowadays trends are changing. I have heard of parents who encourage their sons to fall in love with some girl. If all the parents have that broad thinking then split ups will reduce drastically. In India still parents want to control the life of children. We cannot blame that too. Our parents want us to be happy. We need their blessings to pursue a happy life.'

'Yeah, that is true'

This is not the first time he is blaming women for everything. I had several times observed that he had some grudge over women and he never prevents himself from expressing it. Whatever may be the reason this is not something to be encouraged. He has to change his opinion.

'What true?' I taunted 'Let me ask you one thing. You love a girl so deeply but your parents are not accepting her as their daughter-in-law. What will you do? I am sure you will dump that girl like other men do'

This is not the first time he is blaming women for everything. I had several times observed that he some grudge over women and he never prevents himself from expressing it. Whatever may be the reason this is not something to be encouraged. He has to change his opinion.

'No. I will not do like that. I will try to convince my parents to accept her' he said firmly

'It is not as easy as you think. I am asking you straight. You are given two choices, parents or girlfriend. Who will you choose?'

I looked at him for the answer. His hesitation clearly implied he would say nothing or say parents.

'I will not let it happen in my life' he said 'I will try to convince my parents'

'This is not the answer to my question. You are not able to convince them no matter how much struggle. You even threaten them to commit suicide if they don't accept. Even then they don't accept. Then who will be your choice'

He did not answer. How dare he can blame women like that!

'I said I will marry the girl' he said

Did I hear anything wrong? What did he say?

'Come again'

'I will marry the girl'

'What about your parents then?'

'I trust them. They will be mad at me for some time but one day they will forgive me. My parents will not leave me forever. If I don't make right decision, I will lose my girl.'

'I know for arguments sake you are giving answer like this. In reality, you will not leave your parents for your girlfriend.'

'I don't want that to happen in my life. I will surely make my parents accept her. At least I will not marry any other woman other than her. Me and my girlfriend will wait for our parents' approval and get married but definitely I will not leave her. Not only me no man will dump his girlfriend if he truly loves her. He will do anything for her.'

'So you are so dared to act against your parents' wishes?' I mocked him 'If you leave your parents for your lover, won't they get hurt? As a son is this what you will do for them?'

'If I leave my truly loving girl-friend, she will also get hurt. How can I let that happen? For me both my parents and lover are equally important.'

Is he serious about what he is talking? What did he say? A man who loves a woman truly will do anything for her? Were Aradhana and Shradhdha not loved truly loved by their lovers?

I am noticing for the past few days and I am not able to understand few things about men. According to them who are beautiful women? A girl who is slim, fair with proper tooth, who leaves her hair in free style, wearing make-up, lipstick, mascara, eye shadow, dressed in tight outfits exposing her entire body structures and curves. What is the pride these men get if they expose themselves as a friend of such a girl?

I did not notice that girl until his eyesight followed wherever she went. I have heard him talking about many of his girl friends (myself and Ashwin always have a doubt whether they are his girl friends or girl-friends) but this is the first time I ever noticed that his eyes following some girl so vigorously. Not only in one or two occasions, I have seen several times that girl waves a 'hi', gives a light smile and when the girl comes to him to talk with him he almost forgets the entire world around him. One day when we went to Cafeteria together for coffee-break, he almost forgot that I am accompanying him and started to behave as if I don't exist there.

'What is going between you and that girl? I often see you with her?' I asked him.

'A new friend. Got introduced some days back.' he said

Why I am getting angry for this? Why I am so concerned to know about what is going on between them? As usual a negative feeling started in me. I hated when I saw his face turned red on seeing her. Oh My God! He is blushing.

'Do you know one thing? I have seen a woman blushing for real. One day when she was introduced to me by my friend I said 'hi' to her and immediately she blushed. I was so excited. A girl blushes on my presence.' he told me enthusiastically.

I did not want to smile.

'I have seen several times both of you talking with each other forgetting the entire world around you' I asked in teasing tone but in reality I was so furious.

'What else I can do? You see, women are fond of talking with me and I usually never disappoint them. I always find happiness in making others happy. But it is not easy to be dream boy of girls. If I don't pay attention to them or if I pay more attention to some other girl I will get into trouble. Somehow I have learned to manage the technique of making all women feel that they are important to me than anyone else.'

'Great talent' I mocked him.

I cannot blame him alone. Nowadays women have become so stupid that they cannot recognize who is genuine and who is faking.

'I have to say something. That girl is not interesting me at all.' He said

It is not something I have to wonder about.

'Why?' I pretended to get surprised

'She always says men are trust-worthless. She never trusts any men and thinks men are not good'

The respect for the girl increased in me within few seconds. I don't know if her judgment about men is right in general but judgment about this guy is absolutely perfect. I have to appreciate for sure.

'Why did she come to conclusion?'

'She says men talk to her normally only for few minutes. Then she blames that they are calling for coffee in next meeting and then they propose in subsequent meetings'

I just wanted to end this horrible topic. I hated both him and that girl like anything. Men or women everyone is considering themselves as Prince charming or beautiful princess and having an impression that everyone is after them. This guy has nowadays become so proud of himself that he is thinking that all women want to be his close friend or girl-friend.

I have to admit few things here. In last few days I am very much wondered about myself and the feelings which is developed in me. I am not happy at all. No matter how much I am happy, this guy is taking away my happiness from me. Even if I try to gain my confidence and bring my happiness, the moment I see his Instant messenger popping with a message from one of his girlfriends, I lose it.

'Ganesh ji, why you never get any IMs from any guys? Only girls flood with messages.' teased Ashwin

'What can I do? It is the general problem faced by an extremely handsome guy. All the girls wanted to spend time prince charming.'

Shameless creatures. I thought angrily.

'It is fine for a prince charming to facing these troubles. I wonder why you are facing these troubles.'

'Boss, you people don't have idea of how young girls are standing in queue to become my friend and come close to me.'

'Even in railway ticket counters I have seen young girls standing in queues. Does it imply they wanted to become friend with the ticket issuing staff?' I teased him

'Ha! Ha! Ha! Very funny'//

'Even I have seen young women standing in queue outside the ration shops.' Said Ashwin

'I have seen many young girls standing in queues outside movie ticket counters' I said

'You people are jealous of my huge female fan following. No matter you people accept or not you cannot deny how much I am wanted by girls around me'

I should blame the girls around him. Though I will not say this guy is a handsome prince charming but sure he is cute. The problem is he looks cute not only to my eyes but also to eyes of many other girls. Adding to fuel to fire, my mood got spoiled when he waved hands at the new sensation girl.

'Looks like you both of them have come so closer' I asked him hiding my irritation

'Kind of'

I did not like the smile in his face

'What is her name?'

'Sanjana'

'Age?'

'May be 27.'

I got shocked

'27? But you are 24.'

'So what? She is hot.'

This is current trend. It does not matter for men about the age of girls if she is hot and sexy. What makes him to think that I am not? Even I am of same age as hers. Don't I look hot? Am I not looking beautiful? Why he is not noticing me?

Wait a minute! What the hell am I thinking? I want him to notice me and appreciate me.

'You consider the girl elder to you as hot?'

Rubbish! My thoughts are going in wrong direction. What bothers me if he thinks some random girl as hot or cold!

'What is wrong in it? Nowadays men are falling for women who are elder to them. Actually even I prefer to marry an elder woman. I will not have to worry about anything. She will take care of everything and I can lead happy life without responsibilities' he said.

My heart started to beat fast. I got back to my work immediately.

'Do you know? I am leaving from this project' he said with joy

'Oh' What feeling is that? Whatever it is, I did not like it. I somehow tried to hide it from getting exposed in my face.

'When?' I asked

'Not sure' he said 'Our manager told me forward my resume suddenly. I asked him the reason and he told me. Two members are moved out of our project and I am one among them'

So he is going to go away from here forever. I felt so sad for that.

What is there to get sad about?

Nothing, I consider him as my friend. Don't we feel bad if our friend leaves us?

Is it the real reason?

What other reason could be?

Are you sure?

Yes. I like him very much and if he is going to leave me sure I will miss him.

I recalled the words which I told my mother on that day

> *He should be mischievous making people around him happy. The mere presence of him should make atmosphere so lively. Everyone should miss him when he is not around and not feel happy.*

I don't remember missing anyone in my life. All those whom I have met were mere passing clouds till then. Somehow I started to realize that this guy is more than something he means to me. His project transition process started and moved so fast and he was released from the project the very end of the month.

'So you will be moving to some other place? You may start to work with new people and ou will forget all of us' I tried to be so casual and unaffected by his movement.

'I don't know. I am so excited about this migration. As you said I will be working with new people. I will be more happy if I can find some pretty girls over there. I have been working only with older people'

My eyes grew wider.

'Excuse me?'

'I mean, you and Ashwin are older than me, is it not?' he stammered

'We are elder to you not older' I said

'Yeah. I wanted to work with my age group people.' he said

I got angry and did not speak to him then.

He came to my seat and asked 'You got angry huh?'

'No. You go wherever you want and work with whomever you like. Who cares?' I tried to indifferent

'Alright! I get it. You are taking things so seriously. I was just kidding' he said

It has become universal habit of everyone. Every one of them will speak whatever they wanted to and in the end they will finish the topic by saying 'just kidding'

'Still angry?'

I did not talk to him for a while. I can very well realize that this guy is creating an impact in my life. It will be better if I stay away from him as much as possible.

'I guess I won't be going away from this place. I am moving to another project but I am reporting to same manager. So chances of my going from here is very less.'

I was not able to control the happiness inside me. It was very hard for me to control my expression. I tried to maintain the angry expression is my face.

'Ok. I think you upset with me. It is my duty now to cheer you up. Let us go for a break. Today's snacks is my sponsor.' he said

God! Please save me.

When somebody notice what I am doing they will shoot me with at least thousand 'Why' questions. But I am asking those why questions to myself

'Why I am so excited about his birthday?'

'Why did I come to this gift shop?'

'Why I am looking for some birthday gift for him?'

'Why I am thinking that he will look so cool in the cap?'

'Why did I buy it for him?'

This is not something which I usually do for anyone. Earlier my job gets over by just contributing money to the gift for colleague's birthday. One another would take responsibility of buying the gifts. This is the first time I am investing my time and breaking my head to find what gift of mine would impress him?

'Happy birthday'

'Thank you so much'

'Do you like my gift?'

'Oh! Thank you but I have this cap with me already. You have wasted your money unnecessarily.'

'Oh! You don't want it then?'

'You should have asked him before. What is the use of having same kind of caps?'

'I thought you will like it'

'I like it but I don't need it'

Nowadays my thoughts have become so pessimistic.

'Happy Birthday'

'Oh! Thank you so much'

'Here is my gift'

'Oh that is so cool'

'Do you like it? It is very simple but I was not sure what can I buy for you?'

'Yes. This is the best gift. Thank you very much'

This is positive thinking. Gifting is important than the gift. Sure he will ….whoa

Too much of imagination is not good for health. Today is his birthday. I wish I could gift him by myself and see how he expresses himself on seeing my gift. How true it is! Man proposes God disposes. Always God disposes all my proposals. Otherwise I would have noticed the slippery wet marble staircase and walked carefully without getting slipped injuring my back. Now I have to wait till I am cured from my pain which may take around four to five days.

When I fell down, I did not feel anything serious but within few minutes my position became horrible that I cannot take even single step without a support. I was rushed to the first aid center in my organization. I was not able to stand without being supported by someone. Ganesh offered his hands to me for support but I was bit hesitant to hold his hands because of a small incident happened a some months back.

It was during one day a blood donation camp was organized in our company campus. Ganesh volunteered to donate his blood and he was not feeling good.

'I am not able to lift my hands at all' said Ganesh

'Why what happened?' asked Ashwin

'I don't know whether the doctors knew how to inject needle in one's body. I feel like my hand had become numb'

'Show your hands' I told him

Blood got clotted in the place where the needle was injected.

'Not a big problem. If the place was rubbed for few seconds blood flow will start once again' I said to him.

I wished to do the rubbing by myself however I pulled Ashwin and asked him to rub. I don't know why I wanted to rub the hands. Is it out of pity or out of care or out of something else? Later in the evening he felt the same pain in his hands but at that time Ashwin was not available and hence I rubbed his hands but he pulled his hands away.

'It is ok. There is camera over there. People will get us wrong.'

I gave an angry look.

'I was just rubbing your hands'

'I am feeling little uncomfortable if you touch m hands' he said

'Perhaps you have forgotten a thing. I am elder to you in age. I am like your elder sister. Will you feel uncomfortable if your elder sister touches your hand?'

He did not say anything but he did not feel good when I touched his hands. That incident made me little hesitant to take help from him and hold his hands. He may feel uncomfortable but no one was there to give me support till the cab which was going to take to my home. I had no other go other than to grab his hands.

What kind of feeling is that? I wish I could hold his hands without leaving it forever. I held him so tightly. It was not the first time I am holding a guy's hand. In my school days I have held the hands of my guy friends during a dance function. Even now my father wishes me to hold his hands while crossing the road so that he is convinced that I am safe under his protection. There is nothing different I have to feel about. I felt so protected and secured while I was holding this guy's hand. The feeling did last only for few seconds as one of the female nurse offered her hands for me to hold. I had no other go but to get rid of the protection feeling as I had to protect my dignity there.

I felt so happy when I got a call from him when I reached home

'How are you now?'

'Not good. Not able to stand'

'Take rest and take care of your health' he said to me

I was so moved by the care he showed.

I did not sleep that night as I was very much excited about the birthday. I thought of sending him message at midnight 12 am but somehow I felt that I am giving too much of importance.

'Call me once you reach your seat' I dropped a message to him

I was waiting with restlessness for him to call me. I am not sure if he will like the gift or not. It is not something so costly or unique. Just an ordinary gift. He has lot of friends and they will gift him even iPads/iPods or any other expensive gifts. I don't think it is going to impress him much. I am wondering why I am bothering myself about meaningless things. I should not bother even if he does not like. As a colleague, I am gifting him for his birthday. He likes it or not that should not be my concern. My duty is over. If wears it or throws it, that is none of my business. Suma, stop thinking too much.

Mobile rang. Call from him.

'Hello' I said

'Hello, now only I saw your message. How are you?'

'Yeah. Fine'

'You went to doctor?'

I liked the concern he showed on me.

'I have to go.'

'Why you have not gone still? Go to doctor soon and get it cured.'

I smiled this side.

'Sure Baba sure. I will go. I called you as I needed a help from you.'

'Yes. At your service Madam'

'Can you open the second draw in my seat and take a cover?'

'Just a minute'

I heard the sound of draw being pulled that side.

'Which cover?'

'The one in violet color. Take it and you can see a packet inside it. Take it outside.'

'I see some gift wrapped stuff inside'

'The same packet. Take it outside'

'Yeah, taken'

'Wish you Happy Birthday' I wished him with little excitement.

There was silence for few seconds

'Oh' I heard him exclaiming 'Ok. Thank you so much.'

'I bought it for you. Thought of giving it you today. But everything turned upside down'

'It is ok. Thank you so much'

'Opened it?'

'Opening'

After some seconds 'Oh! Cool. Nice gift'

'You like it?' I asked in excitement

'Why not? Who will not like a gift like this? Thank you very much'

I felt very happy on hearing this.

'Ok. That is it.'

'Thank you for the gift and the surprise'

'No problem. I wish I could have been there.'

'Will you come tomorrow?'

'Not sure'

'Take care. Go to doctor as soon as possible.'

'Yeah. Bye.'

It was a very nice conversation. I felt so happy and excited. He liked my gift. How caring he is! But in the corner of my mind I felt little sad.

Days were rolling so fast. I felt I joined the company few days but one year has passed by. I have to surely admit I enjoyed my days like anything except for few occasions. That is my marriage.

'Suma, we need to discuss about one alliance.' Said my mother

Once again started.

'The groom is from New Delhi. He is PhD in Chemical engineering. He is working as a professor. As you demanded, he is more educated than you and he earns more than you. He is owning a flat at Delhi. Can we fix a meeting with him?'

I did not reply her.

'Say something. This time you cannot say excuses. This seems to be good alliance.'

'Should I leave Delhi if I marry him?'

'Obviously. What non-sense question it is?' asked my mother

'Is it ok for you if I settle somewhere?'

'Not somewhere. You will be just 3000 kilometers away by land and two hours of flight journey. It is not big problem. Look already you have rejected so many potential alliances for some reasons. We are not going to send you away from this planet.'

'Amma but...'

'Suma, remember choices are getting narrowed down. If you demand too much, you have to stay single for your rest of your life. The groom looks smart and he has hair in his head. I checked it again and again as you were so adamant of not marrying the groom who was bald.'

'Don't blame me for that.' I said angrily 'He is almost a mental patient. You want me to marry an insane?'

'Let us not talk about it right now. I will speak to his parents and arrange for meeting through Skype. Is it ok for you?'

'Do as you wish.' I said to her.

Anyway meeting someone in Skype alone cannot fix a marriage. What harm in chatting with some guy? Amma is so nervous and tensed whenever a new alliance comes across. I have told her many times not to stress herself much. I started to hate Indian system of arranged marriage.

Groom's parents are complaining that brides are so arrogant and brides' parents complain that groom's family is arrogant. Parents on both sides are too much choosy and they always search for best for their children. I am not sure if every groom's parents are aware what they expect from their would-be daughter-in-law. One fine morning the groom's family shall wake up and understand the reality. By that time their sons would have crossed 35+ years of age and they will accept whatever proposal come in their way no matter bride is of different caste, religion or even divorced/widowed. The same is the case with brides but age alone will be little advanced i.e. 28 or 29.

As a matter of fact, I have stopped all the demands which I had earlier. I rejected many alliances as one or other demand was not satisfied. I am not feeling like getting married. I want my parents to looking for alliance and leave me as I wish. It will never happen for sure.

I have to admit one more thing here. For the past few days I am not behaving normally. I am feeling so irritated and depressed. I feel like I have lost something or losing something. I don't remember exactly when it started but one day I was angry for the rest of the day on seeing a thing.

It was during our regular coffee-break time. Ganesh and the new sensation Sanjana were seated in the reception couch laughing and chatting there. I tried to get glimpse of Ganesh but he was not ready to turn his eyes away from her. I wished he looked at me but is not ready to turn away from here. It was Sanjana who looked at me and waved a 'hi' towards me.

'Are you going for a break?' asked Ganesh

'Yes. I thought of calling you but it looks like you are not free' I said with irritation though I smiled outside.

'We were just talking.' He then turned towards Sanjana 'She is my Tech Analyst Sumana and she is Sanjana.'

'I know her. She was the one who spoke very boldly in our ODC during that oratorical contest' said the girl Sanjana.

I remember that day when there was an oratorical contest was organized. Four contestants including me spoke one after other on the topic 'Technology is a boon or bane'. People in the ODC have to vote who is the best for next level round. It was a happy day for me as I came to know people loved my speech and way of speaking more than others. This girl Sanjana came to me after I spoke. To be honest I was jealous of her as Ganesh noticed her over me and I did not like to speak with her.

'You spoke very nicely' she said

Oh God! How can I get angry on some girl who appreciates my talent? All the anger and grudge which I got on her vanished in few seconds.

'Thank you'

'I am Sanjana'

'Yeah. I know. You are Ganesh's friend is it not?'

I cannot understand why she is blushing on uttering his name. Is blushing her general nature or this is because of Ganesh? If latter is the reason, I will surely kill her.

It is how we both introduced. I cannot why but somehow I did not like when Ganesh spoke with any girl. Often I see both of them chatting together. Nowadays I have become too possessive. I don't like the way I am behaving. II am getting angry and jealous and most importantly becoming possessive. I have started going in wrong path.

That guy is not willing to get up from the couch at all. It looks like he wishes to continue his chat with her rather than coming for regular coffee break with me. I stepped aside the place angrily. Ashwin invited Sanjana to join with for coffee with us.

I laughed within myself on seeing the expression of that girl. I remember Ganesh saying how she would get angry if any guy invites her for coffee. I was able to see the irritation in her face.

'It is ok. You carry on' she said to him

'Just join us. For today.' said Ashwin

'No' she said hesitantly. 'I don't think it will be nice if I come with you all. My team mates will not feel good.'

'What is there to feel bad about? You are our hero's friend' teased Ashwin

Why these guys are straining themselves in inviting her when she is not willing.

'Come on. Join. See you have female company too.' said Ganesh

I had to grin fakely. He uses me to drag her to have break with us. Now only he is reminded that there is a soul name Sumana.

The girl finally consented to come with us for coffee-break. While on our way to cafeteria she herself came close to me which I did not expect it from her.

'Hi' she said

I smiled.

'You go to coffee-break with them often'

'Quite often. Almost daily'

'Ok' she said.

She wanted to ask something to me. I did not ask her anything and waited for her to start.

'How are these guys?' she asked.

I frowned.

'I don't get you'

'How about this guy Ganesh?'

'What about him?'

'What kind of character he is? Good bad best worst'

What kind of question is this? What bothers her if he is good or bad, best or worst? Why is she so concerned as if she is going to marry him? Or has he proposed her? She wants to get details about him to know him better so that she can decide if she can accept or reject him. Why should I not reveal the truth of his playboy nature. She will sure run away.

'He is a very nice guy.' I said 'Why? What is the matter?'

'I just wanted to know. How does he behave with girls?

What should I say for this? Should I open about his sister friends to this girl?

'He behaves with me with respect and discipline. I think he is good in behaving with girls'

'I have been talking with him for few days. I will feel comfortable if some girl certifies him to be good guy. I don't like when guys invite me for coffee. I got angry on both of them when they invited me. Had you not come with us, sure I would have not joined you.'

It was very hard for me to control the laughter on hearing what she said. I felt little proud because she came because of me.

'I believe those guys will not invite me for the coffee alone right?'

God! Please give me strength to control myself from laughing.

'Why do you get worried if they invite for coffee?'

'You don't know about these guys. You cannot believe them. First they will invite for coffee like a friend. In subsequent coffees they will start to propose. I am sick of these. That is why.'

How can I take this attitude? Is it childishness or pride or arrogance or what else? She is allergic to guys' love proposals.

'I am not sure about Ganesh but Ashwin is married with a child. You don't have to worry about him'

'That is cool' she exclaimed happily.

'What is your age?'

'27'

She is elder than me. I started to like her on hearing this.

'Ganesh is three years younger to you. I don't think you have to worry about him too.'

'Need not be' she said 'Nowadays boys have no norms about age'

I remembered the words of him few days back.

> *Actually even I prefer to marry an elder woman. I will not have to worry about anything. She will take care of everything and I can lead happy life without responsibilities.*

Did he really mean it?

'Guys why you are talking separately' asked Ashwin

'Some girl talks. There is nothing you guys have to know'

'Ok. Sumana had got a new friend today and she started to keep us aside.'

'Yes. I don't need you people anymore. We will be together and go everywhere' said Sanjana to them and she held my hands so tightly.

Everything was fine and I enjoyed the moment happily.

I smiled not aware the ugly game which destiny has started to play in my life.

All of us ordered their favorite health drinks. I felt so lonely on that day. Both of them were giving importance to the new girl and left me alone. Ganesh was so fond of attracting that girl. He is the one who sponsored for the expenses on that day.

I ate my snacks and health drinks silently. I tried to interrupt on one or two occasions while he was speaking with her but he never seem to care about what I told rather he was so busy to express about himself and impress her. I hated all the three of them in front of me. I wanted to leave the place.

'You seemed to have lot of friends. I have heard a lot about you' said Sanjana

Ganesh smiled proudly.

'Yes he has lot of sister friends' said Ashwin

All of us except Sanjana laughed.

'Yes, even I am also his friend' I said to Sanjana

'Who told?' he asked at me

'What, I am your friend is it not?'

'No. you are not my friend. You are my colleague. She is my friend' he said casually

I was dumbstruck by this reply. I was not able to believe what he said to me.

'Then me?' asked Ashwin

'You are also my colleague' he said again

'Bloody nonsense. You faithless creature' mocked Ashwin. He was not affected by the comment.

Everyone laughed at his comments except me. I was terribly shaken by what he said. He said that I am not his friend just a colleague.

'See, how he is talking' I tried to speak casually.

How could he say like that? I am not his friend but just a colleague. Do I have this much importance in his life? I felt so hurt and bad.

'Hey, what is this? Don't take it personally' said Ashwin.

'Why? What happened? I did not say anything wrong. How can you be my friends? You people are elder than me'

'Even she is also elder to you' I told him

'But she is not my team mate'

'So team mates cannot be friends' I asked angrily

'How can colleague be our friends?' he asked me again

'Why do you think colleagues cannot be friends? Are not we interacting socially and how much fun do we have in our cubicle? We consider you as our friend but you are speaking like this.'

I cannot suppress my anger further.

'This is not fair. You should have not told like that. Say sorry' said Sanjana to him

'Why should I apologize? I did not say anything wrong'

'But she took it offensive.'

'That is not my problem. I told my opinion. I am not responsible if she is offended.'

'He is not ready to realize that what he told and way he told is wrong. What is the point of talking about this? It is not his mistake but mine. I should have not cared for him. I really deserve this.' I said angrily.

'I really don't understand what is there to get offended. I just told the truth. How can you be my friend?'

'I told is it not, not to talk about it further' I said

'This is totally unfair. You way of speaking is so harsh and you are not realizing that. Apologize to her' Sanjana insisted

'Apologies should be asked from bottom of heart. It should not be demanded' his tone was so arrogant

'See, I told isn't it. It is waste of time to talk to him' I said

'Guys, please don't fight. Suma, it is his opinion. You don't have to take too personally. Leave it'

'How can he say like that? Is it how we are all dealing with each other all these days? He very well knew how much I care for him. Do colleagues care for each other?'

Ashwin smiled at Ganesh. None of my words seem to affect them.

'Can't you keep quiet?' asked Ashwin to Ganesh.

It was very casual and funny scold. Ashwin never cared about how I feel now.

'I think he tried to convey some other thing but some misunderstanding happened. It is not a big deal. You people can stop quarrelling.' said Ashwin 'He did not convey it properly. Forget it'

'Boss, you have to justify. We are all working together. Can I behave with you in the same way as I behave with my friends? According to me, friends have a difference definition. It does not apply to you both. That is what I am trying to say.'

'It is ok. See this is a communication gap. We don't know what your definition of friendship is and that is why she feels bad. I think both of you can stop this here.' said Ashwin.

'See how her face turned!' Sanjana said to him. She turned to me and said 'Please don't feel bad'

'Alright. I am sorry' he said

'See, he apologized. You forgive him.' Said Ashwin

'I don't need any sorry which is asked out of compulsion. Apologizing should come from heart realizing one's mistake. He is apologizing out of the pressure which you are putting on him.'

'Nobody can pressurize me. I never do anything on others insistence. I do it out of my own accord.' he said

I did not say anything.

'Boss, you told me to apologize and I did. See, how is behaving' he said angrily

'Sumana, just leave it. Don't fight for silly things' said Ashwin

'This is not something silly. You cannot understand how bad I feel now. He still persistent that what he said is not wrong. What is point of the apology here?' I burst angrily

'I am apologizing because you are offended by my statement. I did not mean to hurt you and that does not mean what I told is wrong. I am strong in my point.'

'Ashwin, let us go. I will not blame him. I am a real fool for considering him as my friend. Yes, I am not your friend. I am after all your colleague. Are you happy now?'

'She is over reacting' he said angrily

'People who got hurt and most of all made fool will react as I do' I said

'Ok. Relax. I have a call to attend shortly. Let us go' said Ashwin

On the return way, I and Ganesh did not talk with each other. Sanjana held my hands and said 'It is ok. Don't feel bad'

'How can he say like that? You know how much I showered affection on him. This is not my character at all. I never develop bonding with my colleagues or friends. I somehow considered him so special in my life. He made me feel like a fool.'

'Are you crying?' she asked me in surprise

'I will not cry for these silly things. My tears are not that cheap to get spilled for a worthless guy like him.'

'I am telling you this today. Don't trust the boys. They always let us down and they will never care about it. Stay away as much as possible and that is how you can live peacefully.' she told me.

The same advice was given by my parents several years when I joined my job in my first company. I really deserve this for not obeying them.

Entire weekend got spoiled because of the crap happened on that day. I cannot still digest the way he spoke.

'I don't see anything wrong in it' said my father

I angrily glared at him.

'He is right. How can colleagues be friends? You people are going there to work and not to have fun. There is nothing you have to get angry about'

'You men are not giving respect to emotions. Don't you people think of how the person in front of you will get hurt by the way you express your opinions?'

'Why should one care about your feelings? What bothers the person if you are getting hurt? No one can hurt us except us. We are hurting ourselves because we give importance to things which is not relevant to our life. When a thing does not mean anything to us, it cannot hurt us. I cannot find fault in that boy's statement. He is your junior. Imagine the situation like this. If he tells that he is your friend but suddenly you deny and say that you are not his friend but his colleague, how he will become a fool. So he stayed in safer zone. I am fully supporting him. What he had done is correct.'

I did not want to talk to my father on this further. Men always support men no matter what they have done is fair or not.

'Suma, we have several times told you stay away from men. If you get close to them, you will have face this kind of embarrassing situations.' said my mother

'Don't give importance to people. If you do, you have to face the consequences. Why you giving this much importance to some random boy's statement? I don't get it.' said my father

I kept silent.

'Suma, I don't want you spoil your mood and ours. We are not okay with the way you behave with that boy. You are grown up and we don't want to advice you on this. Forget everything and plan for the Skype meeting tomorrow. Do you get it?'

I nodded like 'Ok'

'I wish this alliance gets fixed for you. The groom-bride drama should come to an end'

I did not say anything.

'Are you fine with the meeting tomorrow?' asked my mother suddenly

I continued my silence

'What is wrong with you Suma? You are getting upset for non-senses like this. You are spoiling the entire mood of ours. Do you realize it?'

No one can understand my feelings and emotions. Everyone is persistent in their opinions. What my father asked is a good question. Why am I giving importance to some random guy's opinion and get my mood spoiled?

'Shradhdha?'

'Yeah. Tell me' she answered

'Where have you gone? I am trying to catch you for past three to four days? Your network always said 'Not reachable'.'

'I went to Haridwar'

'Haridwar? But your mother told you are in Bangalore'

'Is there any rule that you should not travel to Haridwar from Bangalore?' she replied irritatingly

I felt little awkward

'What is up in Haridwar? Any pilgrimage trip?'

'Please don't tell this about to my family. They are not aware of my Haridwar trip.'

I was bit surprised

'What is up with you? You are so unusual today. I called you to know how you are feeling now. Are you alright? Did you come out of all the pains and sorrows you had?'

'How easy it is for everyone to advise others to come out of heartbreak? Only heartless people can give these kinds of suggestions' her voice still showed the frustration.

'Very well any one can understand that you are still in pain. Actually you don't want to come out of pain.'

'How you all expect to get rid of everything so soon. It has been just few months I had my break up'

'Everything is over. Why are you not accepting the truth and moving on?' I asked her angrily.

How I am going to make this girl understand.

'I truly loved him' her voice broke and I am able to hear the sniffling from her side. 'I cannot let him go.'

'But he left you forever' I said to her

'No, he will not leave me. He will come to me. That is my purpose of visit to Haridwar.'

'I don't get you.'

'I heard from one of my friends that if we do some prayers our lover will come back to us. She took me to one of the priests who does these kinds of prayers. I went there so that I can get back my love.'

The most humorous thing I have ever heard in my life. A prayer can bring the love back.

'Are you making fun of me?' I asked angrily

'No, it is serious. I mean it. I went to meet the priest there and he asked me to do some prayers. I was there for three days and completed the rituals. The priest told my boyfriend will come back to me within a week and beg me to accept him in my life. I am waiting for him to call me. I will not accept him so easily. He has to go through all the punishments for breaking my heart before he can marry me.'

'Shradhdha, how can you ever think like this? You are an educated girl and how can you be so innocent to keep your beliefs in these superstitious stuffs.'

'Why do you think it is superstitious? Don't we pray to God and ask for wealth, health, prosperity? Have not you heard about people performing prayers at home? It is similar to that.'

'I have never heard that God gives something what a devotee asks for in a week. You are so confident that your lover will come back.'

'We have some prayers for that in our ancient books. If we do it with full sincerity we can get what we need'

'You have not informed your parents about this?'

'I asked for their permission to conduct that prayer but they got mad at me. That is why I came all alone to do it.'

'I don't think you are going in correct path. How dare you leave your home without informing about your whereabouts? What if something unwanted has happened to you? Why you are so blinded like this? I am very much worried about you. I feel you are slowly becoming insane'

'It is not insanity. I am following my heart'

'Rubbish! Leaving somewhere to do some stupid things and you say your heart tells you to do this.'

'It is the power of love. Once you are in true love, your brain will stop functioning. It is the heart that makes to live your life. Our heart will never betray us. If you follow your heart sure you will succeed. Brain always doubts on everything. It will confuse you but heart will correctly direct us. In a relationship there is no place for brain but only for heart'

What can I say for this? This girl is completely blindfolded with love. She is persistent to get her love back and it looks not even a single word will enter inside her brain

'According to me, the main functionality of heart is to cleanse the impure blood and pump it to all parts of the body including your brain. Heart does not think my dear. Brain is the one which makes your to think'

'You are wrong. If we face break, it is not our brain that feels the pain but the heart.'

'It is all your imagination' I yelled

'You have not fallen in love with anyone truly. If you fall, you will accept what I say'

'What do you want to say ultimately?'

'Always follow the heart. Others heart may betray but your own heart will never let you down.'

'Do you think your lover will come back to you?'

'I told you, is it not? My love is pure and true. It will bring him to me'

I did not hear any of her words what we spoke except this one

Follow your heart. It will never let you down

I am not normal for the past few days. When I found the reason, I was not happy. I recalled what happened in last two months.

To begin with, I am not normal when he is around me. My heart beats faster than usual if comes near to me. I am getting jealous when he talks to other girls. I don't like when he utters the name of any girl. I feel a burning sensation in my stomach when I see any girl walking beside him. I feel happy when he notices me and says I am beautiful. I get happy when I see any message from him especially when his WhatsApp status changes from 'last seen' to 'online' and delighted when the status changes from 'online' to 'typing…'

Why did I buy gift for him on his birthday?

Why did I want to surprise him with my gift?

Why I was feeling happy when he liked my gift?

Why did I feel sad when he talks about other girls?

Why did I feel jealous when he flirts with Sanjana?

And why I am getting hurt when he said I am just his colleague not his friend?

I Wish I Could Hate You

'Suma, is this your final decision?' asked my mother once again

'I told you many times.' I said

'He is a suitable match to you. Just because he wants to settle in Australia you are rejecting him'

'Amma. I am not interested in Australia. Moreover he plans to settle with his entire family. How can I leave you all and go there forever?'

My mother did not say anything. She looked at my father for help.

'Don't look at me. It is her decision. Is she is not willing there is no point in persuading her.' said my father

I turned to them

'Appa, it is fate of every woman to depart to her husband's house once married. That does not mean she has to get rid of her parents and family. Practically you both cannot accompany me to that country. How can I accept this? I am your daughter. I cannot leave you and settle there.'

'I told already that your decision is final. If you don't like we are not compelling you'

'Thank you Appa'

'I was eagerly expecting this alliance to get fixed. I did not expect this turn. Everything was fine with him' my mother lamented.

'Let us not talk about it further' I said to them

'We have discussed with another groom's parents is it not? Tell her about him' said my father

'Everything is fine with him except that he is six years elder to her. Is it ok for you?' asked my mother to me

‘Six seems so high’ I said

‘Even we felt the same. Large age difference was fine in our period. Nowadays you people are more adamant in age difference also.’

‘Better I will marry a guy who is younger than me’ I said to them and looked at my mother’s face.

‘Don’t talk rubbish’ yelled my mother. ‘Why are you bluffing like this? Don’t even dream of such things in your life? We are not living in such a society. This thinking looks so awkward. What is wrong with you?’

‘What is wrong in this, Amma? There are many people who have married guys younger than their age. You can take examples of Aishwarya Rai, Sachin Tendulkar and many other people.’

‘You are not a celebrity. They got married in unconventional way and there is no such rule we can follow their foot-steps’

‘What is wrong in it? Indian Penal code never mentions it as an illegal marriage’ I raised my voice.

‘Your thinking is wrong. Our society is not used to such cultures. Moreover our ancestors formulated rules of husband being elder than wife for a specific reason. It is not so easy to accustom with a person and live with them for long time. There should be physical balance and emotional balance between them’ explained my mother.

‘At one point of time men will not be psychologically matured. Women mature so early than men. A 27 year old man and 24 year old woman will have balanced emotions whereas 24 year man and 27 year old woman emotions will not be balanced. The same is applicable in physical balance also. I cannot explain about it to further. You find it by yourself’

‘Where there is a will there is a way. When the celebrities can live with that emotional balance why an ordinary person can't? By the way, celebrities are also human beings. They did not jump from the sky suddenly.'

'Don't argue with us Suma' screamed my mother. 'I don't like the way you speak. I am not encouraging these kinds of thoughts.' said my mother firmly.

Everything is finished. I thought of preparing my parents psychologically but everything turned upside down. Suma, all your feelings have no meaning. You cannot do anything in this.

My Monday started with irritation. It is not usual one which every employee in this world face rather I am irritated because I have meet that stupid. Even my father is supporting his statement. How I am going to face him as if nothing had happened. Had I was normal I could have let it go. But now when I developed unnecessary feelings for him which I am not supposed to. I cannot forgive him so easily.

He did not turn towards me like usual. You are showing your attitude to me. Even I have attitude and I can show it. The ice did not break for a long time. I turned towards his side. He was looking at something about his favorite star Ajith Kumar. He is an ardent fan of him. He was browsing through some pictures of that actor. I turned back to my desktop.

'Good Morning' I heard a terrific suspense voice from that guy sat in the next cubicle. He joined very recently and was occupying a seat in our cubicle. His name is Prakash

'Good Morning' I imitated him.

'You look so bright today' he said to me.

I looked at Ganesh. He was so busy in browsing his actor Ajith Kumar pictures. I got an idea at that moment.

'Yeah. I have a reason to celebrate' I said to Prakash and I looked at Ganesh. 'I got my marriage fixed'

Ganesh immediately turned towards me.

'Wow! That is great news' said Ganesh to me

Ganesh is happy to hear me getting married to someone. This expression created a pain in my heart. I thought he will feel sad on hearing about my marriage.

'Who is the groom?' he asked me

I got angry on him.

'He is a professor from New Delhi' I said with irritation

'So you will be leaving Delhi then?'

Again this happiness gave me a pain. Does not he supposed to feel sad on my departure from here?

'You are feeling so happy about my leaving?' I mocked him.

'Of course. Who will not be happy to hear when someone is getting married? And moreover after you leave I can expect a beautiful girl to occupy this place so that my days will go interesting'

When I heard him leaving the project and moving somewhere else I felt so sad but this guy is happy about my departure.

'When is the marriage?' asked Prakash

'Not fixed yet'

'Congratulations' said both of them. I did not like Ganesh wishing me for my wedding.

He is supposed to feel sad not happy on hearing my wedding news. This is not fair.

Stupid! You have unusually developed feelings for him. How come you can expect the same from him? He behaves normally like everyone and you find fault in every movement of him.

I smiled at both of them. A silence occupied in the cubicle for some time. I waited for Prakash to leave the place and I turned towards him.

'You are so happy about my departure from here, is it not?' I cannot control the anger in my voice.

'Why not? You are getting married. You are going to quit the company to migrate along with your spouse after marriage. It is good news.'

'Is it a good news for you? You will not feel bad about me quitting this organization. After all I am just your colleague not someone important to you.' I tried to speak indifferently but it did not work.

'You have started again' he voice showed irritation.

'Do you know how I felt bad right from that day? How cruel it was to hear such a statement from your mouth. You consider someone who is known for few weeks as your friend but you know me for more than year but I am after all your colleague'

'I never said after all. Don't add extra words as you like' he replied with anger 'You are not ready to understand what I tried to convey. I even apologized as you felt very bad. What else you want me to do? Do you expect me hold your legs and apologize once again'

'Even now you are not ready to understand what you told. You confessed in front of her that I mean nothing to you. Do you know how hurting it would be?'

'I did not mean like that'

'You said she is your friend and I am your colleague. What is the meaning of that?'

'Listen. According to me friends are someone with whom I share lot of comfort level. I never give any respect to my friends. Friends are someone with we can take a lot of advantage. They are the ones who will allow us to take them for granted. Can I take you for granted? Can I take advantage of you? I have a lot of respect for you and that is what I said'

'Oh! If this is your definition of friendship then you mean to say you will take advantage of Sanjana. You will take her for granted? You will not give any respect to her?'

'Sure. I will not give any respect to her. I don't have to give respect to her. She means nothing to me. I don't have to care how she thinks or how she feels about me.'

I am not convinced.

'I cannot break open my heart to show what kind of place I have for you in my heart. I have lot of respect for you, care for you and affection for both you and Ashwin. I cannot treat you both like I treat my other friends. This is what I meant.'

'Your definition of friendship is rubbish. You can have friends and you can respect them too. We don't know about your friendship definition and neither do that Sanjana. You have degraded my status in your life in front of her by giving more importance to her than me.'

'Don't just blame me alone. Even you did the same'

I gave a surprise expression.

'Don't stare. For how many days you know that Prakash? You shared the important information of your life to someone who you know for few months. Am I not the person who is supposed to know this first? You shared your happiness with him and not with me'

Mission successful

'Huh! Now can you realize what you did to me? You felt bad that I gave importance to him than you. You did the same thing with me on that day. Now understand how I felt on that day.'

'Alright. What you want from me? You want me to accept that you are more important to me than her, is it not? Don't worry. Next time when we all meet for the coffee break I will convey this to her. Happy now?'

I did not like the way he spoke. What I am expecting from him? I don't understand.

'I am sorry' I said to him 'I was so sad about your behavior and I burst in anger. All I did because I am valuing you more than others.'

'I can understand. I know, for you I mean something more'

Both of us grinned.

'Let me tell you something. No two swords can be in one sheath. I am not coming to coffee- break if Sanjana joins us. Whenever she is involved you are getting excited. You wanted to impress her and you are not caring about how others feel. Hence it is either we three of us or you three of you.'

'You are taking things too seriously' he said

'No. I am not backing off from this. I am not coming if she comes and she should not come if I am in. Deal?'

'Ok Deal'

Ashwin was out of office on that day. So we two of us alone went for coffee-break. I felt very bad and sad as we both of us started to fight frequently.

'I usually never share any bond with anyone especially with my colleague. I know attachments will lead to disappointments.'

'I accept your fact. It is not good thing to develop any kind of feelings. Especially with colleagues'

I looked at him with surprise.

'Do you know? I had break-up in my life'

This guy always has a habit of shocking me. Break-up? I cannot imagine.

'Before joining this company, I was working in a BPO for few months. She was my colleague there.' He said

'She was my very good friend. We had good rapport with each other'

'Who proposed first?' I asked him

'She proposed. One day she shed tears saying that I am not feeling as she feels for me. She is very much hurt by my behavior. She said she was not able to tolerate it. She said she wants me in her life forever'

'What did you say? You accepted immediately?'

'No. I did not feel the way as she felt at that time. I did not accept to it. I said 'ok' after a month'

'How long you have been in relationship?'

'Two years. We were madly in love with each other. I can say that I have not loved anyone in my life before that'

'Then why did you break?'

'It was not me. It was her who broke our relationship' he said with anger

'Why?'

'Because of bloody astrology'

I frowned

'I took our horoscopes for matching. I got to know my life will be in danger if we marry. When I said to her she broke up with me'

'What?' I exclaimed 'Two years of intimate relationship broke because of horoscope? Unbelievable' I said

'Yes but that is the truth' there was a bitterness in his voice

'I don't see this as a reason. Do you people believe those things so deep?'

'She told that her family will give lot of importance to horoscope matching. If there is no match, her parents won't consent for marriage'

'Did not you convince her in any way?'

'It is not just convincing. I begged her to not to go away from me but she was stubborn in her decision. I was not able to stop her'

I don't know what to say

'I even told her I will come and meet her parents. She did not consent to it. She told her parents will think badly of her if they come to know that their daughter was in relationship'

'Wasn't she aware of it while she proposed you?'

He smiled.

'I was not able to believe how could she do this to me? Do you know when I was in training I got ill one day. We both were in different cities. She travelled from her to the place where I was staying via bus. She called me standing outside my training center and told she came to meet me. I felt I am the luckiest guy in this earth.'

'Her parents were aware of this?'

'She lied to them and travelled far away to meet me. I cannot accommodate her anywhere. Hence I accompanied to her return for few kilometers and then returned to my place'

'How come a girl who loved in-depth broke up with you? I don't understand'

'Yes. It is the truth no matter you believe it or not'

A little tear droplet peeped from my eyes. I wiped it before he saw it.

'Her name?'

'Swati'

'When those things happened?' I asked him

'A year back.'

It was the time I joined in this company.

'Did not you contact her after that?'

'Why should I?' he asked angrily 'She broke up with me mercilessly and left me devastated. You cannot imagine how much my heart was broken when she left me'

I felt so sad for him.

'Some eight to nine months back I was with my friends on a trip. I got reminded of my love and break-up. I cried very heavily and tears rolled like water flowing from dam.

I usually never cry for anything. But it was just for few minutes. I convinced myself that I should not cry for her.'

I kept listening to him

'When this is the truth we have to accept it. I was not normal for few weeks after this breakup. I did not feel like working at all.'

I remember that cloud which I saw in his eyes when I joined this project team was not actually an imagination. This guy drowned himself into sorrow of his breakup. Now I understand.

'You never shown yourself affected by this much deep pain. You were so happy and cheerful'

'What else I can do? I don't believe in sharing my pain with everybody and make others to show pity on me. I thought the only way I can make myself happy is by making others happy'

'Do your parents know about your relationship?'

'It is a big war story.' He said 'When I opened up about my relationship with her to my family, everyone got shocked. Probably they might have not expected their son falling in love with a girl. My parents did not talk to me properly for many days. I tried to convince them for our marriage but they were not ready to accept us. However everything came to an end and I did not had to strain myself to convince them'

Something started to stir my abdomen. An astrology prediction separated a couple. It is a ridiculous thing. AS a matter of fact, I also believe in astrology but I never take it too seriously. My father used to say most of the astrologers have the habit of scaring us so they can earn money by suggesting any remedial solutions. May be astrologer whom he consulted might have said like this to scare him and make money. Why the girl took it so seriously? Even if there is threat to his life, can't it be rectified? Had it was me in her position I would have got ready to fight like a Savithri to save Satyawan's life.

I looked at the face of Ganesh and I felt so sad to see the pain in it. I have unnecessarily made him to recollect the unwanted things and made him to feel sad.

'I am sorry. I don't know what I can say' I told him.

'You don't have to. All are over. Nothing can be reversed. When I am not feeling sad why do you want to worry?' his tried to show indifference in his voice.

'I want to say one thing. I don't think that girl left you because of this horoscope issue. I feel she has found this as a reason to leave you. For example, she might have told her father about you and her father would have strongly opposed and threatened or her parents found some other potential groom than you or anything else. If she loved you truly she would have not cited this as a reason'

'Who cares? She left me and I don't want to analyze why she did like that. There is no use in crying for spilt milk'

He looked at his watch and said 'I got to go. One of my friends is performing on stage today. I have to attend it. Catch you later'

My heart started to feel heavy.

It took me a lot of time to return to normal mood. I don't know why I am feeling so bad for him. Is it out of sympathy or something else? I was not able to eat properly for some days. I was able to realize one thing for sure. Day by day my affection towards him increasing with drastic speed. It is disturbing my regular life very much. Nowadays I don't feel like talking to anyone around me rather I like to sink myself into the thoughts about Ganesh. I felt something pleases me when I think about him. Each and every minutes of day is occupied by his thoughts and actions.

I cannot exactly figure out when I started to feel like this but the feeling started to eat me like anything. After he opened up about his past break up the feeling for him in my mind doubled. I had a chance to know more about his love the same day when we met while we were returning to our home in train.

'I really don't want to make you feel bad but since you shared your story with me I am asking you' I asked him hesitantly

He smiled at me

'What if she comes again to you apologizing for her acts Will you accept her in your life?'

He smiled more

'What do you think I will do?' he asked

'That how do I know?' I asked with smile

He did not answer for a while

'I will never think of taking her back in my life. It is all over'

'What if she repents for her action?'

'I don't want to think about it. First of all she will not come again. I am sure about it. Even if she comes I am not interested. Once was quite enough' he said with irritation.

'Why do you think she won't come?'

'Do you know what happened before our break up? We finished our relationship over phone itself. She was not even interested to meet one last time before we finally split'

I did not say anything to it.

'She blamed for me for spoiling her life. She told me that I was the reason that she was not able to pursue her higher studies in abroad. How cruel it is!'

'What did you say for that?'

'I did not say rather I blasted. I taunted her like anything. How can she blame me for something I am not responsible. I did not stop her to pursue her higher studies.' He said angrily

'Did you meet her after your break up?' I asked

'Why should I?'

Good question.

'Did you at least saw her anywhere?'

'No. I don't have to see her. I have nothing to do with her.'

'I think you should know what she is doing now?'

'I don't think I have to'

'Do you still love her?'

'No'

'Then you have to definitely do this.'

'No need. I don't care where she is or how she is. I have self-respect which I cannot get rid for anyone in my life'

'I am suggesting you to do this because even if you have some feelings for her, if you know if she is married it will get washed away. You can be free.'

'I cannot do that. I cannot tolerate on knowing that she moved on with her life without any guilt. The very thought of imagining her as someone's wife will make me crazy' he said

I felt very bad to hear this. He still loves her.

'So you love her still?'

'No'

'Then there is nothing you have to feel jealous about. If you don't love her what bothers if she is someone's wife. Once you meet her you can get rid of all feelings for her'

'I am fine as I am now.' He said firmly

'You are cheating yourself' I told him

'May be. But there is nothing I am losing. You know one thing. Have you ever observed one thing with me?'

'What?'

'I used to get up from my seat one station ahead my actual station'

Even I do that usually. I always have the fear to missing my station and hence I used to stand one station ahead of my actual station. What is special in it?

'Is it so? I have not'

'Yes. I will stand like that and there is a reason for it'

'What reason?'

'That is the station where I and she have spent lots of quality time together. We meet mostly in that station. Whenever train crosses that station I will get reminded of all my memories with her there.'

I did not know how I smiled on hearing this. I felt like someone is squeezing my heart and sucking away all the blood from it. My stomach burned with jealousness and it was very hard for me to react normally on hearing them.

'I don't know about this' I said 'Even now you do it?'

'Even yesterday' he said casually and irked

I wish I could push him away from the train.

'I don't understand what you are gaining from this. Don't you think it is something ridiculous' I asked angrily

'I don't think. I had spent my time with her there and what is wrong is remembering it?'

'You are suffering the pain'

'No, I am not'

'You are wasting your time.'

'In 24 hours of a day, what I am going to lose just because I spend one or two minutes reminding my old memories'

'Again I am saying you are cheating yourself. It clearly shows you still love her. I think you can try your luck once again'

It was not easy for me to give this suggestion. No one can ever understand how possessive I felt when he spoke about how he loved that girl. I cannot control the jealousy which secreted in me.

'No way' he said firmly. 'Do you think I don't have self-respect at all?'

'There is nothing called self-respect in a true love'

'That is your opinion. You don't know how much I begged her to save our relationship. She did not listen to me at all. Why should I go and beg her again?'

'You are suffering out of pain' I said

'It is your assumption. I don't have any pain'

'I was able to see you pain when you told about your break-up.'

'Go and check any eye-doctor' he said with annoyance.

This topic is going weird. I think I have triggered pain once again. I have to do something. It is my responsibility to console him as I started the topic. It was because of me he is feeling about his past love.

'Alright! Let us talk about some other thing instead talking about this stupid girl. I don't want to argue further onto it' I said

What kind of reaction is that? Am I imagining or he is looking at me angrily for real?

'I don't like this' he said

'What?' I asked.

His voice was somewhat so scaring

'What you told about my girlfriend now?'

'What did I say?' I asked

'You told something about her just now.'

'I don't remember'

'You mentioned her as 'stupid''

'May be I have told. So what?'

'Don't say that again' he told

'Why?'

'I don't like it'

'Why?'

'I am not feeling good when someone scold my girlfriend. I will not encourage it' he said

'Are you getting angry on me for a girl who dumped you? She left you and hurt you. What is wrong if I scold her?'

'See, I am saying that I am not comfortable on hearing someone scolding her. Since it is the first time I am not making this as issue. I expect you to not to repeat it. I will not take it easily' he said angrily

What nonsense! He is getting mad at me. How can he do this to me?

'See, I scolded her because she left you. I felt bad for you. It is out of the care and affection on you I taunted her' I tried to console him.

I felt so bad on seeing him getting angry on me.

'I don't want you to care for me. I am there to care about myself. Just don't do it hereafter.'

'You are so mean. You are not concerned about how much I care for you' I asked him sadly

'Even she began saying that she cares for me. That care turned my life upside down. I am done with care and affection of everyone. I am fine with the care which I have for me. Moreover my parents are there to care about me. I don't want anyone to waste their care for me'

For the first time ever I have ever seen his ruder side. Somehow I did something and triggered his anger. I cannot tolerate the very thought of him angry on me.

'Alright! I am sorry.' I said to him

I did not turn towards him and looked at the window only.

'What you are angry on me now? He asked me

'No' I said

'No you are. I can see. If you get angry you won't look at the person's face.'

Even I do not know about this. I smiled at me. He knew one thing about me which I don't know. It made me happy.

'See, it is your duty to respect other people's feelings. Why are you taking things so personally?'

'You threw away my care and affection for you. You know how it hurts me'

'I did not mean to hurt you but at the same time I cannot express more politely than this. Seriously I don't want you to waste my time on me. I feel so bad when someone cares for me.'

'What is there to feel bad about?'

'See, you scolded my girlfriend out of the care you had which I did not like.'

'I don't see anything wrong in it. She left you and you still get angry for her. What makes you get mad at me if I scold her?'

'Yes it is. I feel since I am the person who is directly affected, I am the only one who has rights to scold her and not anyone else'

'But she left you' I reminded him firmly

'That is my problem'

Bloody hell! What kind of a creature you are!

'I am not talking about it again. I am sorry' I said angrily

'You are getting angry for small things. Let us close this chapter now. You are getting hurt very easily'

'You are hurting me very easily' I replied angrily

'Ok, I am sorry. Happy now?' he asked

I reluctantly nodded like 'Ok'. I was not able to hold my anger for a long time and I started to laugh.

'You should not get angry on me if I say something bad her. You have to allow that is how I will understand you value me'

'I cannot accept that. Again I am saying that I was the one who got affected by her and not you. I have the rights. If you want me to be friendly with you please don't do it?'

So the girl who dumped him is still more important to him than the one who cares and shows affection on him. I felt so sad. But on the other hand the respect which I had for him grown further. He is surely a great lover.

'Why are you laughing?'

'I cannot say that to you. May be one day when I leave this company I will tell on that day.' I said

'No. Tell right now' he insisted

'You will take me wrongly'

'No I won't. Come one, tell me. No suspense'

I gave a pause and looked at him. I again laughed.

'Had you been elder than me, I would have married you?' I told him

My heart started to beat fast. How he is going to react for this? Or he is going to get angry? What if he scolds in front of everyone here? God please save my honor.

Thank God he did not as I scared. I was surprised on seeing him smile

'Thank God! It did not happen' he teased

'What do you mean by thank God? Am I such a bad looking girl?' I asked him with fake anger.

'No. I did not mean like that. I cannot manage a girl like you. That is why.' he teased me.

'This is even more damaging. You are hurting me'

'See. That is why I say. If I we are together, I have to spend my day in saying sorry alone and you have to spend your day getting hurt.'

I laughed on this. He stood up from the seat. I saw the station and it was the same station which he told that he used to spend his time with his girlfriend. I gave a scorching glare at him. Had I got super powers he would be turned into ashes.

I felt very sad on his behavior. His heart still beats for a girl who dumped him a year back. How lucky she is! He does not even care to hurt people around him for her. I can surely say one thing. I don't know why did she dump him but it is her most terrible mistake of her life.

Nowadays the world around me has become so boring. Nothing around me interested. I was so sad for no reason and I did not find anything which could make me happy. My daily routine continued with waking up in the morning, brushing, bathing, eating, commuting to office and then again getting back home, eating and sleeping.

Reading books used to be my hobby. I stopped reading books and hated it like anything. I am an ardent fan of Hindi television soaps. I watch them mainly for the costumes and accessories which the women used to wear. Even it failed to make me happy. I used to watch Hollywood movies during my leisure time. I am very fond of the screenplay and CG used in their movies. It failed to entertain me. I used to sleep a lot when I feel bored but the very thought of sleep makes me angry. Even the delicious food failed to cheer me up. I lost interest in hearing music, watching TV, reading books and magazines and I even hated to meet people around me. I wanted to shout at anyone who come and talk to me. The only thing which makes me happy is the very thought of him. I felt happiness whenever I recall all the conversations we used have at our office.

There is no use in asking the 'Why' questions as I knew the answer already. When I realized the reason I did not feel happy. It was from that day my darker days started in my life. I lost all the joy which I had in my life.

It was not easy for me handle the truth. I got shocked when I realized what is going on inside me. I told myself several times that it is not possible. I cannot happen with me. This is not something I can encourage.'

No use. I am slowing losing my control over my mind. The more I suppress my thoughts and feelings, the more I felt the suffering and stress. Some feelings are not meant to be shared with the people around us. Love stress is an important among them. It was first time ever I have come across the negative feeling in my life and I struggled very hard to handle it.

'Suma, do you like this ear ring?' asked my mother to me

Had I was in a normal mood it could have surely impressed me. I was not in a position to admire it.

'Looks nice' I replied without any interest.

'Do you want to buy any more ear rings? Just have a look at these rings. I feel that ear droppings would suite you well.' said my mother and she looked at everything with excitement.

Nothing seemed to impress me and interest me. I stood like a robot beside her and tried to take part in her excitement.

'It was long time we planned to buy the silver container. I think the price is reasonable. Let us finish the purchase' said my mother.

I got irritated with this plan. I wanted to go home and immerse myself in the thoughts of him.

'Suma, come and have a look at this?' said my mother. I did not take much interest to see the stuff.

'We have chosen this container. I will present it to you for your marriage' she said with excitement.

I got angry on her. Why is she speaking about my marriage all the time? The talk of my marriage makes me crazy which no one understands. I don't want to get married to anyone.

'Suma, look here' my mother pointed to some things in the display area. 'When your marriage gets fixed, I have to buy all these silver stuffs for you. They are generally kept in the nuptial night room of the couple' she gave a mischievous look.

I got angry on her

'Is this the way you talk with your daughter? Indian mothers never tease their daughters like this. I feel so bad.' I yelled at my mother

'I just made fun of you. Why you are getting angry for this?' my mom yelled at me again. 'What is wrong with you Suma? I have observing you for a long time. You are not showing interest in anything. We came to this jewelry shop to buy ear rings for you but you are not showing any interest in it. Even now you are not excited about what we bought. Why you are always so sad and worried?'

What can I say to this? I know the reason for my behavior but I cannot share it to her. I cannot imagine how she will react if I say why I am abnormal.

'Suma, I don't want you to be like this. Come and have a look here. You can choose anything you want. We will get it for you' said my mother.

'I don't want any of these things' I said with irritation 'All I want is happiness in my life'

My mother did not say anything after that and she continued to look into the stuffs in the jewelry box. Even after returning home she did not ask me anything. I started to long for solitude.

'Excuse me Boss' said Ganesh 'please have this. I am cordially inviting you my family function coming Sunday'

He gave the invitation card to him.

'And this is for you' he said to me and gave a card to me.

'I think let us ask what gift we can buy for him.' I told Ashwin 'We can buy something which he intended to buy for a long time'

'I wanted to buy a car' said Ganesh

'I will not buy you even a toy car' teased Ashwin 'We have to first decide the budget. We will decide later. Is it possible for you to buy the gift?'

'I don't think so. I will try anyway' I spoke as if I am not interested to strain for him.

'I don't think so. Let me try after it is the family function of our team member.' I spoke as if I am not interested to strain for him.

I took the responsibility with utmost happiness. I found myself so happy when I do something for him. I know the happiness is short lived and has no meaning but I don't want to lose it. I don't want to miss a single chance to offering my service to him. No matter how many days we will be together, until then I have to let it continue.

I tried my level best to buy suitable gift for him so that on seeing it every time he will get reminded of me. Out of all the gifts I found, one floral bouquet attracted me a lot. On the previous night of the function day, I felt so excited about meeting his family.

Stupid! Why you are so nervous and enthusiastic as if you are going to meet them to become their daughter-in-law? You are going there just as colleague not as his girl-friend.

I did not like when my conscience pointed the actual truth to me.I am not his girlfriend but what is stopping me to think myself as his girlfriend and attend the function?

On the day of the function I was not able to take my eyes from him. Where ever he went my eyes followed him. He looked so cool in the usual traditional costume of Dhoti and a red shirt. He looked like a groom to my eyes. The ceremonies got over and photographers were clicking pictures of family members. I too wanted to stand one among them beside him.

Day dreaming is not good for health. The sole right of standing beside him for the family picture is meant to some other lucky girl in this world and definitely it is not me.

I can very well realize how much I have changed in last few months. Everything has turned upside down. I cannot believe if it is me doing all the things. Why I am doing this? I know it is not correct. Developing feelings for a guy who is younger than me. If any one finds about my secret I will lose my respect. I am not in a position to think about it. I have bitten by the love bug. I am not able to find the cure for that but the actual truth I don't want to cure that. What if he finds out that I have this kind of feeling for me? He may feel so bad or he may think badly about me. May be he will feel bad about himself for behaving in such a way that triggered this wrong feeling. No, I cannot think of degrading myself in front of him. This is my secret feeling which belongs only to me. Until it remains within me, I am not going to lose anything.

No, this is not correct. You have open up your feelings to him. Let him decide if he wants to pursue or not.

How it this possible? Who will like to date a woman who is elder than him? He is not going to accept it anyway. When I know the result why should I make this dangerous attempt?

What if he accepts your proposal?

What if he does not accept? I will lose my respect.

You should try once.

No. I am fine as I am. I know I will lose.

You lose really when you don't try

I don't want to try.

You have to

No, I won't

You will regret later

I am not cared

Try once

No

Only once

No

I threw the purse in my hand outside the cafeteria out of rage. I did not notice people standing behind me. It took me sometime to realize the surrounding and where I am. I looked at Ashwin who was wondering about my behavior. I controlled myself and took my purse back. I was not in a position to talk with any of them right now. I ran from that place as quickly as I can. It took some time for me come back to normal.

'Are you alright?' heard a voice from the side. It was Ashwin

I nodded like 'No'

Ashwin sat beside me.

'I am watching you for past few days. I can very well see something is eating you. If you can share with me, you can' said Ashwin

I wished someone would hear all grieves in my heart.

'Is everything fine at your side?' asked Ashwin

'I am not mentally stable. I am in lot of stress' I told him

'If you are willing to share your problem I am fine with that. I am ready to listen' he said

I hesitated for a while but it is not time for that. I cannot struggle with the secret with me alone anymore. I don't care how he thinks of me.

'I am in love with a guy. I am not able to express it. That is my problem' I said

'Why do you think so? May be he can accept'

'He won't. No man in this world would'

'You are so sure about it?'

'The guy is younger than me. This is not something allowed in our society.'

'You are not talking about Ganesh is it not?'

I got shocked on this question. He managed to guess the person in a single clue. I looked at him with scare. He smiled.

'Why you are so much stressing yourself for these silly things?' he teased me.

'I have not come across this kind of situation. I feel so bad about myself. I have fallen for a guy younger than me. I think I have some psychological problem' my voice broke down and tears rolled down from my eyes.

'Sumana, there is nothing you have to feel guilty about. The feelings are so natural. Every human being somehow or other feels it on someone. This feeling has no caste, creed, religion or age and nowadays there is no sex restriction also' he said and we both laughed.

'As far as I have observed I don't think that guy feels the same as you do. So there is no point in thinking about it further. You have make up your mind and move on. Why do you want to invest your time on him?'

I did not say anything.

'Again I am saying there is nothing you have to be guilty about or ashamed. It is a natural feeling. We have to decide how we should handle this. You are aware that this is not accepted by our society right now. Few years later, falling or marrying younger guy can become so common but not now. Instead of stressing yourself better let it go and get back to normal.'

Get back to normal. It is not as easy as it is said. I have to get rid of all the feeling which I developed in myself. I should not allow the feeling to grow further. Had I was able to do this already why I am suffering now like this?

'Are you getting my point? When you cannot change something you have to accept it. You yourself know that it can happen between you too. Then why do you want to stress yourself and suffer. The more soon you accept it, the more it will be good for you'

I nodded my head as 'Ok'

'Let me say something. No one in this world can hurt us. It is us who actually hurt our self. We have to decide to whom we should give the power to hurt us. Stop hurting yourself and start to live your life.'

'Yes'

'Are you alright now?'

'Somewhat'

'Then come on. We have lot of work to do' he said

'Thank you Ashwin for listening to me patiently and helping me' I said

'Only then you will concentrate on your work. We have a delivery today is it not?' he teased

I smiled. I knew he is kidding. I was very grateful to him as in the current world no one cares to hear the grief of the people around them. Being my colleague he don't have to listen to my sorrows and pain yet he spent his time for me. My respect for him grew a lot.

He is right. I should not stress myself on something which I cannot change. I have to get rid of all the feelings which I have developed for him. Ashwin should be first and last person who knew my deeper heart.

I should not share my secret to anyone else and especially Ganesh should never know this.

It was not easy for me to follow my decision. The more I tried to suppress my feelings for him the more it grew. Each and every minute of mine is consumed by the thoughts of this guy. I am trapped in the love net. I hated myself for being like this. When I tried to control my feelings I felt my head start to ache and explode. I was able to realize that I have lost myself completely.

'I am not feeling well. I am leaving home now' said the hero.

I wanted to give my care and affection for him. I was about to open my mouth to subscribe some remedy for his illness but I stopped in the middle. It is not my concern. He has lot many people to take care of him at his home. I felt like getting headache as I once again tried to suppress my emotions.

'Do you like to join for coffee?' I asked him

'Why not?' he said

I felt happy. I know I cannot be with him forever at least I can save the memories of the moments with him. I am not going to lose even single chance of spending my time with him of course as a friend.

'Can I ask you one thing and you should not get mad at me?' he said

How can I get mad at you?

'Sure I will get angry.' I said

'Ok. Let me not ask'

'Alright! Ask'

'I can see that something is eating you. Is there anything that I can do to help you get out it?'

Only you can do something to get me out of what is eating me.

'There is nothing that you can do' I said

'May be I can give a try. You can share to me your problem. I can give you solution'

I smiled. I ordered a coffee and he ordered a sugarcane juice.

'You finish your coffee and we can share this juice' he said

I wish I could share everything with you.

'Now tell me your problem. I will solve it'

I gave a mocking look at him

'Sure I can give. You know I am professional psychologist'

I laughed. What I can say to him? I wanted to say to him that you are the root cause of all my stress and tension. How he will react if I say that?

'I am in love with a guy. I cannot marry him. At the same time I am not in a position to marry anyone whom my parents choose. This is my problem. What solution you think you can give to this?' I asked him

He thought for a while

'Why do you think you cannot marry him? Is he from different religion or caste and your parents won't accept?' he asked

'In order to marry him, first he should consent. I know he won't'

'You are already aware of that then why do you want to stick to that guy?' he asked

I did not answer

'Who is he? Any of your school friend or college friends?'

I wanted to shout it is 'You'

'Forget it. It doesn't matter' I said

'Don't get angry on me. I will surely say you are wasting your time. When I see you I get reminded of one of my friend.'

'Similar to you she fell in love with one of my friend and she even got permission from her family to marry him but the main person who should consent did not love her at all. The girl is so persistent about marrying him but the guy is not at all interested. She is not changing her mind and vows to win his love and marry him. How funny it is!' he said

I felt so sorry for that girl. I am not the only fool in this world and lot many existing in this world already.

'You persistence sounds similar to her and funny. Somehow you know you cannot marry him. I think you better move on'

What an idea, Sirji! I got this advice from one person who is elder than me and one person who is younger than me. Only a new born is left to give this advice.

'We should feel like loving someone when we meet them. That guy is not having any feeling for her yet she is stubborn. I have already you how I loved Swati but she left me. That does not mean I will not fall in love again. I will sure fall in love with someone whom I feel like loving'

I smiled.

'So you will fall in love once again in your life?' I asked

'Sure. As I said if I feel like loving that girl'

'What if a girl comes to you and proposes you? Will you accept her?'

'If I like her, I will accept'

'If you don't like her, how will you express it?' I asked with nervousness. Why I am asking this question him. The conversation is going in dangerous path.

'I will say I am sorry.'

'Politely or harshly'

'Politely. I cannot be harsh to her'

'Will you continue to be her friend even after you reject her?' I asked

'Why not?

'You will not ill-treat her. You will be normal with her?'

'I will be very friendly to her'

Suma, please don't do it. Control your tongue. Run away from the place.

'You asked who the guy is, isn't it.' I asked looking at his eyes straight. I can very feel my heartbeat rate going rapid like a race horse.

'Yes'

'It is you' I said and I did not stay there even for a single second after that. I ran as fast as my legs could carry me.

I started to sweat as if I had ran ten kilometers in one minute. I cannot believe what I did. I exposed the important secret of my life to the person who is not supposed to know it. Now what am I going to do. I have spoiled everything.

Stupid! What the hell you have done? How can you ever face him again? He is your colleague and he is seated beside you and how awkward he may feel on seeing you. Suma, you have spoiled everything. You are unfit to maintain secrets. Everything is finished. Your honor, your reputation, your respect ... He already told he respects me a lot. From today onwards everything is gone.

My mobile phone ranged. It was him. No way. I am not attending the call. I am sure he is going to scold me in all the bad words in the language. I disconnected the call. The phone ranged again. What I am supposed to do? Should I talk or disconnect again? I got so tensed and my heart bet so fast.

Suma, you have sowed and it is you who should reap. Attend the call and get the scolding from him.

I pressed the 'answer' button.

'Hey, look if you are going to scold me I will disconnect the call now' I said

'Why did you run so fast?' he said 'Did I not say I will share the juice with you after your coffee? I was waiting with the juice for you but you vanished.'

What he is saying? Did not hear what I said or he is kidding me?

'I am sorry. I behaved very foolishly. Please don't take it seriously. Forget it' I told him.

It was the worst moment ever in my life.

'It is ok. No problem.' He said

I got my breathe back.

'I am leaving now. We will talk about it later' he said 'You should have tasted the sugarcane juice. Do you know how delicious it was! You missed it'

I smiled. He is definitely a sweet guy. He is consoling me and making me feel comfortable. No wonder my heart fell for him.

'See you tomorrow' he said

The call got disconnected. Now what should I do? Feel happy or feel sad? What did I do? I proposed him or just exposed my feelings? What is going to happen?

I was trying remind when I got scared this much in my life. I am scared of a man who is younger than me. I should ashamed of myself. As a matter of fact, I did not do anything wrong nor I behaved indecently with him in public. All I did was just expressing my feeling for him. Did I do the correct thing or not? What did I gain out of it?

'Are you in this world, Madam' asked Ashwin

I smiled.

'Yes Sir'

I know the reason of my fear. I am afraid because I fear to lose him. It is not silly fear. He does not belong to me how I am supposed to lose something which is not mine.

Message tone popped in my mobile. Message from him in WhatsApp. Once again my heart started to beat fast. Why is he messaging now? I opened the application with all the fear of the world.

The message read

Ganesh: You are so clever. You cross verified with me on how I would react and then expressed your feelings. On that day in train when you said that you would have married me if I was elder than you I got disturbed a little. Today you disturbed me a lot

Sumana: I did not propose you. I just told you my thoughts. I know it is a waste of time. I liked a person who thinks like me

Ganesh: How can you think that I will scold you? Do you think I can do that? What to do? I born after you.

Sumana: I don't know how you will react. I may have become cheap in your eyes now. But I am relieved from the burden of hiding the truth from you.

Ganesh: Is it how you have known me? I felt so bad when you said I will scold you. I would have not scold you even if you said 'I Love you Ganesh'

Sumana: But I am feeling so bad. I misbehaved with you. Sorry.

Ganesh: I feel happy that you were relieved from unwanted burden.

I got relived on seeing his messages. He is a nice guy for sure. How many men could react so decently after this much happened.

Sumana: Don't feel bad for these silly things. I will not like if you feel in front of me. To be honest I got shocked at first. But I am happy to know that you like me so much. Thanks for that. Now I don't feel the difference between the Sumana in the display picture and one I am chatting with.

I smiled at the message. I had one of my childhood picture as my display picture for my profile

Ganesh: You have a heart of a kid. I will never consider you as a cheap. I am happier to have a friend like you. Tomorrow as usual talk to me with smile.

Sumana: It is ok. You have said sorry in a polite and decent way. It will take a long time to accept the bitter truth. I am not lucky enough.

Ganesh: Truth is I am not lucky to be your guy.

Sumana: You are a nice guy. That is why even though I knew you are younger to me I feel for you.

Ganesh: No. It is me who is unlucky. I am not as nice as you think. Every one of us have darker side. Even I have one.

Sumana: Why? Are you womanizer?

Ganesh: No.

Sumana: Are you a drunkard?

Ganesh: Not at all

Sumana: According to me these factors measure darker side of a man.

Ganesh: I am not as good as you think

Sumana: I don't care. I don't know why I wanted to buy you a gift for your birthday. When you said you liked it, I felt very happy. When you told Sanjana is your friend but I am your colleague I felt very sad. I think that is how my feelings started to develop.

Ganesh: I think I should have not opened about Swati. I think this feeling is out of sympathy you have one me.

Sumana: No. Swati is not the reason. It started much before. Do you know why I got mad on you on that day? It is because I was not able to tolerate that Sanjana is more important to you than me.

Ganesh: It is a waste of time for you thinking about me. Don't follow your heart. Follow your brain. I don't want you to get into unwanted pain. I like you and I care for you.

Sumana: I know I have degraded myself as low as possible. Why do you think it will not work between us? Is it because of Swati?

Ganesh: Swati is one of the reasons. Important reason is I cannot manage you. I never take things seriously. But you are not like that. Chances of us breaking up is more.

He says Swati is one of the reason. Jealousy again started in myself.

Sumana: I am so angry on Swati. Had she married you I would have developed feelings for you. I would have not been bluffing like this.
Ganesh: You felt so much and you are saying it as bluffing?
Sumana: Had you accepted these are feelings. Since you are rejecting these are bluffs. I am real fool. Remember there is always a place for you in my heart.
Ganesh: I did not reject you. We are not in America. We are in India and that too south side. How it is possible?
Sumana: I have to confess one other thing. It was me who took your key chain.
Ganesh: OMG
Sumana: I know it is silly. I know I cannot have you in my life and so I thought of start collecting your memories. Sorry again for behaving like this
Ganesh: Ha! Ha! No problem. Leave it.
Sumana: I will return your keychain tomorrow. I still feel like I am in dream. I don't know how I opened my mind and told you this. Let me complete my mission properly so that I don't have to regret later. I Love you Ganesh

Ganesh: Oh No. Is this my colleague Sumana? I cannot forget this day. Thanks for everything
Sumana: Ok.

The WhatsApp status turned from 'online' to 'last seen'. I can surely say this is the best and most memorable day in my life.

'Hello Madam' called Ashwin

I came back to earth on this call. For a while I was not able to realize where I am.

'What happened?' he asked 'your face looks so bright'

My face turned red.

'I told him' I said

'Oh'

What kind of expression it is?

'What happened?' I asked

'I think you should have not.' he said

'Why?'

'Just thought of saying' he then turned back to his work.

Why is he saying like this? It is too late to think about. I expressed my feeling to him and he forgave me. Chapter closed. I should not think about it again. I have to return the keychain to him.

How nice it would have been had he was elder than me and there was no one in his life before. Everything would have been great in my life.

I felt my mind turned so light like a feather. I pray to God that we both of us should not fight for anything and hate each other at any cost.

Ganesh did not recover the next day and did not come to office. I placed the keychain back in his place. I felt my day was so dull on that day without hearing his voice and without seeing his cute little smile. Though we settled down the matter forever, I still had some fear on how to face him.

'Your face look so bright today? Anything special?' asked my mother during our dinner.

What can I say for this? If I say the truth... No. She is very proud about her daughter and her character. Let me not spoil it. When this feeling has no future why should I worry her?

'Nothing special' I said

'When I see you like this, I feel so happy. Always keep smiling like this' she said

IT is true. The feeling love and being loved makes a person the most happy in the world. Even though I am not loved by him, the very thought of him makes me smile.

My mobile sounded the notification tone. My face so bright on seeing the sender that entire city can be brightened. It is from Ganesh. I did not know I would feel this much happy when I get message from him.

Ganesh: Hi

Sumana: Hi

Ganesh: Too bad. You have confused me. I am in dilemma.

Sumana: For what?

Ganesh: It is not the first time I am dealing with women elder than me. I somehow have to

express few things about you which was in my mind.
Sumana: What is that?
Ganesh: you should not get angry
Sumana: No. I won't
Ganesh: I had different feelings for you. I feel so shy to say what it is

What does he mean by different feeling?

Sumana: What is that different feeling?
Ganesh: you are matured girl. Don't make me to say everything. Understand

The word 'different' has lot many meaning. Which meaning I should take?

Ganesh: I have called women who are elder than me as sister but somehow I did not feel like calling you like that.

What a coincidence! There were days where I used to get scare at him. On the day of Raksha Bandhan I got scared whether he would ask me to the tie the sacred thread on his hand like his elder sister. Thank God still South side of India does not follow the practice non-South Indian festivals.

Sumana: Why you did not want to call me as sister
Ganesh: I told you isn't I had different feelings for you. If I say what it is you will lose all respect for me

What feeling it could be? Does he want to say he has love feeling? Not possible.

Ganesh: I have to say one thing. According to me, love is something which is meant to end in marriage. But in our case it is not possible
Sumana: Yes. It is known truth
Ganesh: What can we do?
Sumana: You have to say.
Ganesh: Even if I fall in love with you I cannot say 'I love you'. That is my problem
Sumana: Ok. What can we do?
Ganesh: We can be together as long as we can and part away when our path comes. Is it fine for you?
Sumana: I don't get you
Ganesh: I like you a lot. But we cannot be together. We are not meant to be together.
Sumana: Do you mean 'Friends with Benefits'
Ganesh: No. We can be together and close but within limits.

Seriously this is an unexpected offer. I can spend my quality time with him until I get married. I will not regret in my life later.

Sumana: You mean to say we can be close till I get married?
Ganesh: Not till you get married till you get engaged.

There are no words to express how happy I felt at that time. I cannot afford to lose even a single second of my life from now on. I wish I could preserve these seconds in my life somehow.

Sumana: Done. But we should not expose it when we are in cubicle. We have to be normal as usual and we can chat as we like in WhatsApp. Is it ok?

Ganesh: Done

I prayed God that my marriage should get delayed at least for six months.

The next morning it was so difficult for me to face him directly and say a 'hi'. Either of us showed our feelings in our cubicle. I now got reminded of my first day in this company and the orientation happened on that. No employee is supposed to behave unprofessionally no matter even if they are husband and wife. When licensed couple denied romance rights, non-licensed couple should not even think about it. We are not even non-licensed couple rather temporary illegal couple. Not even a couple.

WhatsApp message popped in my mobile. Nowadays I feel as I am living every second to receive message from him.

Ganesh: I wanted to give something.

Sumana: What?

Ganesh: You have to turn back to see it

I turned back towards him. He smiled at me showing the thing in his hand. It was the key-chain. The same key-chain which I stole and returned to him.

Sumana: That was the gift of your friend, is it not?

Ganesh: It is ok. You took and returned. I thought of giving it to you by myself

Sumana: Thank you so much. This is the best memory I can have from you. I wanted to ask you a question

Ganesh: Yes

Sumana: Do you like me or not? I have heard about accepting a relationship or rejecting a relationship. Third kind I have heard is 'Friends with Benefits'. What kind of relation this is?

Ganesh: I like you but I cannot marry you. This is the truth. You have to accept it.

Sumana: Your parents won't accept is your concern. Assuming that your parents accept me. Will you love me? I don't care if we marry or not. I want to know what kind of feeling you have for me. I will be happy at least I was able to impress a guy and win his heart in my lifetime.

Ganesh: I know you as my senior staff. I have not seen you as a lover. I don't what kind of a woman you are. Hence I cannot say that I love you or not. As I said already, love is something which is meant to end in marriage. We cannot marry and I won't call it as love.

What a confusing answer! What is he trying to convey? He likes me but does not love me. His feeling for me is not love because he according to him we cannot marry. I can understand one thing. This is fourth kind of relationship 'Friends without Benefits'

Ganesh: I like the way this is going. I feel like I am a celebrity

Sumana: Celebrity?

Ganesh: I feel so happy and energetic when I realize that I am loved madly by a girl. Thanks to you.

Sumana: But you are not giving that happiness.

Ganesh: I said I like you is it not?

Sumana: But you are not saying I Love you

Ganesh: I told you already.

'What is this, Sumana?' heard the voice from the side.

Ashwin was looking at me.

'I am frequently seeing you with mobile. Please focus on the work' he teased me.

'Yes' I said and got back to work.

Ganesh: Ha! Ha! Carry on with your work. I will message later.

I smiled. If I had the power to freeze the time, I will surely not let the moments pass through my life and become my past. I have seen how people become so mad when they are in a relationship. This is a fake relationship. No it is not a relationship at all. Yet I am feeling so happy. How much happiness would be in a real emotional relationship! Now I understood why Aradhana and Shradhdha were so stubborn and persistent of not letting their relationship break and made them to take extreme steps.

'Sumi, it is getting late. I have a meeting early morning today. Hurry up'

'Yeah. Just five minutes.'

'I cannot wait for even two minutes' he was taking his bag and car key'

'Hey, wait a minute. Drop the girl to her bus stop. I will make her ready in two minutes'

'I cannot do it today. You drop her' he was in hurry

'Come on. Don't you know I have to take care of the baby? It is already late for his food. Just two minutes. I will get her ready'

He looked at me with irritation.

'What?' I asked 'I am asking you drop your own daughter to school not some neighbor's child. Don't give me that stare. Is your job is more important than your daughter?'

'Today my job is important than my daughter. You get it' he yelled at me.

I smiled

'Alright! Just two minutes.'

'Only two minutes. Then I will fly away. Got it? Already one minute passed by'

A baby crying sound is heard from the room inside. I looked at him with scare. His face turned red like a tomato. Now what should I do? I have to beg him more.

'Please cradle the baby sweetheart. If I go there, I cannot attend the girl' I begged him.

'That is it. I am leaving. You do anything to manage your kids'

'That is not fair. They are your children too. You are their father. Is it not your responsibility to take care of them?' I asked him angrily

'I was not ready for this at all. Marriage is a big burden and moreover you made me to father two kids at a very young age. People are raising their eyebrows when they come to know I am married with two children'

'Oh, come one. You know world's youngest father was thirteen years old. He takes care of his kid with more love and affection than you. And I did not make you a father by myself.' I mocked him

He tried to hide his smile with an angry look but I saw his eyes sparkled before he changed it

'Your one minute is running out. I swear I will leave in forty seconds' he warned

'Ok! Ok!'

I gave one final touch up to my daughter's hairdo and took her school bag.

'Come on, baby, come-on. It is getting late for your dad.'

I handed over the girl and her belongings to him. He carried her and ran as fast as he could.

'Bye baby' I said to them.

He did not say a bye to me. I felt little sad. Nowadays he is so focused on his job and he has forgotten that he has a wife who loves him a lot. I turned away to attend the little guy in the room.

Hey! What is that? Something is grabbing my hand so fast and something is pressed in my cheeks. It is a kiss. I wondered for a second before I realized who is standing in front of me.

'Bye. Love you' he said and ran away once again.

I felt so delighted.

'Love you too' I said

I closed my eyes to feel the kiss once again.

I was not able to open my eyes at all. Somehow managed to open the eyes and looked at everything around me. What is this? Where is the cradle? Where is the baby? Where are my daughter's school things? Where am I now?

I was lying down in my bed and the room is semi-dark with the light ray of sunlight passing through the window. I am in some room at some house. Whose house is this?

It took me some seconds to realize that I am at my own home. I saw my parents sleeping near to me.

It is a dream. Clock showed time as 6.05 am. I had dream of having a family with my beloved. I am married to him and parenting two children, a daughter and a son.

I can say that it was the best dream I ever had in my life. I wish my dream could come true. I felt sad. Day-dreams never come true. It is going to be a dream forever. I am visioning a life of some lucky girl in my dream. He would have dreamed the same kind of life with Swati when he was in relationship with her. It remained a dream for him too. Who knows if destiny turns things may be his dream can come true.

I took my mobile and checked if I had received any messages from him. For past few days I have got addicted to WhatsApp. Once in five minutes I started to check the messenger.

There is a message from him. I got it around 1.30 AM. He was awakening till midnight.

Ganesh: Slept?

What else I would do at 1.30 AM? I should have been awaken and replied him. This is not going to last long. One day I am going to stop receiving messages like these. The very imagination of that scene made me horrified. I am developing too much of feelings for him daily. What am I going to do?

Suma, just stop over-thinking. Live your day today. You are happy on seeing his message. Enjoy this second and you will never get it back. In a few minutes, I am going to meet him. Time was 6.15 am. I have still one three hours to see his face. Why the clock is too slow today?

I dropped a message for him

Sumana: Good Morning

He was awake at mid-night and he would be sleeping now.

Time showed 8.00 am. I boarded the train in my station. The train stopped at his station. I was looking for him but I was not able to see. I looked at my WhatsApp. The tick mark turned in blue color. He has seen my message but did not reply. I felt so sad. It was very much enough to spoil my entire mood for the rest of journey. What is he going to lose if replies my message?

I frequently checked my WhatsApp. One or two times his status was online but he did not message me at all. I got angry on him. I switched off my mobile data then. I am not going to talk with him today.

I did not say 'hi' to him and carried on with my work. The IM popped up in my screen

Ganesh Shankar: Come to WhatsApp

All the anger I had for him for past few minutes had vanished like a snow exposed to sun. I switched on my mobile data. Notification popped up

Ganesh: Good Morning. What doing?

I felt like thousand roses fell around me in few seconds.

Sumana: Hi, I had switched of my mobile data. Saw your message now only.
Ganesh: It is ok. Are you busy now?

This is what we call it as fate. I was fully loaded with work. If Ashwin sees me with my mobile sure he will not hesitate to break it even. The little time which I got in my life is running out.

Sumana: Yes. It is ok. I will manage. Actually I wanted to ask you one thing. I don't know how you will take it. You should not get me wrong.
Ganesh: I won't.

I felt little hesitant and embarrassed but I cannot afford to miss the chance.

Sumana: No. You will get me wrong. I cannot ask from you
Ganesh: Tell me.
Sumana: A kiss?
Ganesh: In hands?
Sumana: No.
Ganesh: Cheeks?
Sumana: No
Ganesh: then?
Sumana: Lips
Ganesh: OMG. Is it my TA talking to me like this?
Sumana: No. It is Sumana
Ganesh: you are making me to feel shy.
Sumana: It is ok. Just kidding. No need
Ganesh: My morals is stopping me
Sumana: I told it is OK. No problem

The conversation had to interrupt as my manager called me to meet me. It was a new experience for me. I had never asked like to anyone before. I cannot believe if it was me who dared to speak to a guy like this.

I was gathering all my happy moments in my life every second. This is not something I would get in my life again. We behaved like normal colleagues in front of everyone and like lovers in Instant messenger. Had I not told my feeling to Ashwin he could have not definitely found out what was going on between us. Life was so beautiful for me. I was the happiest woman in this world. On that day it was the most memorable and peak day of my life which gave me the ultimate happiness of the life.

It was Friday. The next two days I am not going to meet him. I wanted to jump the Saturday and Sunday in time machine. Let me not spoil my Friday now. It was during the evening when no one was present in the cubicle.

'Can we go for a walk?' I asked him

He blinked for a while. He looked so hesitant.

'Don't worry. I will not rape you' I teased him.

He smiled

'Why not?' he said

We went for a walk in the campus area. As usual my heart started to capture the memorable moments. He walked with me but he maintained a distance from me.

'Can you hold my hand?' I asked him

He got surprised and hesitantly held my hand.

I got angry on that hold.

'Leave the hand. It is better you keep away' I said

'Why? What happened?'

'I don't feel your touch at all.' I complained to him

He grinned. He took my hand and held tightly.

'That is my boy' I said

We left the hands when someone crossed our way and again held the hands when there was no one. I felt like flying on the air.

'I am still so surprised. I did not know you would behave with me like this. I thought you will get angry at me when I opened my mind to you' I said

'How can I get angry when I myself had feelings for you?' he said

'Then why you did not open up?'

'Good question'

We walked further in the campus. We were not able to hold hands for a long time as one or other person was crossing our way.

'Hey fools! Why do you want to roam here always? Can't you go to elsewhere?' said Ganesh with fake anger

I smiled.

We went to cafeteria together and had coffee break. Seconds passed so fast and my heart was catching everything in it. After all one day, the memories are alone going to be with me.

Suma, don't think about future and lose your current happiness. Enjoy your moments.

We returned to respective seats. I wanted to travel with him today. I wished none of his friends should come and take him away from me. Thank God, it did not happen as his friends left for the day well before. We spent some time together in cubicle. We wanted to hold our hands but the CCTV camera right above the top stopped us from doing.

'Do you remember earlier I asked you one thing?' I asked

'What?' he asked surprised

'I asked you a kiss'

He smiled 'Yeah, I remember'

'Possible?'

He gave warning look at the camera and I grinned at him.

'Ok then' I said

'Just a minute. Come close to me' he said

My heart bet fast.

'Why?'

'Come near me.'

I was ready to jump from the seventh floor at that time. Getting close to him was not a big deal. I went towards him. He held my hands tightly and kissed my hands.

First kiss ever in my life even though it is in my hands. These are golden moment of my life. I kissed him again in his hands.

'I wanted to ask you one thing' I said

'Another kiss?' he teased

I laughed

'I wanted to go on bike ride with you. Some long drive' I said

He thought for a while

'Done' he said 'Where do you want to go?'

'Some long distance'

He said one place

'That is too far away. You will become tired. Some short long distance'

'We will go next Saturday' he said

'I will be waiting for that day from this moment'

'I feel something odd' he said

'Why?'

'I think what we are doing is correct' he said 'I feel so guilty. I feel like I am using you. I am not doing right thing'

According to Indian society it is not correct.

'Let us not think about it. We know we are not meant to be together in our life. Set aside those thoughts' I said

He held my hand so tightly. I was happy with the time in the cubicle and did not know a jackpot was waiting for me.

We started to our homes together. For next two days I am not going to meet him. He told that next Saturday we can go for bike ride. I had to find some reason to convince my parents. I should say that I have work in my office. What else I can do?

Inside the shuttle bus we sat together and we continued to hold our hands. Though I was happy I felt very awkward for misbehaving in public. I felt all the co-passengers are looking at us.

'Can we sit at last? I am not comfortable here. Shall we go at last row' I asked him.

Maybe we also felt like that and consented to go there. We shifted to last seat and I prayed god no one but us should occupy that row.

'I cannot say how excited I am' I exclaimed happily 'Hold my hands'

He held my hands. I wanted to lean on his shoulder for the entire journey but I was not able to.

'Hey turn your face towards me' he said

'Why?' I asked

'Turn I say' he insisted

I turned my head.

Oh My God! What is happening here?

Oh Time! Please stop right here. Don't pass away. I wanted this moment to be like this. I closed my eyes so tightly and I felt a pair of lips pressing gently on my lips. First kiss of my life.

I got tears in my eyes out of extreme happiness. But it did not last even for five seconds. He backed away from me.

'The guy in front is watching at us. I don't think we can pursue further' he said

I was not able to talk for a while. I was trying to rewind the seconds in my memory.

'Did you like it?' he asked me

'I am so disappointed' I said

'What?'

He frowned

'No' I said 'I wish it could have lasted at least ten seconds. I was not able to enjoy the kiss fully'

'You did not enjoy the kiss at all?' he asked me.

Is he disappointed with me?

'No. I meant to say. It is first time in my life. I was so scared and when the moment my scare gone away and I start to enjoy it got ended. Not even five seconds'

I tried to console him

'It is OK. We may get another chance. I am sure it will last longer' I tried to cheer him up.

He did not say anything. He is angry on me. I think his ego is hurt by my answer. I should have told 'Yes' instead of truth.

We boarded the train together and sat opposite. I was so scared if I had made him disappointed.

'I don't know what I can say' he said

'About what?'

'Whatever is happening? I am deviating from my morals. What I am doing is not correct'

I acknowledged him.

'Can I ask you one thing?'

He looked at me.

'I am not asking you to marry me. But if your parents consent to marry me will you?'

'I don't know what to say for this' he said 'To be honest I cannot lie just to satisfy you. I don't feel like marrying you'

I did not expect this reply. All I just thought was he cannot marry me because his parents won't accept the relationship but he says he does not feel like marrying me.

Why do you think so?' I asked concealing my pain in my heart. 'You don't think I am attractive'

'It is not about attractive.' He said 'You and me are of different character. It is not easy for me to manage you and it will not be easy for you to manage me.'

'Why do you think so?'

'I am easy go lucky person. I never care about anything in my life. I am not perfect but you always look for perfection.'

I kept listening to him.

'It does not matter' I said 'No one is perfect in this world. Somehow one person has to tolerate the other and get going. That is how a marriage works'

'I cannot live with a girl like you' he concluded 'You are not meant for me. You are so strict. It will not work with me'

It is a harsh comment. I got angry.

'I am not as you think.' I said 'I have to be strict because of my job demands. I can be lenient too if required. I never meant to be strict.'

'Anyway it is not going to work between us. It is of no use in talking about it. We decided to be together as long as we can and part away when time comes'

I was so sad about it. I did not want him to go away from my life. No matter how much he is imperfect I am ready to tolerate him. How can I make him understand?

'You know what? I once had dream about us' I said

He looked at me with surprise

'In that dream, we are married and we have two children. One daughter and one baby boy. You are rushing for office to attend meeting. I am fighting with you to drop our daughter to school. We argue on how to take of our children. While I make our girl ready, our son starts to cry and we again argue on who has to cradle the baby'

His eyes showed mixed expressions.

'Somehow I am convincing you to drop our daughter to school. You rush away to office. I feel so sad that you did not say 'bye' to me. But suddenly you kiss and say 'I Love you''

'You are making me feel so bad' he said 'I never thought you would love me this much. I don't think I deserve this love'

'It was so real that when I woke up I was not able to believe it is a dream. It was like 'Inception''

'Don't dream too much. It is surely not going to happen for real.'

'What is there in dreaming?'

'I feel so guilty. You very well know it cannot happen. Why you are taking so much pain? The day when we part away you will suffer a lot' he warned me

I looked at him sadly. I don't want you to go away from me, sweet heart.

'I did a great mistake. I think we should end this' he said

'No need. You don't have to worry about that. I am fine'

'No. You are not. You don't know how it feels about parting away after being so close. I am senior to you in love. I don't want you to invest your life and waste your time on me. I fear that if I am close to you, you won't move on.'

'That is my headache. I will move on. I don't want to miss these moments with you' I pleaded him

'Then you have to promise me' he said

'What promise?'

'That you will marry someone and settle in your life. You have to throw all the memories and thoughts about me from your life'

It is so easy for you to ask such a difficult promise but I cannot. All my memories of you cannot be erased even in other births.

'That is so silly.'

'You have to do it' he insisted

'My parents won't allow me to be single. So you don't have to worry'

'Are you sure? I don't want to feel guilty in future. If I see you not married and if I am the reason it will kill me for the rest of the life. Adding fuel to fire if I have settled and you have not, I cannot live my life even a single second peacefully' he said

There is a very easy solution for this which you are not ready to listen. What I can do?

'You don't have to. I will marry' I said

I wanted my dream to come true.

'Forget it. Let us talk about coming Saturday. I am so excited about the bike ride with you. I was not able to enjoy the kiss. On Saturday you are kissing me again'

'I have to re-think about the Saturday' he said 'I don't think it is a good idea to have that plan. I suggest we drop it'

I was fed up. Why he is behaving like this?

'Come on! I told I will marry and move on in my life. Why are you spoiling the things?' I yelled.

'Are you sure?'

'Yes. Sure'

He de-trained in his station. I felt happy today because he did not get up from his seat until his station came. Somehow I made him to forget his routine re-cap. He has started to think about dropping the plan. Eight days more for my dream day. I wish nothing should drop the day's plan. God! Please help me.

For the next two days, there was not even a single second I lived without thinking about him. I held my mobile phone in my hands where ever I went. Even in washroom I kept it with me. I was so addicted to WhatsApp.

I did not get any message from him for a long time. I got scared. Did he change his mind? Yesterday I talked too much to him and that is why he is angry on me? Then I have to apologize.

Sumana: Hi

I dropped a message. I did not get any reply at all. What should I do now? Call him and apologize. Every second passed away with terror and fear.

After few minutes I heard the most beautiful sound in the world. Message notification sound.

Ganesh: Yes

Sumana: Are you angry at me?

Ganesh: Not at all

Sumana: I feel so guilty. I think I indirectly insisted you to marry me. I am sorry.

Ganesh: you are confusing yourself too much

Sumana: If you are not comfortable with what you are doing, let us stop everything. You be as usual.

Ganesh: Can I call you Sumi?

He wants to call me Sumi.

This is a special right which I want to give my future husband. Only he can call me Sumi and no one else.

I remembered long time back I said to him. Honestly speaking I am ready to give him the rights to call me like that forever. If he calls me, Sumi then even my future husband will not have that right to call me like that.

Sumana: Sure. You can

Ganesh: I will never do things which I don't like. No one can make me to do anything. You know how it feels to be madly loved by a girl. I have to thank you for that.

Sumana: I am a fool I started this and confused everything.

Ganesh: Sumi, you are in love madness. Enjoy the moment fully and when we part away everything will be alright.

He is always thinking about parting away. I am dying here to be with him forever but he is not ready to give me a chance.

We then chatted that day and next day. I was not close to a guy before. Day by day my love for him increased. Like he said, when we part away I am going to have a tough time. But I am sure before I part away from him I will try to extract as much as possible from him so that I will not regret later in my life. Will destiny be in my favor?

I have to take special training to handle men in a relationship. I did not know that my small disappointment will turn into a disaster on that day. I tried to remember what wrong did I commit but everything got ruined in minutes.

To being with, I should have not browsed Facebook on Monday morning.

I should have not seen status which said

'What is the difference between I like you and I love you

Buddha said

When you like a flower you pluck it, when you love a flower you water it'

I got so disappointed one seeing that. I recalled how Ganesh treats me. He treats me like a flower which he wants to pluck and not to preserve and water it.

Next big mistake I should have definitely not done. I forwarded the status in WhatsApp to him. All I just wanted to make him understand that I wanted to be his flower which he wants to preserve but not to be plucked by him.

Ganesh: Wow! What a great quote. So you think that I am ruining your life, isn't it?

Sumana: When did I say like that? I just wanted to share what is actually going on between us?

Ganesh: Fine then. If you feel like that, then we don't have to continue this at all. Let me be as usual like your colleague. I don't want any lover Sumi. I am fine being with my TA Sumana itself

Sumana: I did not mean to say like that.

Ganesh: I don't want anyone to feel so bad about me. Even I have morals and I am not interested to ruin any girl's life.

Sumana: So what you want to say? You want to break up with me?

Ganesh: Let us all wind up everything

Sumana: don't get angry. I am sorry if I had hurt your feelings

Ganesh: Certainly you did hurt. How can you say like that? Did I ever do anything which you are not comfortable? You want to say that I am using you?

Sumana: I wanted to be the flower you want to preserve.

Ganesh: Even preserved flowers are plucked one day. You don't have to act like smart. Whatever you want to say, convey it straight

Sumana: Ok. Let us talk about it in out desk. You are so angry.

Ganesh: There is nothing we need to talk. Everything is finished. Let us get back to normal. I don't want to talk about this further

Sumana: You are over reacting

Ganesh: You are making me to. I did not know this is so complicated. It is stressing me a lot. I don't want to continue like this.

Sumana: You have decided finally to end everything?

Ganesh: Yes. I have every right to decide what I should do. It is my decision. I won't change it

The fight continued for some more time. I felt so bad for my act. I don't know how I am going to convince. When I met him in my cubicle he did not turn towards my side. I waited for him come to me and speak but he behaved as if I did not exist there.

It is not going to work. I started and I have to end it.

'Are you mad at me?' I asked

'No'

'I am sorry. I was trying to convey something and it turned it some other way'

'We already discussed about it. Just leave it' he said

'I want you to give second chance. I don't want to lose the moments with you'

'What is the use in it? This is not correct at all. I feel like I am crossing my limits. When we are not meant to be together why should we be like this?'

'If you give a chance we can be together forever' I said

'That is not possible at all'

'It is possible. I can surely be good partner to you. I won't say that I am perfect and nice. I cannot be cool all the time but that doesn't mean I am bad'

'You very well know it cannot happen between us. No use in talking about it'

'First reason is our age. Three years difference is not something accepted in our society' he said

'I know. Nowadays no one takes this seriously. There are living examples which you know'

He did not reply immediately

'I am ready to face any consequences rising out of it. I am ready to convince anyone. I am ready to fall in the feet of anyone. I can fight against the whole world if you want to' I said

'You are making me feel bad again. I feel so guilty' he said

'I am saying the truth. I will not leave you like your ex-girlfriend did. Trust me. I will be with you till my last breath'

It was almost a begging

'Why don't you understand?' he said in frustrated tone. I can very well understand that he is trying to control his anger.

'I am not the guy for you. It will never work between us' he said

'We can try to make it work. I have that confidence'

'See, all I am seeing is the problems alone. I don't want any problems in my life.'

'Are you sure?'

'I am fine as I am. I have my own path to go and you have yours. Let us travel in our paths. We will stop it here'

'But…'

'Please. I don't want to discuss anymore. We will stop everything'

'Just think once. If you don't want to marry me at least let us continue as we decided'

'That is not required. It is not correct thing. I am spoiling your life'

'No. You are not. I don't want to have distance between us' I said

He did not say anything.

'I am not compelling you. Take your time and let me know your decision as soon as possible'

'Alright. I will let you know. But whatever is my decision I want you to accept it'

'Yes' my voice did not raise at all. My situation has become like a student who is waiting for university exams result. Am I going to pass or fail?

All the day I did not focus on my work. At times I used to turn at him to see what he is doing. He was working as usual. Nothing seemed to affect him. He looked so casual. Here deep inside my heart everything got collapsed.

I recalled everything happened between us. In past few days I was begging to him each and every second. I don't know why I am doing this? I am not able to convince him to accept me. I got angry on him for a while. It was him who started everything and now he wants to move away from me.

I have to Thank God that Ashwin was on leave on that day. Otherwise I could have not faced him with such sorrow and grief in my mind.

I was not able to control the tears from my eyes. All I did on that day was crying, crying and nothing but crying. Where my destiny has brought me? All I wanted a man whom I loved in my life the most. I have never loved anyone in my life like I love him. But I am not able to have in my life.

I was scared to talk to him. The seconds which passed so fast earlier is now passing in slow speed. I was scared to talk with him. Each of his moments scared me. He did not talk to me at all the whole day. He did behave as if I do not exist beside him. It was so easy for him. How long should I wait for the result?

Notification sound was heard from my mobile. My pulse rate increased to a great speed. What was according to me the most beautiful sound once upon a time has become the most horrific sound today? I opened my WhatsApp. As expected message from him.

Ganesh: I have decided. Let us stop everything

I felt as if someone is trying pull the heart away from it place.

Ganesh: I don't want this. I feel like I am doing a cheating. This is not correct. I think you will understand

Sumana: It is ok.

Ganesh: Listen. I am an emotional guy. If I want to love someone I wanted to do it at fullest. With them I can be closer as I want. This is correct.

I kept seeing the status as 'typing…'

Ganesh: I am not able to involve with you fully. I am not much into this relationship. So if I come closer this will not be good.
Sumana: Ok
Ganesh: I know how it hurts you. But you have to accept the truth. I like you and I have lust on you but bitter truth is I don't have any love for you.

Tears already started to flood in my eyes. I was not in a position to see what any letter in the messenger.

Ganesh: For me to be closer with any girl I should love her madly like anything. Only then I can do dating and mating with her.
Sumana: Then why did you drag to this much level. You could have ended on that day itself. Why did you kiss me? Your kiss was also out of lust?
Ganesh: Please understand. I like you. I have lust but I cannot love you. I cannot marry you. When I cannot marry you I cannot be close with you.
Sumana: You could have finished it on that day itself. Why did you drag this to this much level?
Ganesh: Stop typing and listen to me. I don't want to hurt my parents again.
Sumana: You don't have to hurt anyone. I am also respecting your parents. My only concern is you could have ended this on that day.

Ganesh: I am not able to get emotional with you.
Sumana: You are not emotionally attached to me. That is the only thing which is hurting me.
Ganesh: I have emotions on you. I like you a lot. But I don't want this. I am feeling like a sugar patient. You are a sweet. I like sweet but I don't want to eat it.
Sumana: You don't have to.
Ganesh: I like you. I called you Sumi out of my own wish. But something is stopping me to come closer to you. Please don't mistake me. I know I am hurting you. Let us not drag everything. I saw the true love in your eyes. I am so happy about it. But this is not going to work between us. I am sorry. I don't want to misuse your pure love. Next birth surely we will marry. Is it fine?

Everything is over. He had thrown me out of his palace of heart and closed the door permanently. I saw him standing at his friend's place laughing and chatting with him. How come he is able to be so casual? Does not he realize he has broken a heart?

I rushed away from that place.

It has been a week that he officially ended everything between us. No one except me can express how my life turned after everything had happened. Few days before I hated the sunset which used to separate me from him and loved the sunrise which will get me to him. Now I started to hate both sunset and sunrise. I kept my mobile beside me expecting to get any message from him in WhatsApp.

It has become my routine to smile in front him and shed tears when I am away from him. It was very painful to see him so unaffected by whatever happened in past few days. I did not know relationship is so cruel. He behaved as if nothing has happened but it was not that easy for me. I lost focus on everything in my life. Nothing in my life had capability to bring smile in my face.

'Suma, I need status of the task assigned to you. It was supposed to be completed a long time back. When it will be completed?' asked Ashwin.

I cannot complete this in this birth.

'I will finish it soon' I said to him.

I was tired of crying and wiping my tears. The more I controlled my tears the more it secreted especially when I see him behaving so casually. Nowadays I can clearly observe that the distance between us has increased drastically. I felt he is trying to avoid talking with me. Earlier when we meet at morning we used say a 'hi' and when we leave for the day we will bid a 'bye'. Everything was stopped.

I was not able to tolerate his presence beside me. I can neither keep away from him nor go near to him. The pain in my mind increased day by day. I wish I could express him how I feel of losing him. I did not feel like eating and sleeping. I did not want to come to office. All I want was romantic messages from my love. Many times I browsed my WhatsApp during nights only to see his status as 'Last seen' which will be few minutes ago.

'Can we go for a coffee-break?' asked Ashwin one day to all of us.

'I cannot come, Boss. Having lot of work' he said

He does not want to have coffee-break with me. He is deliberately avoiding me. Ashwin did not care much about it.

'I really have to learn the secret of acting like busy when you don't have any work' he teased him.

'Boss, I am having work really.' he said

Both of them enjoyed the fun of pulling each other's legs.

I was not able to involve in it. At the cafeteria I said 'He is not having any work. He is deliberately avoiding to come with us. He does not want to talk with me' I said sadly.

'Oh My God!' said Ashwin in frustrated tone 'Why are you still sticking to it? You should always let go of the things which you cannot control'

'I cannot let it go.' I said

'Sumana, you have to learn to accept the truth. If you keep thinking about it, you will feel the pain more. No one can hurt you except you. Don't hurt yourself. You have to be strong and you make efforts to come out of it' he said.

I remembered the day when Aradhana lamented about her love failure. Like how I am suffering today, she suffered the pain on that day. I did not care to listen to her and heal her. I easily told her to forget everything and move on. It is not as easy as it is told.

'I am so hurt by his distancing behavior. Why can't he be normal?' I asked angrily 'I know very well he does not want to see my face. For the past two days he is not talking to me normally.'

'Who is he to you?' he asked me

He is everything to me. Screamed my heart

'Don't think about things which cannot control. He may have genuine reasons also. What bothers if he talks to you or not?'

Ashwin is behaving in the same way as I had behaved with Aradhana. I was not affected by her pain and did not care to understand it. It was very easy for me advise her to come out of the pain. Destiny is avenging me in the form of Ashwin. I cannot expect him to feel or understand my pain. It will be better if I stop talking to him about this.

I felt so lonely for next few days. Every routine chatting between us stopped. I hardly found him in his seat. Ashwin was on leave due to illness. Fourth seat in the cubicle was vacant. I was all alone left in the cubicle. I browsed the internet on ways to come out of the love failure. It said eat well, sleep well, talk with friends, go for outing, and go for jogging or gym etc. etc. etc. None of the techniques worked. Our interaction almost stopped and there were many continuous days where we both seated beside but not even uttered a single word.

I regretted for creating this confusion. Had I kept quiet about my feelings for him at least he would have been my friend. Now I lost him not only as a lover but also as a friend. This was my pathetic situation at office. At home I almost stopped talking to my parents and sunken myself to solitude. I did not do anything at my home except one thing. CRYING

'Suma' called my mother

I wiped my tears quickly.

My mother sat beside me. 'Suma, I know you are not fine for past few days. I did not ask you anything. Whatever problems you have you will come and reveal it to me by yourself. What is wrong with you now?'

That is it. Now I have no other go other than to pour my heart to her. I was little scared as my father was also present with her. How will my parents react if I say everything to them? I lay down on the lap of my mother and started to cry again.

'Suma, crying is not going to help you anyway' said my mother 'Whatever is your problem share it with us? We are your parents. We can help you'

I was not able to utter a single word to her. My tears blocked my eyes and voice all at a time. My parents were watching me helplessly not knowing the way to stop my cry.

'Suma, you are scaring us. Is everything fine? Whatever big is your trouble just share everything.' said my mother anxiously

I narrated how I was attracted to Ganesh, how I felt so possessive and jealous about him, how I was stressed on finding about my feelings, how I said I liked him etc. I carefully censored the incidents of our WhatsApp chats and the kiss which we shared.

'I think the chapter is closed. He is very clear in what he wants. Who will like to marry an elder woman than him? You have to stop crying and forget everything' said my mother

'I am not able to forget it Amma. I am so hurt' I said

'Suma, you have done one of the biggest mistakes in your life. You used to consult with us for every small matter. This is the matter of your life. Why you did not reveal to us about what you felt for him?' asked my mother

What question is this? I have never heard of children consulting parents on love matters with them.

'Suma. Men are supposed to open up their minds to the one they love. Women should not do this. They will become cheap in their eyes. You fell for a guy who is younger than you. This is so awkward. I cannot believe that a strong girl like you had done such mistake' said my mother

My father sat beside me

'Whatever has happened let it be. But now let us focus on what should be done by you' said my father

I looked at both of them

'We have given all that we can. But this is something which is beyond our control. We cannot buy you for him. You have to forget everything and move on. A man will not want to marry a woman who is elder to him. It looks like he is so adamant about not hurting his parents. You don't have to waste your time. Forget everything'

Every one of them is repeating the same dialogue. Forget everything and move on. Not even a single soul is ready to feel my pain and support me.

'What do you expect us to Suma?' asked my mother 'Do you want us to go to talk to his parents?'

I looked at them with new hope. He said he does not want to hurt his parents. What if I properly approach him for marriage? May be this could help.

'I don't think their parents will accept to this' said my mother 'We are not happy with your choice but for the sake of your happiness we are ready to take this step. For that he should give consent. Only then we can take next step'

'May be I can talk with him about this.'

'Suma, first I want to meet that boy. I can judge if he will be willing to move your relationship to next level or not'

'I can bring to our home, Appa. I will talk with him' I told him

'Your struggles are meaningless.' Said my mother

'No Ma. He told that his parents won't accept and he does not want to hurt them. Perhaps I can convince him in this way.' I said.

A new ray of hope glittered in my eyes. My parents looked at me with some mixed expression. I did not pay attention to it. I was not ready to leave my last hope to get him in my life.

It was not so easy for me to re-start the chapter once again. I was so scared. At the same time I convinced myself that we did not part away due to differences and we did not fight with each other. However I was so tensed and anxious. How he will react if I am trying to open the closed chapter once again. No matter whatever happens I have to make this attempt.

He gave a warm smile at me. I was able to hear my heart beat.

'Are you free now?' I asked him

'Not really' he said 'Why?'

'I just want to talk something important to you'

'Yeah. Tell me' he said

'I may even become your lifetime enemy if I talk about this once again but I had to re-open it again'

My heart beat raised further. I cleared my throat and said 'On that day you told that your parents will not accept to our relationship and you don't want to hurt them'

My voice trembled and I spoke in low tone

'Perhaps if you can take me to them I can convince them. I can even ask my parents to talk with them. What do you say?'

I can very well understand that he is trying to control the temper.

'First sit down and listen to me' pointing to a chair beside.

I sat on the chair he pulled

'Do you know? When I told my father about Swati how did he react?'

I looked at him.

'He immediately started from the home and told me to show her home to meet her father. Not for fixing alliance but to insult her entire family. He was so angry that he was in rage of humiliating entire Swati's family. I was so terrified on his reaction on that day'

He was so angry that he was in rage of humiliating entire Swati's family. I was so terrified on his reaction on that day'

I kept silent

'In fact, I and Swati belong to same caste. Yet my father got furious on knowing my relationship with her. My mother was totally broken on knowing about my love affair. She used to cry at late nights imagining that she has lost her son forever. I did not knew it for a long time.'

What is he trying to say?

'Listen to me. My parents are not used to this kind of things. I already hurt them enough and I don't want to repeat again. My father will not accept any daughter-in-law from other caste. It is of no use in talking with him'

'But though I am from different caste we both still belong to same Brahmin group'

'Swati belonged to same caste we belonged. He did not accept her. I just told you. He is totally against love marriage. I am going to marry only the girl whom my father accepts. This is final. That is why I did not involve myself with you fully.'

'You can convince them right. On that day you told you will try to convince your parents for the girl you love' I said

'That is true. Even now I am saying the same thing. I will try to convince my parents for the girl who I love deeply. I can even fight with him for her. Why should I fight and argue with my parents for you?' he yelled at me

One knife got stabbed in my heart straight.

'I will fight for Swati. I will not fight for you'

Second knife got stabbed.

He is ready to fight with his parents for the girl who dumped him but he cannot do it for the girl who loves him truly.

'Let me share you another thing. There is a girl who is in love with me for the past four years. She is from different caste. That is why I did not entertain it. It will not work at all.'

Third knife.

'That girl loved you when you were in relationship with Swati?'

'Yes. She made an attempt when Swati broke up with me. I did not allow going further'

'Do you love her?' I asked him

'I like her a lot. I cannot marry her'

'Did you kiss her like you kissed me?'

He nodded his head like 'no'. Is he saying the truth?

'You cannot imagine how much I can love you. It is more than sky or universe. I love you more than my life.'

'That girl loves me for four years. Do you know how she would care for me? If I get ill, she will be the first one who cares for me a lot. I don't think your love is more than hers.'

Fourth knife.

'What do you mean by not more than hers? You don't know how much you mean to me?' I said anger and tears 'Do you have any scale to measure love?'

He frowned.

'Listen. Don't compare me with someone. I don't know how to explain what is in my heart. I never been like this before. I cannot break open my chest to show what is that I have about you.' I said

'You listen to me first.' he yelled. 'I have lot of things standing in line in my life. To begin with, I am going for higher studies to US. I am preparing for that. I have to go abroad, complete my studies, get placed in a big company etc. etc. etc.'

'It is ok. What is stopping you from doing this? Even I have ambitions. Both are different things. I am not going to interfere in your career. I can support you for everything in future' I said

'That is not as easy as you think. Right now I am not in a position to think about getting married. I am too young for that. I cannot take care of myself. How do you expect me to take care of you?' he screamed

'I trust you. Someday you will become more responsible. I will manage until that'

He did not make attempts to conceal his irritation.

'I have never begged to anyone for anything before. This is the first time.' I said in begging voice

'You are talking to a wrong person' he said 'Yours is a wrong choice. I am not your man and you are not my woman. I don't know how can I make you understand this? I did a great mistake in my life. I should have not opened up about my break-up. All your feelings for me is because of sympathy'

'It is not sympathy or infatuation. I started to feel for you even before that. I don't know how I can make you understand how much I want you in my life' I pleaded 'I am ready to adjust as much as possible for you.'

'You don't have to do that. You can be as you are. I don't want anyone to change themselves for me. I am not expecting that'

'Have you heard a saying? You will be so happy when you marry someone who loves you more than someone who you love. I can even sacrifice my life for you. Just give me a chance. I will show how much happiness I can bring in your life'

'You will sacrifice my life for me but I will sacrifice my life only for Swati. I cannot love any other woman like I loved her'

Fifth knife

'Anyway you will love your wife in future, isn't it?'

'That is my personal life. It is none of your business. I know how to live my life. No one need to teach me'

Sixth knife

'See. My father toiled himself a lot during his young days. He was the responsible person in his family and he did not allow any kind of disturbances in his life. Being his son I wanted to be like him. There is no way I am getting committed to any woman in life without my parents' consent. Even if next time I fall into live with some girl first I will ask my father if I can pursue only then I will propose that girl'

I was not in a position to speak next word. My vision was blurred due to the tears from my eyes

'See. Please stop crying. It looks so awkward. You are a matured girl. You should know to handle things.' He said with irritation

I was not in a position to feel ashamed of myself.

'You are comparing my love with some other girl. You are doing injustice to me. You don't know how much I feel for you. There is not a single moment I am living my life without your thoughts. One minute'

I opened my drawer and took the greeting cards from it.

'I wrote these for you. These are all not cards but my heart. I have done all the foolish things I could.'

His face showed that he is not affected by them.

'I don't want to stretch it further. Let us close the topic today. You are wasting both of our time. I clearly explained my point. You have to accept and move on. Don't you understand how much you are making me feel bad?'

'You even stopped being close with me. I was happy that even though I cannot have you in my life I can be close with you for a while so that I will live that memories.' I said

'I have dignity and morals. I am not supposed to do that when I know that we both are not going to be together. You are not my wife. I cannot be close with you like my wife'

'You were like that before'

'I realized my mistake and that is why backed off. I did what is correct. I don't want to ruin your life.'

'There is nothing that you are ruining my life. I am not able to let you go.'

'Your behavior is so senseless. There is nothing that we cannot change. Ten years later you will feel bad for what you are doing now. You may even laugh at that time thinking about how funnily you behaved today. Time can change everything. It will change you.'

'I am hurt and broken. I don't know how I am going to face you daily after this much happened'

'May be I can wear a mask on my face. Will it help you?' he teased me angrily

I looked at him desperately to understand my feelings but his face became rock like.

'Imagine. You are three years elder to me. Three years! What will society think of us?' he asked

'You have now become everything to me. I wanted to give you a happy life and live with you happily. I did not care about the age when I started to feel for you. I cannot forget you.' I said with utmost grief and sorrow from heart.

'You just imagine that I am in a relationship. Your problem will be solved.'

What a cruel suggestion he is giving me! How can I ever think like that? I cannot imagine him to be someone's man.

'What I am trying to say is...'

He interrupted 'I wanted to end this once for all and you are beginning again. Enough is enough. I don't want to talk about it anymore.'

Once again he kicked me out of his heart forever and closed the door. No. I knocked his door to enter inside it but he kicked me out. He is ready to die for the girl who dumped him but he is killing the girl who is ready to die for him.

'Suma' called my mother 'Are you alright?'

I did not reply her. I was not in a position to talk to anyone of them in this world. I was silently doing my routine work. My entire dream home, dream wedding, dream life has got shattered in few minutes. Everything is destroyed except one thing. The truth. He is not mine and he will not be mine forever.

I tried to console myself and that I am in middle of some nightmare. No, this is real. Everything is over. He has thrown me out of his heart and has shut the door completely. He has not given any hope of knocking the door in future.

As a matter of fact I should not feel bad about it. I know it is going to happen one day but I did not expect it so soon. Though I knew it is the actual future of my relationship I had prepared myself to face the truth.

I don't know what should be done now. The truth is threatening me now. I now realized how much I love him. How can I let him go? I cannot tolerate on imagining that he is not going to be in my future and I have no place in his life. I cannot think of living of my life without him. Why this is happening to me?

'Suma, look at me' screamed my mother

It took me some minutes to come back to the actual world.

'How many times I am calling you? Why are you not answering' asked my mother angrily

How can I answer? Tears are ready to flow down from eyes. I am not in a position to cry in front of them.

'Yes Amma. What happened?'

'Come and take your food. I have lot of work. I cannot bring it there' she said.

I behaved like robot and did whatever she said. The food used to be my favorite dish. Had it was any other time I would have not let anyone but me to finish it. Today each and every spoon of food looked like stones to my eyes. I was not able to swallow anything. I felt some uneasiness in my whole body and was not able to function normally. I felt some bitterness in my taste buds, something smashing my organs in my abdomen and someone is squeezing my heart. Every part of my body ached. I was not in a position to talk to anyone. I quietly detached from everything and did lay down in my bed.

'Suma, you are so dull today. You did not eat properly. I cooked your favorite item and I was thinking how to protect the food from you. What is wrong with you?'

This is the problem with my mother. She is watching me all the time. Even a slight difference in my tone will make her smell something is wrong with me.

'Nothing Amma. I feel so feverish. I don't think I can go to office tomorrow'

'Is it so?' she was surprised and worried. 'Let me see.'

She touched my forehead and cheeks and checked my necks.

'Your body is little hot.' She said 'You can take leave tomorrow if you are not feeling well'

'Take some anti-biotic tablets. You will be better by tomorrow evening. You take rest now' said my father

I closed my eyes and pretend to sleep. Thank God. They believed me. I don't have to any of them till tomorrow morning. The lights were switched off and everything became dark in the room and in my life as well.

I cannot lead a normal life hereafter. It is time for me to decide my next course of action. An action which could relieve me from all pains and give me peace forever.

I woke up very late in the morning as did I not sleep for very long time. I tried to find peace in anyway but my every attempt failed. I finally decided a way to finish this chapter in a most peaceful way. The moment I decided it, I was able to feel a calmness occupying my mind.

'Suma, how are you feeling?' asked my mother

Tears peeped into my eyes. She got tensed on seeing me cry.

'What happened?' asked my mother

I wiped my tears immediately.

'Nothing Amma. I am still not feeling well. I wanted a deep and permanent sleep' I told her

'What?'

I got tensed.

'I meant to say I want to take rest'

'Ok. You sleep as much as you can. If you are not cured we can visit doctor today evening' she said 'I have prepared food for you. Take an anti-biotic once you have your meal. I will now leave to my office.'

I smiled at her. Today evening some unexpected guests are going to be in his house. When she was about to leave me, I grabbed her hand.

'What?' she asked me with surprised

I gave a tight hug to her

'What happened to you today?' asked my mother with surprise

'You are the best Amma in the world' I told her 'I love you, ma'

She smiled but it disappeared very soon.

'Your behavior is so strange right from yesterday. You are not normal at all. Are you fine?' she asked me worriedly

'I am fine, Amma' my voice broke 'I am feeling so feverish'

Her eyes looked worried.

'Take your tablets soon and sleep well. It is getting late for me' she said

Tears oozed from eyes. Both my parents left home. It is the time for me get into action. I took a paper and pen.

Dear Amma and Appa,

I am very sorry for being so selfish but I am not able to live with this pain anymore. You are the best parents in the world but I am not a good daughter. I promise at least in next birth I will be a good daughter and make you proud.

Goodbye

I kept ready the sleeping pills beside me. I googled about how many tablets would suck the life in how many minutes. I remember the day we bought this medicine at the pharmacy. The pharmacist was not ready to give this sleeping tablet without a doctor prescription. Even when we provided the prescription he was not willing to give more than ten tablets. The tablet which was supposed to relieve me from depression is now going to relieve me from my pain forever.

I got bewildered on hearing the calling bell ringing four times. It is the usual ringing code of our family. No one other than three of us ring the bell in that way. I quickly closed the video and kept the tablets back into its place. I opened the door and became surprised. It was my mother and father standing outside. How it is possible? Aren't they supposed to be in their offices?

'What happened? You are back?' I asked them

Both of them did not say anything.

'Did you forget anything?' I asked them

'No. We took leave today. I don't know why but something told me to come home. I did not feel good to leave you alone. Surprisingly your father also felt the same way like I did.' said my mother

I did not expect this turning point at all. Both of them felt unusual and returned home. How true it is 'Blood is thicker than water'. Something made them to sense wrong and brought them home.

Suma, look how your parents love you a lot. How did you decide to take the stupid decision of taking your life! They are showering you tons and tons of love and affection. Why are you running behind the love which one stranger is not ready to give you? You are the real stupid in this world.

'Had your meal? Did you take your tablets?' asked my mother

I blinked

'You have not taken your food still?' screamed my mother 'What were you doing all these time?'

What can I say? I was so busy in looking on the ways to end life.

'I was browsing Facebook'

My mother looked at me angrily

'You are not supposed to browse computer when you are so unwell. You have your food and medicine and get back to sleep.' she told finally.

I silently followed what she said. I took the food and medicine and went to sleep

'Suma, are you alright for sure?' asked my mother

I looked her with shock.

'Yes Amma' I told her 'I am fine. I will be completely fine soon'

I tried to talk normally

My father came near to my bed. Both gave a deep stare at me. What is wrong with them?

'You are sure that you are fine?' asked my father

'Yes Appa'

The reaction from my mother was not really so unexpected. Tears started to roll from her eyes so fast. What is wrong with her?

'Amma, what happened? Why are you crying?' I asked her worriedly.

I looked at my father and shocked even more. His eyes too shed tears in equal speed to that of my mother. What is happening here?

'What happened to you, Appa? Why you both are behaving like this today? What is wrong here?'

'If you are alright then what is the meaning of this?' asked my mother pointing to something

Oh My God! She has the suicide note in her hand. How did I forget about it? I kept in the showcase of the drawing room so that it will be visible to everyone. I did not think of clearing it away from there. What am I going to do now?

My whole body trembled with fear.

'I was so worried by your behavior today morning. I have never seen you like this before. I know something is eating you right from yesterday. I am observing that you are not normal for past few days.' my mother's voice broke.

I was not able to look at her face to face

'I have to really thank the almighty for making me to sense the abnormal situation around me. I believe we returned at the correct time. Otherwise I cannot just imagine what could have happened?'

My mother exploded her emotions. Both of them cried like anything. What can I do now? I did the worst blunder of my life today. How can I set it right?

'Amma, Appa, Please stop crying' I begged them 'There is nothing that you have to get scared about. Nothing has happened here. I am fine and see I am alive with flesh and blood. Trust me.'

My mother tightly hugged me and my father held my hands so tightly. Both of them sat at my both sides.

'You are alive because we came home at right time. I am sure you were doing some non-sense thing to end your life when we are on our way. Is it true or not?' my mother screamed with anger and fear 'Who knows? Had we not returned on time you might have succeeded in your mission. We would have seen your lifeless body.'

She was true. I was doing the foolishness when they rang the calling bell. If I say the truth how would they react?

'Amma. You are wrong. I did not do any such thing' I lied to her

'What is the meaning of this letter then?' she asked me angrily. 'Why did you write it? What were you doing when we are away?'

'I was browsing the internet. That is it'

'Then this letter. I know your handwriting. Why it was there?'

I was not able to answer her questions.

'Suma, Whatever is in your mind open up everything to me. I know what made you to come to this horrific decision. Is it that boy?'

I kept silent. Tears started to roll from my eyes.

'You decided to end up your life because of that boy? You did not think about us even for a second?' asked my mother angrily

'Suma, what happened to you? Why you wanted to give us the lifetime punishment? Don't you know how much you mean to us? You are not only our daughter but everything to us. We are living every second of our life only for you, only to see you living happily with no sorrows.' said my father as tears rolled from his eyes.

I very well remember when my father last wept in his lifetime. It was during my grand-mother's death. I felt so guilty. How selfish I was!

'Do you think we will survive in this world after you have left us?' asked my father

'Appa please don't kill me with your words. Please listen to me. I don't want you to take that letter seriously. It is a mistake. I did not do anything. Trust me.' I told them

I grabbed the letter from my parents and tore into many pieces.

'You still have not answered to our question. Don't ever think you can escape from us by tearing that paper. We want the exact answer. What happened in last few days?' my mother asked me angrily

For the next few minutes the whole house turned silent like a graveyard. All the three of us looked at each other's face with tears. My parents did not leave my hand at all. My mother followed me till the restroom and neither of them were ready to leave me alone. I did not have guts to stop them after this much happened.

'Tell us Suma. We wanted to know each and every truth from you. You told you have forgot him and moved on when I asked you last time. Now what made you take this decision?'

I recalled the horrific moments of my life in last few days. God made me to enjoy the best day of my life and worst day of my life within last seven days.

'Suma, we thought you just liked him. We did not take that so seriously other than infatuation.'

'It is not an infatuation, Amma. I love him so much' I screamed

I got fed up. No one is taking my feelings so seriously.

'What do you want us to do?' she screamed 'We are not fine with the idea of marrying off you to some younger boy at the same time we cannot afford to take risk with your life. We will go and talk to his parents if you like him so much'

'There is no use' I said with tears

'Why?'

I was not able to answer. I cried heavily

'Tell me everything, Suma. We need to know every single thing happened.'

'He does not want to marry me' I told her 'He said that his parents won't accept their relationship. He does not want to hurt them.'

Every word from his mouth flew like thousand knives and stabbed my heart.

'And so you wanted to leave us forever. A useless coward has become important to you than two people who were living for you like fools, isn't it?' shouted my mother

'Amma, I told you not to take that thing so seriously. It was a mistake' I begged her

'The real mistake is that I have trusted you so much. Today you broke everything. I am so scared to leave you alone even for a second.'

'You fear is unnecessary' I screamed 'I told you several times. You both are harassing me'

'You are scaring us.'

I got fed up. It would have been better if I ended up my life. No way could I convince them here after. I am sure going to regret for this my entire life time.

'Now what you want us to do?' asked my mother 'He is not ready to marry you and you are not ready to forget him. You are punishing us for being your parents.'

I felt ashamed.

'Suma, tell me the truth. You are not able to bear the rejection or something more has happened between you too. Do you get what I mean?'

I wish I could tell everything that happened between us. No. It is not going to help anyway rather they will feel bad about me. They are so proud about their daughter being raised as a disciplined and well-mannered. They should not know that the love which clouded their daughter's mind changed her completely.

'Nothing has happened that I would regret in my life'

'Suma, you are doing dangerous things in our absence. No one except you wants this to happen. It is practically not possible. Forget everything and move on. Promise us that you will move on in your life. Do you realize that you are sucking our life also?' Said my mother.

I kept silent.

'You have already sucked enough of our life from us. Don't think we are not watching you. I already knew that it won't work but you did not listen to us. Suma, I am begging you. Please forget everything and move on. Don't kill yourself and kill us. This family has lost its happiness because of you. From the day you got into this trouble we almost forgot laughing. Only you can bring colors and brightness to this home. Consider this as a sacrifice. Get rid of everything for sake of two souls who has nothing left in this world except you' begged my mother

'Amma, please don't make me feel bad. I will forget everything and move on. I promise you.' I said to her.

The entire home was filled with tears, sorrow, grief, depression and nothing else.

I was not able to lay on my bed and sleep that night. I was not able to stand or sit, walk or jump, cry or laugh, eat or drink, inhale or exhale. I switched on the television and tuned to a children's program. It ran for around two hours. Somehow it had capacity to keep me away from my depression.

'Suma, what are you doing?' asked my mother.

She saw me watching the TV and then looked at the time. It struck 2.30 am.

'Why are you awake?' she asked

'I cannot sleep.'

She saw me helplessly. She knew no one can heal the pain which I am going through. Even though she is ready to heal the sorrow she knows no way to heal it. When I myself do not know the healing way who else I can blame.

'It is OK. You watch the TV here in the room' she said

'I will watch it here itself. It will be disturbance for you there' I said

'No problem. You watch there as much time as you want' she compelled me

I knew the reason behind it. She did not want me to be alone even for a minute. I was not in a position to do any kind of activities. I did not go to office the next day too. My mother tried her level best to take off but she could not. My father stayed with me that day. After that incident my parents were not ready to leave me alone even for singe minute.

'Suma, where are you going?' asked my father

I got angry.

'I am going to washroom' I yelled at him

'Don't shout.' My father yelled at me. 'You don't have any rights to raise voice after all what you did?'

I felt very bad.

The whole day I did nothing but seated alone on my bed looking at something. I tried very hard to stop my thoughts haunting me but I couldn't it. Same dialogues ate my brain.

> *I can even fight with him for her. Why should I fight and argue with my parents for you?*
>
> *I will fight for Swati. I will not fight for you*
>
> *You will sacrifice my life for me but I will sacrifice my life only for Swati. I cannot love any other woman like I loved her.*

The moment I recall the above lines no matter how much attempt I make I cannot stop the tears from my eyes. My heart got squeezed whenever I reminded it and I felt like knives are stabbed in my heart once again.

'Suma, you had your food?' asked my father

I hated everything in the world. All I wanted is stay alone in one corner of room and cry for rest of my life.

'No Appa. I don't want anything to eat' I said

'There is no use in starving yourself. The bitter truth in front of you will not change.' said my father angrily.

'Please Appa, don't force me. I don't want anything to eat' I said firmly

He did not force me after that. Afternoon he came to me and said 'Can we go out somewhere? I would be somewhat a good change for you'

I agreed. We both set to the one of the biggest shopping malls in the city. I saw a thing which wounded me further. It was a poster of actor Ajith Kumar, the next superstar of Tamil cinema after Rajnikanth and Kamalhaasan. The favorite hero of my favorite hero. Nowadays he has become my favorite hero too. I started to watch his movies and feel connected to my beloved through it. The moment I saw his poster it reminded me everything which I wanted to forget. I wiped the tears from my eyes.

I roamed around the shopping mall and stepped into every shop in it. Like many other women shopping used to be my favorite hobby. Today none of the products managed to impress me. I entered into one of the biggest brand textile showroom which belonged to famous superstar of Bollywood.

'You buy whatever you like' said my father

I understood his attempt of making me to forget my pain. I know even if I purchase for one lakh rupees he won't mind paying it. I felt so proud of my parents and thanked God for making me the daughter such a good people. I don't know how many parents can digest their daughter falling in love with some stranger. My parents were ready to marry me off to a guy of my choice. They are not bothered about caste, religion or even age. All they wanted is their daughter's happiness. They did not try to take control of their child's future completely. They are ready to respect her feeling and desires. I was so proud to have a father like him.

I recalled what he said.

> *My father toiled himself a lot during his young days. He was the responsible person in his family and he did not allow any kind of disturbances in his life.*

Even my father was so responsible son to his parents. He also did not let any disturbances ruin his life. He puts his child's happiness over the society, honor and every other thing. To him his daughter is more important. Not all is blessed with father like mine. He is not like few fathers who consider social status and caste more important than the child's happy future.

I am sorry, Appa for hurting you and Amma so much. You are the best parents in this world. I am ashamed to call myself as your child. I was so selfish only to think about myself.

I was able to see the pain and sorrow in his eyes no matter how much he tried to be normal. For him there should not be anything in this world which he cannot get for his daughter. What to do Appa? I know you are very sad because you are not able to buy the thing which your daughter needs desperately.

'Appa, I wanted to resign my job' I said to him

He did not reply immediately and looked at me so sadly. I tried to control my tears as much as I can.

'I cannot be normal hereafter. I feel like each and every moment I am living in some hell. I wanted to come out of it.' I said

'You cannot come out that hell till you serve your notice period. What you are going to do?' he asked

'I don't know. I cannot stay there anymore watching him daily and behave as if nothing had happened'

'I don't recommend your decision. But if it can make you feel better I have nothing to say. Go ahead' he said

I did not make the decision so easily. The relationship between him and me is going to last only for next 90 days. Then I am a stranger to him. He will erase me off from his life completely. He will behave as if I don't exist in the world.

I resigned my job the next day. My manager tried to convince me to retain here but I was not in a position to breathe in the place where he existed.

'I have a good news for you' I told him

His expression was not normal when he turned towards me. He is feeling warned and he was like ready to counter-attack me if I open the topic again. He will not care to hurt me and rip my heart into million pieces. Only God and I know there is nothing left in me to rip-off.

'What good news?' he asked

'I am leaving' I tried to smile

He frowned.

'I am quitting the job. I am going away forever' I said with fake enthusiasm.

He did not say anything

'I think you will be the happiest person in the world. You will not have to face me at all after 90 days. In few days you will be relived from my tortures' I tried to tease him.

How he will feel? Guilty, sad, sorry. I will be happy if he feels sad about my departure.

'If you think your words are going to hurt me then I am so sorry. I am not that kind of a person. None of your words is going to affect me. Stop your non-sense' he said in harsh tone.

'I know nothing is going to affect you because only people having hearts can get affected. Only human beings have heart. You are a devil. I won't expect emotions from devils.' I said trying to conceal my anger

'I have to warn you. I will not encourage you talking like this. You don't have any rights to mention me as devil. You don't know anything about me and how can you judge me?' he asked angrily

I got little scared.

'I called you as devil because you hurt me a lot.'

'I am not responsible for you to get hurt. I will not tolerate any more if you call me devil once again' he said in threatening tone 'You have not seen my other side of face which is not so pleasant. Don't make show that'

Had I was old Sumana, by this time I would have broken his jaws for talking to me like this. I would have shown him the other face of Suma if it was not for the love I have for him. I got changed completely. I am getting scared at him. His voice chilled everything inside me.

'I am sorry' I told him 'Don't get mad at me. I want both of us to be friends at least. I don't want spoil the relationship between us'

'I am ready to be your friend but you have to stay in our limits. It will be good for both of us. No one has rights to judge my character. Even my father has not rights to do that. I know who I am. I don't have to prove you or anyone that I am a good person.'

'Why are you getting angry? I wanted you to be in my life at least as my friend. I don't want to lose you. We should be in touch even after I leave this company. I wanted to be your close friend that even I give you a blow behind you head you should not get mad at me'

'I am reminding you once again. If you do that blunder in your life I am warning you that will not any see one who can be worse than me. I am not responsible for whatever happens to you after that.' he threatened me again

'I was just kidding. Why would I blow you?' I tried to speak normally. Best friends?'

'That is not a big problem as long as you respect my decisions'

'I will respect your decision. Will you accept me as your best friend' I just not asked rather begged him. I think he is neither able to say yes nor no. I smiled at him. One thing is for sure, he is not ready to have in his life even as a friend.

Days rolled in a good speed and it was a month since I declared my feelings for him for the first time. That day created a pain in me as exactly thirty days before I got the first kiss of my life.

I wanted to celebrate my first kiss's first month anniversary. I started from my place exactly the same time we started from last month. I entered inside a bus and occupied a seat in the last row where I was seated on that day. I watched the time in my watch. I imagined that he was seated by my side in the place where he was seated and closed my eyes for few seconds trying to recreate the scene. I imagined that he is kissing me again. Had I known on that day that it was going to be my last kiss from him I would have enjoyed it to my fullest. I tried to taste his lips in my imagination.

I won't say that I was happy and normal after the episode. I pretended to be happy in front of everyone especially in front of him. I tried to make myself happy in front of my parents. I browsed internet and found ways to come out of the heartbreak. I tried to follow as many steps as possible.

My parents are scared to send me alone anywhere even now. I remember how funnily my father was accompanying me to my office traveling with me for more than hundred kilometers daily. He came with me to drop at mornings and picked me up at evenings. Literally he traveled for more than two hundred kilometers in a day just to ensure I return home safe and alive. Perhaps they were scared if I might jump out of the running train. I initially laughed at his behavior but as days went on it irritated me. I had to fight with both of them to convince that I will not make the foolish decision once again in my life.

My routine in a day passed with smile in my face and tears in my heart. Sometimes my tears flowed down in my face too. The tears which I shed could have supplied water for our home for a year. There was no one to care about what was the reason for my sorrow.

On the other side of my life, my parents doubled their effort to get married to a potential guy. Like a robot I watched everything happening around me. I observed his face. He was so normal and unaffected. After a long time, the self-respect which was sleeping inside me started to wake up slowly. I tried to be normal and unaffected like him.

He almost stopped talking with me. In few occasions when Ashwin initiates any conversations he would join with that. Ashwin remained a mediator between both us. I was tired of getting hurt. When Ashwin is not available we hardly utter a word with each other. I can sense that he wanted to stay away from me. I tried to wake-up the old Sumana who is currently in coma stage.

Meanwhile I have to mention some great things which I did in last few days. I somehow made up my mind to accept the horrible truth of my life. He is not mine and is not going to be mine anymore. One day when I cleaned my bag a thing fell into my lap. It was his key chain. The one which he gifted me on that day. I got an idea. I thought of collecting his memories and some of the things in his remembrance to preserve with me forever.

My fate played with my feelings like 'Snakes and Ladders' game. I would somehow try to control my sorrow and bring my mood to normal and live a routine life slowly like climbing in the ladder. It won't not last long. I will become the victim of the giant snake and everything would come back to zero.

I did funny things like listening to sad songs of heart breaks, watching movies of love failures etc. I preferred solitude and almost stopped talking with everyone.

One day I watched a Tamil movie "Vinnaithaandi Varuvaaya" which was a blockbuster hit when it was released leading to remakes in other regional languages like Telugu and Hindi. It is such a melodious romantic story.

The story of the movie is 'Hero falls in love with daughter of his landlord on the first sight. She is from different religion and elder in age than him. He madly loves her and proposes her. He convinces to love him but she runs away because she knew it would not work between them as her father will not marry off her to a guy from some other religion. I related my love story to many scenes in that movie.

In one scene, when hero kissed his love in her lips, I remembered how he kissed me.

In another scene heroine utters a dialogue '*I like this but I don't want it. All I see is only the problem. It won't work between us*'. I got reminded of him saying '*I have emotions on you. I like you a lot. But I don't want this. I am feeling like a sugar patient. You are a sweet. I like sweet but I don't want to eat it.*'

In another scene, the dialogue '*My father is a very nice man and I don't know why he is so adamant in this issue alone. I don't want hurt my father. It will never work between us*' reminded him saying '*I don't want to hurt my parents again.*'

On the scene where the hero begs heroine to come with him but heroine refuses I reminded the most horrifying conversation of my life where I begged him to accept me in his life.

In another scene, the hero roams around devastated after he broke up with his lady love and now I am roaming around devastated like him. The only difference between the hero and me was, he does not meet her after breaking up with her but I am meeting him daily.

It was not the first time I am watching the movie. I recalled the day when I watched the movie five years back. I remember saying '*How it is possible for a girl to fall in love with a guy who is younger to her? Doesn't look awkward? The heroine fell in love with him even she knew that she is younger to him. That sounds weird.*'.

> '*It is not correct according to me. You know what when I come to know a guy is younger than me immediately I start to see him like a child. He looks like a kid to my eyes. Even if he is one year younger to me. I cannot imagine such a thing in my life.*'

The memories brought smile in me. I criticized the movie when it showed an elder woman falling in love with younger guy and now the same movie which is relating my life in many scenes has become close to my heart. Had anyone told me on that day that my life is going to turn upside down like in that movie, I would have either laughed at them or strangled them to death.

There is a dialogue in the movie which occupied special place in fan's heart especially with youngsters. The hero would ask himself '*When there are so many girls in this world, why did I fall in love with her?*'

I wanted to ask the same question myself 'When there are so many men in this world, why the hell did I fall in love with him?'

I started to record my love memories beginning with the same dialogue.

I got tensed when I heard the calling bell sound four times. I am having the collections which my parents are not supposed to see. I hid them in my back pack as fast as I could and opened the door. I was very surprised by the person who accompanied my parents.

'Shradhdha?'

I looked at my parents and her with surprise. What is she doing here?

'We met her on the way' said my mother

My mother turned to her and said 'We are leaving now. It will take an hour or two for us to return. You both have your time here.'

'No problem, aunty. I will take care'

I was not able to understand their conversation and I am not able to believe what I am seeing. Is she the same Shradhdha who I met some months back? Last time when I saw her she was in complete intoxicated state behaving like an insane. Now I am very able to see the drastic transformation. All in few weeks of time.

'What are you looking at? After a long time I have come here. You are not inviting me inside.' said Shradhdha

I got back to the world.

'Yeah. You are already in.'

'I can understand there are lot of questions in your mind.' she asked me

I nodded my head as 'Yes'

'Let me come straight to the point. I heard there were non-senses happened in your life in last few weeks. Being a friend it is you who should have told about them to me but I had to hear it from your parents' her voice was in anger

I was not able to look at her eyes. My parents told her about what happened in my life.

'I was not in a position to share my sorrow to anyone.'

'I was very surprised when your parents told that you faced heartbreak. Surprise even shock is an ordinary word to explain how I felt on hearing about this. Suma falling in love is equivalent to me hearing that Sun rises in the West.'

I did not look at her and left the place.

'Suma, as far love, break-up, heartbreaks are concerned I am very senior to you. No one but me can heal you better from you pains. You have heard a proverb right 'A Friend In Need is a friend indeed.'

I smiled at her.

'You are going to heal me from pain?' I asked her mockingly

'Why not?'

'Let me first ask you something. When I spoke to you last time, you said you did some prayers to get your boyfriend back? What happened? Any Good news?'

'Yeah. There is good news. Marriage got fixed'

My face turned bright

'That is cool. Has he accepted you? When is the marriage? You have not told me until I asked? This is not fair'

'Wait a minute. I told marriage is fixed. Not mine. His marriage is fixed with some other girl.'

'What?' I exclaimed in shock 'How it is possible? You told you did some tough prayers to make him accept you. You said you are waiting for him to come back. Your prayer has not worked?'

'I don't know. I waited for him for one week, four weeks, and eight weeks. He did not come back to me. One day I met his friend at a mall. He hesitated and avoided meeting me. I chased him vigorously and caught him. It was then I found my ex-boyfriend is going to get married to a girl chosen by his parents.'

Though she tried to speak casually I was able to understand the pain and bitterness in her voice.

'I contacted the priest and asked why the prayer had not worked. He told that the prayer done by me was not accepted. In order to make the prayer successful I have to do another prayer and it will cost around thousands. I got angry. It was then I understood he cheated me and sucked my money.'

'I already told you these are all not true. You have cheated yourself.'

'I will not say that definitely. When he left me I almost had gone insane. I was not able to live normally even for single minute. When I heard about this prayer, I got a new ray of hope. That hope made me to live for these many days. According to me, the money I spent or wasted is for making me alive. Otherwise I would have taken any extreme step.'

'I can understand how you would have felt when you heard about his marriage' I tried to console her

'Everything is over. He is a coward. I already wasted lot of my energy and money. Enough is enough. Now I am fine.'

'But…'

'Stop! I have not come here to share my sad story. My episode is finished. Let us talk about this.' she said and took something from her bag

It was my diary. I got shocked. After all those incidents happened, I was not able to share grieves to anyone around me. No one had time to listen to my sad story. It was then I decided to pour my pain to myself. I started to write all the incidents which led to the heartbreak in my life. I kept in very secret place as I had written many matters which I have not and which I am not supposed to share with anyone. Somehow I thought I misplaced somewhere and I cannot explain how tensed I was thinking about the whereabouts of the diary.

'Your parents gave me this.' she told me

I felt like getting fainted. How it is possible? How my parents knew about this? It means they have also read it.

'Your face turned pale white in few seconds. I hope now you have understood the danger of writing diary memories. It is the super blunder which you have done in your life. You have trusted your parents so much but for the sake of well-being of their daughter they had to read it'

I felt like I got a heavy blow on my head. I remember how secretly I kept it my bag and locked it in my wardrobe. How my mother managed to find it? Worst of all she had read it.

'Reading one's diary is equivalent to peeping into someone's bathroom while they are bathing. I am very well aware of it. Since your parents themselves gave me permission I read it. Please accept my honest apologies.'

What I can say?

'What is this?' she asked me looking at my collections bag

I got terrified. What if she sees it? It was same time we both of them reached the place where I have kept secrets but I was bit late by a second. She got the bag in her hand.

'Nice handbag. Nice design too. Name also sounds nice. 'Love Paradise''

I gave an embarrassing smile

'I would have not given importance had I not saw your rush to prevent me from taking this bag. I am sorry your reaction to reach this bag has made me to open it and see what is inside'

'There is nothing special in it. I have just put some of my old papers bills, credit card slips. That is it'

'Then why did you rush when I saw it?'

I did not answer to it.

'Suma, I think it is part of my mission to see the contents in the bag. Now if you please allow me to get inside your 'Love paradise' ' she said to me and looked at my hands which was grabbing the bag.

I took my hands from it. She sat on the bed and started to browse it. I her face showed mixed expressions one seeing the stuffs in it. She looked at me with surprise, horror, shock, disgust etc. etc. etc.

'Suma, I am not able to understand what I am seeing. I need explanations from you'

'What you want to know?'

'What is this?' she asked pointing to a pen in her hand.

'It is a pen' I teased her.

'I did not say it is a pin' she asked angrily 'I am asking about the thing at the end.'

The pen was engraved with the name 'Ganesh Shankar'

'I specially ordered it. I thought when I use this pen I will not miss him.'

'How can you use this? When you are writing with this pen and someone asks you whose name is that in that pen, what will be your answer?'

'Not a big deal. I will say the pen belonged my friend. I took from him one day and forgot to return it.' I said causally

She took the next stuff from the bag. It was a calendar and she turned every month in it and looked at me with same mixed expressions.

'It was also specially ordered and designed photo-calendar. When I have this on my desk I will not miss him.' I said to her

'How did you get the photographs for this calendar?' she asked

'I downloaded it from Facebook.' I said

She threw the calendar furiously on the bed. She took the next item and frowned on looking at it.

'This is used tetra pack. It smells bad. You whole bag smells bad. What it has got to do here?' she asked me

I hesitated to say what it is but I know she will not leave me unless I reveal what it is.

'It was used by him. I took it from the dust-bin.'

Probably she got tired to looking at me angrily. I was not able to explain her expression when she took the next item

'Chocolate wrappers?' she said with frustration

'Yes. Same as tetra-pack' I replied with smile.

She took the next stuff.

'Paper cup?' she frowned

I did not see her as I was not able to control my laughter on her expression. How she will react if I say to her that it was the coffee-cup used and thrown by him during one of the coffee-breaks.

She then took other stuffs like comb, then a super market membership card, a photocopy, a certificate which contained his name and a wedding invitation card. She then took a tissue paper and looked at me in surprise.

'Don't say that this tissue paper was used by him' she said to me with be wilderness in her voice.

I laughed on seeing her face.

'Oh My God! You haven't spared even the used tissue paper. Aren't you aware how much germs will be present in it. The germs would have spread into this entire bag by this time. I touched this germ filled bag and I am going to get some disease because of this' she screamed with fear.

It was so funny seeing her screaming like this.

'Did you follow him to gent's toilet and took the tissue paper used by him from there? I cannot believe you did this.' She screamed again.

I was not able to control the laughter.

'Stop laughing. Don't you have any hygiene sense? You don't know in which part of the body he used this?'

She screamed angrily

'Do you know there is a song from movie?'

I sang that song and looked at her.

'Love has no auspicious time and love has no hygiene. You know it right?'

She screamed angrily and her face showed disgust.

'Alright! That is not the used tissue paper. I kept it long time back. It is un-used.'

'Can I trust you?'

Now I angrily glared at her. She took the next thing from the bag and unfolded it. Her eyes grew widen.

'This is a poster of him.' She looked at me but I did not look at her.

'I don't know what to say. Your collections are very much threatening. Which stupid gave you this collecting idea?' She asked

'I saw in a movie.'

'Yes. I remember. Heroine will collect the empty used Coca-Cola tin, chocolate papers, battery cell used by hero and …' she stopped and looked angrily at me.

She took the cover inside the bag and opened it. I got terrified and once tried to grab it from her but she prevented me.

'Step away from me. I don't want you to touch these things until I finish my inspection' she said in a warning modulation.

On seeing me standing there she yelled 'I said step back else I will lock you in that room'

I stepped away from her. She opened the cover and took the greeting cards inside it. I got bored with her expression. The same old shocked one.

She took the first card

'To my beloved from Sumi,

When you read these you may laugh at me thinking that I have gone mad and insane. Yes, that is true. I am losing my mind slowly. You may even get angry at me for my behavior. But if I control my emotions I am afraid I may become a lifeless thing.

Don't you see, I am walking towards point of no-return hoping to hear you call me

'SUMI'

And stop me saying that you will marry me and be my soul mate till my last breath.

Please stop me.

I am waiting to hear your voice. Please stop and rescue from dark of hell'

She threw that card angrily and took the next one. It read

'I Love you Sweet heart

I somehow had courage to open my heart to you once. But after you mercilessly asked me to get out your heart and shut the door I don't have courage to knock the door once again. Please invite me inside by yourself.

For others you are an ordinary human being. For me you are a savior. I am trapped in the hell of dark. Please come and rescue me. Your only word

I love you is the key to open the door of hell. Come soon'

I took the cards which she threw angrily and I read it once again. I started to laugh at her expressions.

Another card read,

'My Angel of happiness, God of my heart. Please accept me in your life

If you reading these cards by chance you must understand that they are my feelings of my heart which I don't dare to show in front of you fearing of losing you.

I am really wounded by the fact that you closed the chapter saying your parents won't accept and you don't want to hurt your parents. Is it really that reason? Or you used your parents to go away from me? What your ex-girlfriend did to you, you are doing the same to me.

I am straight behind you struggling, erupting, bursting, and breaking my own heart? Can't you see that? You begged your girl for eight months but I am not able to beg even for eight seconds. All I can do is just pour my heart in this paper'

'Enough' she screamed. 'I just cannot tolerate this nonsense anymore'

I did not make any attempt to control my laughter. I laughed so much that I got tears from my eyes and my stomach started to ache.

'Stop laughing, idiot.' She shouted at me 'I was in a relationship for two years. Even I did not behave like this. Suma, is this really you who have done all these?'

I did not answer her.

'I cannot just believe that you have scribbled like this. I just cannot breathe.' She said

'You have finished only till the interval. Come on watch the other half of the picture' I teased her.

'No need. I don't want to see even single letter from those garbage. Take it away from me' she screamed.

'But I want it. It has been several days I burst laughed like this. I don't want to miss the fun. Wait, I will read it for you' I told her.

I took another card from the bag and read

> *'Sweetheart, when you will come to me and say 'I Love you'? Why can't you see that I am breaking down right in front of you? Please save me before I collapse completely.'*

She closed her ears tightly. I continued to read loudly.

> *'I am knocking the door of every temple I find in my way. I am begging every God I pass by to pass the message which I am giving you. When I am exhausted with my trials to win your heart I am relying on the Supreme power. What I have for you is not just love but something more than that'*

She tried to walk away from there but I held hands tightly and did the reading from next card.

> *'I don't care even if you throw me the gifts which I kept for you. When did God accept our offerings directly? I am happy that it is for you and always for you. My desire if fulfilled.*
>
> *You are thinking about the girl who left and you are leaving the girl who always thinks about you. Why are you so cruel? Give me a chance. I will make your parents understand'*

'Suma, leave my hand. I am erupting right now. I don't know when I will blast. I am warning you' she said to me

'It is my bad luck that your heart beats for the girl who left you but my heart beats to be with you till my last breath. I know not even single word written is going to change your mind. I cannot give this to you but I pray God that you should somehow read these one day and you will understand who and what I am'

She struggled and got rid of my hold. I cannot help myself from stop laughing on her seeing her face. She got back to the place and angrily threw everything scattered around her.

'The only relieving thing is that he do not know how stupid you were. How he would have felt had he seen these non-senses. I just cannot imagine' she said and looked at me.

I cleared my throat.

'What?' she exclaimed 'I don't like the expression in your face. He has not seen any of these them, is it not?'

I nodded slowly as 'Yes'. Her eyes grew so wide that I was scared if it might roll out from her face.

'How did see this?' her voice was lowered.

'Promise that you will not harm me' I told her. 'I gave him to read it'

Her reaction was so fast that I did not get even a single second to run away from that place. She held my neck tightly ready to be strangled.

'Shameless! Stupid! Idiot! Fool! I am going to kill you' she screamed angrily. 'You are not a human being at all.'

Oh My God! This girl is really in murderous rage.

'Help! Help! Help!' I screamed.

She tried to strangle my neck hard and at one point she got tired.

'You have done a mistake' she told me. 'You should have not used an ordinary ball pen for pouring your heart in those greeting cards. Instead you could have used your blood and written them. You might have got drastic effect'

'Why did I not think of it before?' I gave a sound thought

She looked at me angrily and I was not dared to see her face to face.

'Suma, is the girl who is in front of me is the same who spoke about self-respect, honor, dignity some months back? How much have you degraded yourself! Did not you realize that these are worst behavior by any woman?' she spoke with utmost frustration.

I felt so sad on rewinding those days.

'I was so stressed. I thought he may be moved on reading them' I told her.

'You tried to create sympathy?' she yelled 'Love is not something given out of sympathy. It is something which should come from deep from heart. A Love gained out of sympathy is the worst disgrace for anyone.'

I kept silent.

'Probably he might have come back to you out of sympathy. Is it that you wanted? You know what, making someone to love us using sympathy is like winning in a fight but losing a battle.'

'I told you isn't it? Out of depression and stress I behaved like this. You know how it feels when you lost in your love. He rejected me. I was not able to tolerate. I was not stable mentally. I was not able to do anything. I struggled even to breath'

'But this is too much.'

'Even you behaved like a mad. You went some places for doing prayer to bring your boyfriend' I taunted her

'My boyfriend does not know what I did. In your case, you yourself projected how much lower you can go.'

'Past is past. I know I was wrong. There is nothing I have to regret. During that time I felt it was right thing to do. I cannot change what has happened.'

'At least you can change what is going to happen? Is it not?' she asked me

I looked at her surprised. She took the poster from there and went to kitchen. She came out with something in her hand.

'I don't know why you bought this poster. But we will make use of it now.'

I looked like 'how'

'From what I understood from your diary is that, he has no intentions to have you in his life. Not as his girlfriend and not even as his friend. Am I right?'

I nodded as 'yes'

'We don't need anyone to be in our life who don't need us. Throw him out of your life. Once for all forever'

She gave me the poster and a matchbox.

'Burn this poster. Come one' she screamed.

I got shocked. 'What do you mean?'

'I mean it. Do you remember the movie where heroine will suggest hero to burn down the photograph of his ex-girlfriend. He will say that he feel better after doing that. Similarly you also burn this photo poster right now'

'Rubbish' I said

'No, it is not. You have to do it. Even I did that. I torn each and every photograph of my boy-friend when I heard he got his marriage fixed. I deleted all the photographs of them too. I burned the photo album and you know what, I felt so happy and satisfied as if I has burned him alive. I felt like I got out of some prison and became a free-bird. I suggest you to do this. Burn it quickly' she insisted me.

I stood staring at her.

'Why are you standing like a statue? Did not you hear what I said? Burn this poster this very minute' Shradhdha screamed in high pitch

Her voice would trigger neighbors. Sure one or two may wonder what is going on in our home and start to enquire.

'Suma, I am talking to you now.' He screamed again

'I won't' I said firmly 'I cannot do it'

'You can and you should do it' she said firmly 'That is how you are going to get peace of mind?'

'I am fine as I am'

'I won't accept that' she said.

I looked at her angry expression. She took the diary and flashed in front of my face.

'Whoever reads the diary will not surely believe that you are fine' she said angrily

I turned away from her

'Suma, I am senior to you in relationship. We both were together for two years. You cannot imagine how much we were close on those days. Two years. More than seven hundred days. Even I did not do the foolishness which you did in last few days.' She screamed at me

I did not say anything

'Suma, tell me the real truth. Do you love him still? Are you hoping that he will come back in your life' she asked me

I kept silent.

'Suma, try to understand. He is not worth your love. He does not love you. He never loved you and will never love you.'

'I know' I said

'Then why the hell you are so stubborn about not forgetting him?' she shrieked

'I am trying to forget him' I said

'I don't think so.' She said 'If you really making such an attempt, then what is the meaning of these?'

She threw my collections bag at me. The things inside scattered at different directions.

'Why do you want to have this with you? Why you are hesitating to burn his poster?'

I cannot answer her

'Suma, you don't know how I felt when I read the conversation that happened between you too. I cannot explain how angry I felt when I read it. How can a person be such a rude and mean to a woman who loves him more than her life? He is not a human being at all. He is more than a devil. He is a Satan. Only those creatures can be cruel to innocent people' she spoke angrily

I smiled at her. I thought how Ganesh would react on hearing her praises on him. He would have broken the bones and tooth in her face.

'I was not able to tolerate the harshness of the words he spoke. How did you allow him to behave with you like that? You have written his words stabbed in your heart like a knife. He did not just hurt you. He has insulted you, your love, your care, your affection and everything. The actual fact is he has slapped you with his slippers. Did not you realize that?'

She reminded me the day once again. Tears started to roll from my eyes. She angrily turned the pages in the diary and quoted the lines.

'Look here what he has told' she pointed out the line

'I will try to convince my parents for the girl who I love deeply. I can even fight with him for

her. Why should I fight and argue with my parents for you?'

And here you see what he has said *'I will fight for Swati. I will not fight for you'*

And this dialogue surely no woman will tolerate.

'You will sacrifice my life for me but I will sacrifice my life only for Swati. I cannot love any other woman like I loved her'

Tears flowed from my eyes.

'Suma, You don't deserve this humiliation, sweetheart. You are such a nice girl. You wanted to live with the person whom you love until your last breath. He loves the girl who dumped him mercilessly. Why do you want to go behind such a guy? He is not worth of your love at all. I have never heard if a guy can be so mean to the woman who has done nothing wrong except loving him more than her life. How can he do this to you? If I ever meet him in my life I would sure kill him the very next minute' shouted Shradhdha loudly

Tears kept flowing from eyes in spite of my repeated attempts to stop it.

'Even a woman who has not heard a word called 'self-respect' would not tolerate it. I have seen only this Sumana who would not spare if her self-respect is pinched. Where is she now? Is she alive or not?' she shake my body heavily

'He does not love you. For him you are one among women standing in queue waiting to be loved by him. You are in waiting list. This guy was already proposed by two girls earlier and you were the third one. He has scored three points in his life. This is the ego of a guy. You have quenched his ego. You fell for him and now he is happy that he is capable of impressing woman of any age. He will feel himself like a love God. You let it happen with him'

I continued to be silent

'Suma, known score was two. What is the unknown score? You don't know how many other women proposed him? Perhaps you are not third one may be 30th or 40th one. You allowed him to score one point in his life. You are a human being not a score point. He has seen you as one option not as an answer to empty blank in his life'

I was not able to say anything

'Suma, a woman should be an answer in a man's life not as an option. Why do you want to be an option to one question when you can be an answer to some other question? Can I say one thing? Some girls proposed him in past, you proposed him currently and some more girls will propose him future. He will not accept any of them. He will marry a woman whom his parents choose. While romancing with his wife, in bed, to please her he would utter a dialogue like this *'Sweetheart, You cannot imagine how many women chased your husband madly. He somehow managed to escape from all of them only to get trapped to you'*. His wife will feel proud for having won a man's heart who is lost by many other women. He may utter this to her even to irritate and make her jealous. Or else he would proudly express to his kids about his achievements of how he managed to impress women and make them fall in love with him.'

I recalled the incident with my father where I asked him

> *'Appa, this is too much. You mean to say you were a dream-boy of women of those days. Each and every woman proposed you and you rejected them. What was your score?'*

She is correct. I allowed him to score one point in his life. I felt so ashamed of myself.

'You have wrote some non-senses in those greeting cards and even you let him to read them. I think no woman can do such a blunder in her life. You know what he would say to his wife? '*Many women chased me in my life. One of my colleague who was madly in love with me wrote me love letters in blood*'. You have written the letters in simple blue ball point pen. The blue ball pen ink will change as blood in future. For him, you are just a '*one of*'. Underline the word '*one of*' the women who chased him to be in his life. For you he is memory and for him you are nothing but one random girl in his life. Do you wish to be some random girl in his life?'

Her questions fled like an arrow from the bow. It directly aimed at my brain.

'Suma, right from the beginning he did not love you. You confused yourself with his behavior. I don't know what made you to choose him for your life. Like he said, you have mistaken sympathy for love.'

'I never confuse my feelings with sympathy' I said

'Then what is that you found in him? What made my strong Suma who considers self-respect as more than her life to beg him for love?'

I smiled at her

'What made Shradhdha to take extreme step to leave a place alone and did prayers to win back her boy-friend?'

She glared at me angrily

'I understood how foolish I was. When you are going to realize?'

'Who said I did not realize?'

'Get rid of him then she said angrily

'Shradhdha, please don't scold him. I am begging you'

'Why should I not? He has hurt my friend so badly. I wanted to kill him'

'He may have hurt me still he wanted to do something good. He did not want to ruin my life and so he backed off. He is a good guy.'

'Has he been a good guy, he would have not come closer to you. He would have not kissed you. He would have finished everything in the beginning'

'He is still far better than your ex-boyfriend. Again I am saying I can understand his situation. It is my fault. He clearly told me that he does not want to continue things and closed the chapter. It was me who tried to re-open. He got angry for disturbing him' I said

She frowned

'Imagine the situation in reverse. What I would have done, had someone who tortures me to marry them even after I expressed that I am not interested. Will not I get mad?'

She looked at me with shock

'You still support him. Remember he has insulted you'

'I deserved it. I am not lucky to have him as my soul-mate'

'Absolutely wrong. He is not lucky to have you in his life. I swear, no woman can love him like you do'

I smiled

'What is the use when he is not realizing it? I know I can shower all the love of my life on him. He is not ready to accept that'

'Suma, let me tell you something. A customer visits a car showroom. He looks at two different cars. He chooses less expensive out of the two. That doesn't mean the expensive car is worthless. He cannot afford it. Your love is such an expensive thing like the expensive car. It deserves a place only in the worthy hands. That guy doesn't deserve that expensive thing. Perhaps his ex-girlfriend cleverly realized it'

'No Shradhdha. She dumped him. She is not ready to marry against her parent's wishes' I said

'Have you met that girl?' she asked

I nodded like 'no'

'Then how do you know this?'

'He told me'

'Have you ever heard a film called 'Rashomon'?'

I frowned. Why is she asking about something irrelevant? I said 'Yes'

'A murder take place and trial is going on in a court. There are three witnesses. Each of them narrate their own story in their perspective and none of them proved correct. At the last the final true story is revealed in the perspective of the spirit of the dead. He told you his version of the story about his break-up.'

I did not say anything.

'By chance some you meet that girl in life and if you ask her about why she broke-up with him she would say thousands of justifications which will make her point correct. He was able to break you completely in two days. How much he would have broken her in the years of their relationship. I really appreciate that girl for dumping him. She did not dump him rather she fled away. I am damn sure that she is living so happily after leaving him'

'Shradhdha, stop it' I screamed 'You are too mean. When we don't know what happened actually why should we criticize?'

'I cannot control my fury' she screamed 'He made you to lose yourself. I cannot believe that it was you who begged him like that and to the worst of all you attempted suicide.'

I felt very bad on that. I cannot face her.

'Please don't talk about that. I feel so guilty'

'You deserve it' she taunted me 'Do you remember how you behaved when Aradhana done the same thing? You scolded her that she did not think about her parents not even for a second. You did the same thing now. Assuming that you succeeded in your suicide mission? What would have happened? Do you think he would have owed of never marrying any girl in his life?'

'He would have felt sorry for you. Perhaps if he has heart, he would have felt guilty for few days. Then he will forget about you. People around him will convince that there is no fault of him in your death. Slowly he will persuade himself and move-on. Years later he will marry a girl, have children and live happily. But here your parents will suffer the most irreversible effect of their life. Every year on your death anniversary they will die once again. The guy will live happily somewhere and he will not remember you even on your death anniversary' she screamed

'Please stop.' I pleaded her

'I will not stop. Where has your self-respect gone? Where has your confidence vanished?' she screamed like anything

All I was able to do is stand silent.

'I know what is happening with you. There is no single second that you did not think about him. He is haunting you in your memories. You are immersing yourself in the hell of darkness only to hurt yourself. You will be trying to send messages to him from your deep inside heart but it was not received by him. Most importantly you would have done this for sure.'

'What?'

'You would have set all of your passwords with his name. Is it not?'

She describes everything as though she watched everything every second with me. Like she told, I have set my bank password, office login password and many other passwords with his name. For those who succeed in love, loved ones becomes spouses and for those who fail, loved ones become passwords.

'Your eyes are giving me thousands of 'Yes'' she said

I grinned with shame.

'Sometimes I hate when I am correct.' she said angrily. 'The horrible truth is, on the each and every second when you shed tears thinking of him, he was happy and joyful with someone who is important to him than you. When you cried here he was laughing with someone happily. He is clear in what he wants and he is so sure that he does not need you. Goddamn it you have no place in his life. Are you getting me, you fool?' she screamed in high voice.

I saw her and her attempts to make me realize the truth

'He thinks he can live in this world without you. What makes you to think that you cannot live without him? You managed to survive in this world till now and you can survive without him in coming years too.'

'Everyone has rights to accept or reject any proposals they get. I know I begged him to marry me. I did not want to regret later in my life for not having taking my chance. Now that I have made a try. I am fine that I failed after trying instead of failing by not trying.' I said 'Don't be mad at him.'

'He is no one to me. I don't care who he is or what he is. All I am concerned about is to bring my friend back from the horror she is going through. Follow your brain not your heart'

'Some days back you told to follow your heart and not brain'

'I will slap myself for that. Enough?'

'I will follow the brain. Don't worry' I said to her. I somehow wanted to stop the conversation.

'Then burn the poster and throw away all those garbage.' she said firmly

I stood silent

'Let it be with me' I pleaded her 'I cannot get rid of them'

She looked at me pitifully

'I know it is not as easy as I say. I can help you. I will throw everything on your behalf. Let me throw'

She took the bag in her hand. I angrily grabbed it from her

'Those are not memories' she warned 'They are the poison of your life'

'For now it is not poison to me. It is the medicine which is going to help me to live in this world. I wanted him to be with me in some form. These things are going to fill up the empty space in my life for now. Please don't take it away from me' I pleaded her

She stood silently. I felt so bad.

'Baby, please don't get me wrong. I need time. I cannot let it go easily' I said

'When there are so many men in the world, why did you fall in love with him?' she asked

I looked at her with surprise. She started to laugh at me and I started to laugh with her.

'What about this?' she asked pointing to a gift box

I looked sadly at the box.

'Are you going to gift him?'

'I wanted to gift him but I don't dare to do it. He may think that I am trying to trap him.'

'Then un-wrap the gift.'

'That is the gift for him. I am not going to do it'

She looked at me with surprise

'It is going to be with me forever unwrapped. It is also going to be my memory of him.'

'I wanted to give you an award. 'Foolish lover of the world' she teased angrily

I smiled

'From the love stories of Aradhana, me and you, I can conclude few things. It is a lesson for all the women in the world'

I looked her like 'What?'

'Falling in a love with a man is third mistake. Falling in love with an Indian man is second and falling in love with an Indian man whose parents are alive is not just a mistake rather blunder'

'Falling in love with an Indian colleague is the peak of the blunder' I said to her

We both laughed.

There are many difficult tasks in this world. If someone asks me whether crossing Grand Canyon on a single rope is difficult or meeting the person whom we love and behaving as if nothing had happened, I would say prefer the latter. Meeting the loved one after heart-break is hard task. Meeting the loved one daily and behave as if nothing had happened is harder. Meeting the loved ones only to see him not being affected by incidents happened is hardest of all.

I had go through all the hardest tasks daily. I met him, talked with him and we had all the fun during break time. I wished to spend every second with him and preserve it in my heart but he did not give me much chance. He was so sunken in his thoughts and very busy in his work. All I was able to do is cry, cry and cry. Not even single drop of tear had capacity to move his heart. He is not ready to care about me and distanced himself as much as possible.

I have two options now. Either tolerate all insults of him and preserve the friendship with him or walk away from him as distant as possible. Had it been old Sumana choice number two would have chosen. Current Sumana had lost all her self-respect and preferred the option number one.

I have to surely mention few things. He was caring and soft when I did not cross my limits. We cannot come a conclusion on a person's character. A person who is a villain to whole world will be a loving and caring to his family. A person who according to world is nice and descent shall be a terrific to some people. It all depends on how they behave with us.

He was a very rude and mean to me when I insisted him to accept me as his life-partner. At the same time he was soft to me when he was a caring colleague. I wanted to be his soul mate but destiny denied that rights. I wanted to be his close friend and he denied it

I tried to be his best friend only to demote my importance in his life as just a colleague. He misunderstood my interaction with him as my attempt to get close with him.

'I am not comfortable with the way you are behaving with me' he said

'I was just trying to be your friend'

'I could have allowed you to be my friend few months back but not now. You are not the same person as you were before'

'I wanted to be your friend. I don't have any other intention'

'I have a lot of respect for you. You have a place in my heart. I will surely miss you after you have left. But it is meant to happen. It is good for both of us. I want to keep you away from me. Please understand. Don't make me feel bad' he said

My heart did not break this time as it was already broken into million pieces.

'If you want me to stay away from you I am fine with that. I will not disturb you.'

'Some decisions are meant to be taken for good cause. Don't think I am heartless. I had to make this decision for the well-being and future of both of us. Don't get me wrong'

From then on, I started to distance myself from him. Silence is the loudest cry of any girl in this world. I did not involve in anyway in his activities. I tried to be his colleague alone. I don't think I can lower myself more than this. A guy is not comfortable with me and running away from me. What a great pride for a woman like me! It seemed too much comfortable for him.

'What gift you want for your farewell?' he asked me one day

Tears once again peeped from my eyes. I have now practiced to control tears from flowing down no matter how hard the pain in my heart is. He is so keen to get rid of me. What is use of crying and hurting myself when he is so casual about my departure? He is so unaffected. I tried to be unaffected too.

'It is your wish' I tried to be casual

I rolled the pen in my hands. I bought it as special as a gift for him. It contained his name in it. I was so hesitant whether to give it to him or not but somehow gathered courage to give it to him. He was very focused on something in his system.

'Are you busy right now?' I asked him

'Yes.' he replied in one word

'Can you spend some five minutes of your time?'

'I cannot. I have lot of work' he said

'Just five minutes' I pleaded

'I said I cannot. Can't you see how much I am busy here?' he yelled

'Are you busy really?' I asked him angrily 'If you are so busy then how come you are chatting in WhatsApp? You are talking to Ashwin and to Prakash. You have time to message your friends but cannot give five minutes for me' I tried to ask him politely but somehow anger burst in my voice.

'Don't talk rubbish. You are talking as if you know everything. I don't have to answer you for whatever I am doing. I am very busy here. A person is waiting for me at some corner giving me instructions. I am executing it. Why don't you understand?' he yelled

'All I want is just five minutes' I begged 'can't you give that five minutes for me?'

'I cannot give even a minute to you. Even to president of America. Do you get it?' he screamed

'Why are you so angry? Work is there always. Even I have been busy with my work. I have never been harsh like this'

'You may be Jesus or Buddha. I don't care. I cannot handle multiple things at a time. I am very busy with my work. I don't want to talk to you. Please go away. If you insist me still, then I cannot guarantee how much respect I can give for you. I am warning you'

As usual tears peeped into my eyes. I was able to feel the hatred in his voice which he has for me in his words. I did not talk to him for that whole day.

'Ashwin, look at this guy. How rudely he behaves with me! He is not giving respect to my age' I lamented

'Looks like he is stressed out of something and he is bursting out of it. Better stay away from him.' he said

'Why should I tolerate his stress? Is it the way of behaving with a colleague? I am feeling so bad about it. Please make him understand how much I am hurt by his behavior. He is so stressed yet he talks with respect to you but he is not giving me any respect' I said

'I cannot do anything in this. You are trying to change him. There is no use. It is him who has to realize. I advice you keep away from him.'

I did not talk to him for the whole day. I decided not talk with him for rest of my life until he apologizes for his behavior.

I did not sleep the whole night. I was not able to sleep. I was tired of crying. I cannot imagine myself living a life without talking with him or living with him. But the bitter truth is I have to live. So why should I go mad on him and spoil the relationship? I decided to break the ice next morning.

Sumana: Hi, Are you still angry on me?

I waited for reply from him. He did not reply at all. The message status showed that it was not sent. I was so anxious about getting reply from him. Will reply harshly or politely? Nowadays Ganesh's behavior with respect to Sumana is just rudeness. I dropped another message.

Sumana: Is it really fair? Let us settle down whatever issues we have with us. Are you aware of how much you are hurting me?

I did not get any reply from him still. The train stopped at a station. I got down from the coach I traveled and got inside the coach where he used to travel. I saw him standing there and felt little nervous.

God! Please save me. He should not insult me in front of everyone.

'I came to this coach to meet you' I said

'Oh' he said

'Are you still mad at me?' I asked anxiously

'No. I am not.' he replied.

'I dropped you message in WhatsApp. You did not reply me and that is why I came to meet you'

He looked at the surrounding cautiously and said 'Let us talk in our cubicle'

'I did not sleep for entire night. I was just thinking about this only. I thought of settling things as I am going to stay with you only for few days' I tried to control my weep.

'Let us talk in our cubicle' he said in low voice but firmly

'You are too busy with your work. I cannot talk with you there and that is why I am stressing to settle issues here'

'I was busy yesterday. So I was not able to talk with you. So please listen to me. We will talk in cubicle' his voice was more firm

I had no other go other than to obey him. If I try to talk further he may behave rudely with me. The rest of the journey was spent in silence until we reached our cubicle.

'Why you are behaving like this? What you are expecting me to do?' he yelled at me

'I tried to settle down issues between us. I dropped you a message you did not reply' I said

'That doesn't mean you can behave like this? I am expecting a maturity from you and you are disappointing me. You expect me to feel bad on hearing you saying that you have not slept whole night? Did I ask you stay awake whole night? I was so busy yesterday and I did not want to talk with anyone. You kept on disturbing me. I asked you to go away but you kept insisting me to spend five minutes.'

'I did not know you were so busy. I am sorry' I said

'Do you know how much you are making me feel bad? You always complaint on me. You are making me to feel low. Make me feel good. I cannot tolerate this anymore' he yelled

'Actually I wanted you to spend five minutes so that I can give you this'

I took the pen from my draw and gave it to him.

'I bought this pen for you. I wanted to give this to you yesterday and you got mad at me'

He took the pen from me. What is he going to say? Will he accept my gift or throw it at my face? He looked at the pen and then at me. He looked at his name engraved in the pen

'Thanks' he said

Thank God! He accepted the gift and most importantly he did not insult me. Can I give the other gift to him now? How he will react to it?

'One more thing I wanted to give it to you' I said and I took the wrapped gift and gave it to him.

He looked at me with surprise.

'What is this? You are keep on showering gifts?'

'I bought this gift a long time back. I thought of giving it to you'

His face showed an embarrassing expression

'I don't want this gift' he said

'Please don't mistake me' I said with hesitation 'I specifically bought it for you. I cannot take it back'

'Already you have given me enough gifts. I cannot take this' he said

'This is a very friendly gift. I am giving it to you as a friend. Not with any other intention' I lied to him

I bought the gift with all love in this world. That was not just a gift but all the love I had for him. After my father he is the guy for whom I have spent my money in my life. If I say this, sure he won't accept the gift.

'What is inside?' he asked

'It is a T-shirt'

He unwrapped the gift and opened the content. He gone through the dress several time and showed a disappointment.

'It looks like it won't suite my size' he said

'Try to fit it' I said trying to conceal my disappointment. He is finding reasons to avoid my gift.

'Alright! Diwali festival is fast approaching. I have no time to buy new dress. Let me use it for this time' he said

I felt very delighted on hearing this. He is going to wear the dress which I bought for him for the Diwali. It is a great honor for my love and affection.

'Actually one of my girlfriend bought me a T-Shirt like this yesterday. Till now I got two new dresses. You both have made me to save money by buying me new dress' he said enthusiastically. 'How you girls specifically choose T-Shirt as a gift. You women are alike' he said casually

All the happiness and delight which I had just now burst in few seconds. Another girl bought him dress like me. I bought the dress out of the extreme love I had for him. Some other girl too bought him a dress. It means that girl also has extreme love for him like I do. Never a woman spends money on some passer by just like that. I felt so bad and insulted on hearing it. I wanted to tear the T-Shirt into pieces and burn it this very minute in front of him. Had I known that another girl gifted him a dress, I would have sure not given the gift to him.

My love has become excess rainwater which joins the sea finally. I recalled a small instance in my life few days back. I was returning home and saw few school boys playing cricket.

'Out!' shouted one boy.

'No. The ball did not touch the bat' shouted another boy.

'You are out for sure. The ball touched the bat. I know' screamed the first boy.

'You don't know anything. It was me who batted. The ball did not touch'

The boys were kept arguing about their points and as I went forward one word stopped me.

'Ganesh, do you agree with me? He is out is it not?' asked the boy to another boy standing there.

I looked at the boy who was addressed as Ganesh. Nowadays it has become my habit to have a look at something or someone which named Ganesh. The boy Ganesh would not be more than ten years old. He was so short and wearing the school uniform of nearby government school. I felt so bad to see his shirt torn at two places. He must be from lower middle class or poor family.

I got reminded of that boy that minute. I looked at the guy in front of me who was not showing much interest in my gift. I thought to myself how that little boy Ganesh would have felt had I given the T-shirt to him? Would not his face turned bright and delighted? He would surely know the value of a gift because for him it is something which he cannot afford then. This Ganesh is so cruel that he insulting my gift and hurt my feelings. This big Ganesh neither knows the worth of my gift nor the love which I have behind it else he would have not spoken like this. I felt like an idiot for showering the love on him. Had Swati given him that T-shirt, he would have considered it as a precious possession. Who values the gift of some random girl? He has so many girls in his life who is ready to give anything for him. He does not require any thing from me. I am not supposed to blame him for my foolishness.

After a long time, the self-respect which was in coma started to wake inside me. For me he is someone who is everything to me but to him I am nothing but some random woman precisely a passing cloud. He slowly kills every feeling in me. He has become master in hurting people around him especially me. Perhaps he can author a book in future '1000 ways to hurt people around you.'

'You spend lot of money for me. First this pen and then this T-Shirt' he said

'Love has no price' I said

The love which I have for him is so priceless that if he gives me a chance I will bequeath all that I own in my life. If God gives me an option of choosing mountains and mountains of diamond on one side and Ganesh on other side I would blindly choose him. I lost in all of my battles of winning his love and affection in my life.

I tried to stop the pitying myself. There is no one in this world including this Ganesh to understand how much he means to me. It is all my own feeling which is supposed to get buried along with my soul.

My last working day is fast approaching. I am so worried about my losing him in my life but he is not worried about losing me. After my departure from the office probably we may chat in WhatsApp for few times. Then it would gradually decrease and one fine morning everything is going to stop forever. I will lose him permanently. He will vanish away from my life and remain in my memories alone forever.

I looked at him who was not affected by anything and my departure. He is so normal in his routine.

Time and tide waits for none. Every beginning has an end one day for a new beginning. I still remember my mother said that God wanted me to be here for a specific purpose and that is why he has removed from the place where I was and place me here. In the past few days I understood why I was placed here. Now that my purpose of staying has come to an end finally. Today is the last working day in my company. In few minutes everything is going to end for me here.

I tried to spend as much time possible with him in one way or other. I used to look at him when he is not looking at me. I would pass flying kisses to him when he was busy with his work even though I know it won't be received. I would sit in the chair when he is not there around. Whenever he walks, I would watch him until he disappears from my sight. I did not miss even a single chance to click pictures of him whenever possible.

Ashwin did not know anything about what happened between us on that worst day of my life. He knew that guy rejected me. He was the one who consoled me in those tough times.

'Sumana, there is no use of thinking about something which is not in your control. The world is very big. You have thousands of options, you have to explore before you finally land on something. Let go of things which you cannot change. It is good for your health and life' he said

He is right. I lost control over everything in my life now. All I can do this wait patiently for a miracle to happen. I have to stop playing victim game.

My parents arranged a meeting with a guy once again. All my efforts to stop the occasion has gone vain.

'Suma, you have promised us that you will move on. Why are you stopping us now?' asked my mother angrily

'I need some time to move on' I pleaded her

'The time gap between your engagement and marriage will be sufficient for you.' she said firmly like final judgment.

'Amma, I don't think I can marry anyone else in my life. I don't even want to think about it. What is there in getting married? I am fine as I am now. I will be with you both forever' I said.

'Don't even think of such things' screamed my mother 'It is not as easy as you think. Who will be there for you after our life ends. Do you think your parents got the boon of being immortal? You need someone to take care of you, be with you and support you in tough times, share your life and for many other things.'

'Let me adopt a child from some orphanage. I will take care of you, Appa and the child until I can. Then the child will take care of me after it is grown up.'

'You cannot expect the same level of affection from an adopted child. It is a different blood. You can expect gratefulness not a commitment.' Said my father.

'Then I will have a child through test tube'

'What an idiotic thought! Are you living in western country so that no one questions you for having a child without a husband? Don't forget you are living in India' scolded my mother.

'Amma, I cannot think of living with some guy. I cannot forget him. How I am supposed to live with another person when one guy is occupying my entire mind'

'He is not ready to accept you in his life. Is this our fault? Are we stopping you from marrying him?' screamed my mother.

I kept silent.

'You are not supposed to make decisions when you are in emotional state. One day you will find out the guy who you loved more than your life has settled with another girl. He will live his life systematically with his wife, children and parents but you will be a fool. Do you think he will regret for that? Even if he finds out that you preferred staying unmarried because of him, he will feel sorry for one or two days. Then he will return to his routine. He will not have time to think about you. When you realize you have made mistake, it would have been too late.' said my mother.

I did not say anything.

'In your childhood you have learnt Fox and the grapes story, is it not? When Fox is unable to reach the grapes, it gives up reaching it, thinking it will be sour. Give up for God's sake. He is a sour grape.'

I had nothing to say.

'Listen to me. Your denial makes us to come to only one conclusion. Do you still hope that he will come for you?' asked my father

I got shocked. I was not able to answer

'You will not like to hear this bitter truth. If you ever say to him that you are going to be married, he would feel so delighted. Not that you are getting married but because he would be out of danger. He will feel relieved that you will not chase him, torture him and make his life miserable. Even though you moved out of everything he may still feel unsafe being with you. Do you want to face such a humiliation in your life? A guy wants to run away from you for this kind of reason is not something you have to feel proud about.' said my father

A man knows better the psychology of another man. My father is a man and my ex-dream boy is also a man. I cannot argue with my father that he will not think badly about me. I am not a mind-reader.

'Don't think too much. Let life go in the same pace. Don't disturb him and disturb yourself. Come out of everything'.

Shradhdha scolded me for everything as much as she can. She argues like a lawyer to convince me. She tried to throw away my precious possessions but somehow I managed to save it from her. She said the same thing as my parents said but in different way.

'I fully support your parents. Every word of them is hundred percent right.' she said.

I looked her with surprise.

'I cannot blame them because they don't understand my pain. You are also repeating the same when you have faced a heart break. Was it easy for you to move on?' I asked her angrily.

'When you have no other option, what you are supposed to do? The other available option is dying. I don't want to end my life for silly stupid who did not care about my feelings. Do you want to end your life?' she asked me mockingly.

I stared at her.

'One fine day, in Facebook, he will send a common event invite to all his network friends to attend his marriage. Another day he will change his relationship status from 'Single' to 'Married to' some girl's name. He will post pictures starting from his wedding, honeymoon, his first child's birth, first child's first birthday, second child's birth, their first walking, their first talking, their first day of school, etc. etc. etc. All you can do is 'Like' every picture which he posts. You will have to witness him living happily with his wife while you are sunken in the sorrow of your solitude. Be honest. Will you be happy in living such a life?'

My parents and Shradhdha should have studied law course. All have become experts in arguing and persuading. I thought angrily.

All roads lead to Rome. All advice ended in the three words

'Forget. Come out and move on'

It is very easy for everyone to give the advice but only the wounded soul can realize how difficult it is come out and move on.

I received the farewell gift which he ordered and sent to my home. He gifted me a dart board. When I got the gift, twenty days were left. He gifted me so early. He wanted to get rid of me as soon as possible. Earlier whenever he used to talk about my last working day and farewell my heart ached and now I got used to it.

Sumana: I got your farewell gift
Ganesh: Cool :-) Do you like it?
Sumana: Yes.
Ganesh: Be careful while playing with it.
Sumana: I have to learn to play
Ganesh: I will teach you. Don't worry
Sumana: :-)
Ganesh: I wanted to say something to you
Sumana: Yes Baba
Ganesh: Give me an assurance that you won't get angry. I often find you gloomy. You are looking sad nowadays more often. I know I am the reason for it.

Wow! He finally realized that I am sad. 'Sad' is an ordinary word to express. I am not just sad. The feeling of mine can also be termed as 'anguish', 'grief', 'extreme misery'. However I decided not to play victim game as there is not going to be any use in it.

Sumana: Not really. Actually I am very happy nowadays.

Ganesh: Even I want that. Just felt. May be I could have spoken well and kept you smiling. Sorry to hurt you.

Sumana: You know? A new slipper won't be so strong. Once it is torn and a cobbler stitches it, it will work for life long. I am now a stitched slipper.

Ganesh: You look better than that. I am glad you are positive. As people grow age, maturity comes obviously.

Sumana: I told you already that I will forgive you for everything. I cannot get mad at you. Actually after this much happened I should not speak even a single word with you. But I lost my self-respect long time back. So I am tolerating everything. :-)

I am chasing you to talk to me which I know is not right. I should stop doing it.

Ganesh: No problem. No worries. I wish to be good well-wisher of you.

I did not reply anything. He is ready to be my well-wisher but not as my soul mate and not even my friend.

Sweetheart, what will make you understand how much I love you? Why no God is helping me to make you realize how much you mean to me? I don't want the well-wisher in you. All I want is your unconditional love only for me. I can sacrifice anything and everything if I can get you in my life.

I got tired to praying Gods, shedding tears, hurting myself etc. I decided to capture memories until I stayed there. I tried to behave as if I had moved on and forgot everything in my life.

'I have lot of things to do before I depart for US' he said

I looked at him like 'What?'

'I have to groom myself. I have fix the tooth. It is so uneven. Then I have check my power and change my spectacles. Then lot more things.' he said

I did not say anything.

'I have lot of things ahead of me. I have to complete my Master's degree. Settle in a good job. In between if I get chance I will search for a potential girl from my own caste. I have decided one thing. I will sure marry girl of my parent's choice only. Even if I fall in love, I will love only girl of my own caste and with permission from my father.'

I made a terrible mistake. I should have kept myself as much away as possible. The very thought of imagining him standing beside a girl in wedding costume freaks me out. I don't know if I will be alive on the day when I hear about his wedding news and see him as husband of another woman. He is enthusiastically planning and dreaming about his future. For me, I don't believe have one. I am dead already psychologically. Now it is just my body which is breathing for the sake of two pathetic poor people who did not commit any sin other than giving birth to me and nurturing me.

I was busy with my exit formalities. I wandered to each and every department to get no objection certificate from them. I informed system admin to de-allocate the computer from my name. Even when I was roaming, I did not stop myself from watching him. He was working as usual in his system. Today is the last day I am going to meet him in my life and going to lose him to my destiny forever. I can surely say no one other than him can occupy the place in my heart.

We took several photographs together in our cameras. We went for a get together for one last time. We had fun in the last lunch, last coffee-break and I recorded everything in my mind and in my camera as well.

Finally the time has come. I surrendered my machine to IT department. I got clearances from library, administration department and other departments before my final departure. I spent my last few minutes with him. As usual it passed with pulling legs of each other. I am going to miss it from tomorrow. The final minute came finally. Ashwin, Ganesh and my manager gathered in our cubicle to give last few wordings. The team from Bangalore, Mysore and Chandigarh were connected by conference call.

Ashwin started with a short speech

'Sumana, it was a very good experience working with you. My experience with you was mixed. We had good times and bad times. But today I am wishing you all the very best for your future'

I am already tired of being ashamed for being so weak. I again shed tears after all the only thing which I am doing correctly for past few months.

'I am very happy for working with you all. I am going to miss you all terribly' I said

Ashwin smiled at me.

'Hey, com on. You have to empty your hands at one point of time to hold new things in your life. Be cool'

The farewell call went for a while with good-byes from everyone. Ashwin extended his hands for hand-shake. I had no courage to look at Ganesh but I looked at his face. His face showed a normal expression and a normal smile. I smiled outside but burst with tears inside. I wanted to ask him to give me one last kiss as a token of memory of him but my self-respect stopped me to do so. I tried to control my tears as much as possible. I formally bid goodbye to the team mates over the conference call. Everybody wished me luck and bid goodbye for me.

To my surprise, they threw a party at our cafetaria. People from other teams who I knew for past few months assembled there for my send-off. Sanjana accompanied me for last few minutes. Nice girl.

The main enthusiastic organizer was the hero of my tragic story. I don't know why but I started to feel an hatred for him. I tried to control it but like how I failed to control my love for him I failed to control the hatred too. The same person who was hero to me is slowly turning as a villain to my eyes.

I enjoyed my final minutes in the office there. We clicked several photos. Finally the time to leave the building came. I was accompanied by the folks till the main gate. I looked at him and he was laughing and smiling. I again started to cry.

'Hey, Cheer up' said Ashwin 'Why are you behaving as if you are going out of this planet. We will be in touch. Stop this and set for your new journey.'

I smiled and cried. I hugged Sanjana and gave a handshake to others. At last the most inevitable moment came in my life. I bid goodbye to all until they vanished from my sight and left the place with tears.

'I am very happy for being part of this team. I am thankful for everyone who supported me in work and cooperation extended during hard times. Thank you very much every one and all the best for everyone for their future' I told

I Wish I Could Hate You

When I came out of the building, I felt I have lost everything in this world and I am not going to laugh hereafter in my life. All the happiness has been washed away forever. Now I am just physically exiting this place but still my soul is roaming around the seventh floor of the building looking at him. I frequently turned back and looked at the building until I reached the entrance, no, the exit gate. I turned one last time and gave a last look at the entire campus.

Now I am just physically exiting this place but still my soul is roaming around the seventh floor of the building looking at him. I frequently turned back and looked at the building until I reached the entrance, no, the exit gate. I turned one last time and gave a last look at the entire campus.

My dear company, I am so sorry. It was my dream to come and work for you. I was very happy when you accepted me. I remember how proud I felt when I identified myself to the world as your employee.

I had to leave you now as my soul is heavily injured. Thank you for giving me fresh and golden memories which I cannot forget forever. No matter how many companies I have worked or I will work, you will be close to my heart. It is where I had my sweetest memories to bitterest memories. I wish I could come here once again in my lifetime and at least then you will provide me with only sweet memories for my rest of life.

I did not make any attempt to stop the tears rolling down from my eyes. Whatever happens, life must move on. I don't know for how long I have capacity to remain in the memories of these people and especially the one who heavily injured my soul. Tears occupied my eyes so heavily that I could not anything in front of me. I am terribly confused right now else why would I imagine her standing in front of me?

'What?' she asked 'You are not dreaming. I am standing here really.' She smiled

I looked at her with surprise. How is she here?

'I know how you will feel right now.' She said and looked at the stuffs in my hand.

'Are you relieved?' she asked

I nodded as 'Yes'

'Yeah. All formalities are completed. I surrendered by identity card even.'

She looked at me and asked again 'Are you relieved?'

I frowned and she smiled at me.

'I asked are you relieved.' She said 'from everything'

The smile in my face disappeared. Tears again started to roll from my eyes. She came to me and held my hands.

'I expected' she said. 'Sure something would have happened today making you feel bad. Am I right?'

Tears started rolling so fast and I was not in a position to utter a word. Her hold tightened.

'What happened?' she asked

I was not able to answer. I tried to wipe the tears however I couldn't. Though she smiled I could see the helplessness which her eyes expressed. I took my hands to wipe my tears but she held my hands with hers

'Don't do that, Suma.' She said 'Look, I am not asking you anything now. Let us settle it here in this place this very minute.'

'Suma, there is no point in controlling ourselves when things gone beyond our control. I can see how much you are struggling to control the pain in your heart. You don't have to. Come on, cry.' She said.

I wondered what she is saying.

'I mean it. Come on. Don't worry about anything. Don't care about the surroundings. Forget everything and just cry as much as you can' she said

I stood as if I was under some spell. Tears did not stop from my eyes.

'Come on. Cry! Cry! Cry! You are not a grown up girl now but a baby. A baby never cares about crying anywhere anytime. Similar to that. Cry deep from your heart. This is not just a cry but vomit. When you suffer from indigestion problem, like how you throw out all the food stuff through vomit, puke all your pain, grief, heartbreak, sorrow, stress everything. The cry should cleanse and wash away each and every bad thing in your heart and soul.'

And then I did not make any attempt from stop my tears. I hugged her tightly and I wept aloud. I don't remember when I last cried in my life like this much. The sorrow, the grief, the fear, the dismay, and the pain everything exploded from my heart like a lava from volcano. I did like as she said.

'Yeah. Just like that. Don't stop until you feel that everything from your mind is washed away. Take your time' said Shradhdha to me.

I was not in a position to stop the tears from my eyes. I hugged her so tightly and as minutes started to pass my cry also increased. I did not know how much time had passed. May be half-an-hour or more. I lost the energy to cry and tears secretion stopped gradually. My cry started to decrease as weep. I kept weeping for some more minutes. Shradhdha patiently waited for me to finish crying. She did not make any attempt to stop my tears.

'How do you feel now?' she asked

I was not able to answer. Tears kept rolling down.

'I am sure all the pains from your heart was poured. You are free now. Is it not?'

I kept silent. Honestly speaking I will not say that my pains are washed away. The more I cried I felt more pain in my heart.

'Baby, it is OK. If you want to cry some more, go ahead. But make sure you are not leaving this place until you clear your mind and get ready for big bang moving on.'

'I don't know. I cannot forget anything. I cannot stop myself from loving him. I love him so much. I cannot imagine my life without him. I don't know how I am going to spend my rest of life without him. I wish I could die this very minute instead of accepting the truth that he is not mine' I told her

'History repeats' smiled Shradhdha 'I still remember the same dialogue uttered by Aradhana some years back. She said that she wish to die rather than live without him. The truth is she is now married and a mother of five year old kid now. She is happy with her life. Similarly you will also live happily.'

'I don't think so.' I said

'Where there is a will, there is a way' she said

'No. I cannot do it. Happy married life is not something blessed to me. I have to spend my entire life in grief and sorrow. I cannot give the place of him to anyone in my heart. I am not going to marry anyone in my life. I am going to stay single in his memories forever.'

Shradhdha smiled

'Suma, I can imagine your current situation like this' she said 'You have tied yourself to a big stone and fell into ocean. People who care for you are surrounded by you and they very well knew that you will get drowned if you don't get rid of the stone. Everyone is screaming to cut off the rope and let the stone go so that they can rescue you to the shore. But you love the stone so much that even though you know it will drown you, you want to hold it. Now you have to either you cut off the rope and help us to get you ashore or you drown inside the river and die. You cannot bring the stone along with you to the shore.'

I kept silent and weeping

'What according to you is a stone is a life-saving wood to someone. He is not meant to fill your life and heart with love. He is some other woman's belonging. He is stone for you but wood for that woman. He will drown you but will save her.'

Shradhdha tried to console me as much as possible.

'Suma, failing is not something you have to be ashamed of. Failure is stepping stone to success. Do you know you have not failed in your love?'

I looked at her with surprise

'Yes. You have half-won in your love. Do you know how? It is because you have 'tried''

She surprised me even more

'There are quite a million of people who have no guts to express their feelings to the people whom they love. They have failed by not revealing themselves fearing that they might get rejected. This is the real failure. We fail terribly when we don't attempt something scared of failure. You somehow managed to pour your heart to him. You wrote the exam even though you know that you may not pass in it. This needs real guts and you had that. Failing after a try is equivalent to half succeed.'

Her words started to create a positive feeling in me.

'Had you not poured you heart to him, may be after few years one day you might have felt sorry. You would have thought, had I proposed him, he would have accepted me and I would have married him. You would have regretted for your entire life. Now you are free of the regret.'

I kept listening to her.

'You may have failed as a lover but you have won as a human being. You know how?' she asked me

I looked eagerly

'It is not so easy for a truly loving soul to let go of the thing which it loves. You faced rejection, you faced insult from him and frequently you allowed him to hurt your feelings and yet you have forgiven him. Even though you have tons and tons of love on him you managed to conceal your feelings and faced him daily. You managed to live as if nothing had happened in both of your life. This is not something which everyone can do. Not all of them have courage to face their beloved ones after a break-up or rejection. You have to be proud of yourself.'

I stopped weeping but tears kept rolling down.

'When men face love failure, they immediately start to consume liquor and lament their pains to their friends. Even woman are not able to handle the relationship stress easily. Do you remember how Aradhana destroyed herself by consuming sleeping tablets? I have also consumed liquor to forget my failure. But you did not indulge yourself in such actions. You boldly faced the reality of getting rejected with full conscious. You have heart as strong as a rock.'

I don't dare to recall those black days of my life where I felt I was in some hell.

'Hey! Don't behave as if you are the only one in this world who failed in love. Stop playing the victim game. You are not alone. In this very minute, some girl is dumping her boyfriend and some guy is dumping his girlfriend in some part of the world. Everyone is moving on. You know love is like a chicken pox. It attacks its victim only once in his or her lifetime. Once attacked it gives immunity to the disease. Love can break our heart only one time. Once broken and joined it cannot be broken again. It will become hundred times strong. You heart is now immune to heart break. Even God cannot break your heart again. You have become so strong.'

Her words healed the pain in my heart but still I felt so sad. I did not feel like leaving the place.

'Come on! Cheer up baby. Your prince charming is on the way to come and marry this beautiful princess. He is rushing from some direction of this world. Just wait for few days. Secure all the love which is secreting in your heart for him. Once you get into his life, pour everything on him. When a girl who dumps her boyfriend can deserves happy life, can't a woman like you who wanted to be honest and true to the person she loved deserve?'

I smiled at her.

'Are you fine now?' she asked

'Somewhat' I said

'Good. You will be fine once you leave this place. I can say something which can make you feel better. Have you been to graveyard?'

I got surprised

'No'

'When we lose someone, we cremate them in graveyard and we will cry for them. Thereafter we have to accept that they will not come back to our life. Gradually we will start to accept this and keep going. Imagine the person whom you loved is dead. You cannot have someone in your life who is not alive. That guy is dead according to you. The guy whom you met for all these days is not the same person whom you loved. When you leave this place you have to accept that your lover is dead and he is not going to come in your life again.'

I nodded like 'OK'

'That is my girl.' She complimented me

I looked at the building once again and all the incidents ran through my mind once again.

'Everything is going to be fine soon. What meant nothing to us last year means a lot to us this year and what means a lot to us this year will mean nothing next year. 365 days from now you will wonder if it was you who was emotional. I swear'

Her every word is true. Everything is going to be fine soon. I may forget everything and move on as I don't have any other option.

'Shall we go?' she asked

'Yeah' I said and I looked at the campus again

I got into an auto and started to move away from the place. I kept looking at the building until it disappeared from my vision. When I slowly left the place I got thoughts like this.

I wish I could have asked you one last time to kiss me.

I wish I could have not given you chance to hurt and reject me.

I wish I could have not allowed to developed feelings on you

I wish I could have not met you in my life.

I wish I could I hate you.

The End

Twenty Three Years Later

'The End!' she said and closed the book

'Dad!' she said looking at her father 'I feel this story should have not ended in this way.'

'How do you want to end?' asked the girl's dad without taking his eyes from his laptop

The girl turned the pages again and again.

'If I were author of this book I would have finished like this. 'Few months later she receives a surprising call. He calls her and says 'My Sweetheart! I did not realize how much I need you when you beside me. I am a stupid for having let you go out of my life. Now I understood that I cannot breathe even for a second without you. There is no meaning in my life if you don't stay with me. I want you forever not only for this birth but for each and every birth. Will you marry me my love? She at first gets angry on him for making her cry for months. She does not accept to it at first but gradually he makes her understand how much he misses her. She finally understands that he truly loves her and both of them unite.' This is the way it should have ended. At least she could have married him in this book.'

'So you wanted a fairy tale ending?' said her dad smilingly

'This is surprising.' said the girl 'Mom does not prefer stories with negative endings yet she herself wrote a story with an anti-climax'

'For her, this is not just a story.' said dad

'Yes I know' said the girl 'each time when I read this book, I could feel the pain of her heart. She truly, madly and deeply loved the guy' said the girl sadly

He kept working in his laptop without answering her.

'Dad, you married mom even after knowing about her past. That was so great. Did you read the book before marrying her or after?'

'I did not read the book until your younger brother was born.'

'You have read the book. Then tell me do you really think what that guy has done was correct? He rejected her for silly reasons. He did not value the love of a girl rather too much concerned about society. Was that fair?'

'Why do you think it is not fair? According to him he was correct. His reasons were reasonable. Our society hardly digests unconventional marriages.'

'Dad, I don't think he rejected her scaring of society. He did not love mom at all. He had no feelings for her. Had he felt for her, he would have not worried about people around him. Mom has mentioned that he fought for his ex-girlfriend with his parents. He fought because he loved that girl deep from his heart. He was not ready even to talk to his parents about mom. It was because he did not love her at all. He hurt her feelings. She wasted her time investing her feelings on a guy who did not love her. She was a fool' said the girl angrily

Dad smiled at her.

'Don't be too judge mental. He had his own reasons. You have to empathize before criticizing him. He preferred his career more than her because it was important to him. It is a usual thing for a person to chase his desire and passion. He did the same. Perhaps you have forgot a thing. In one place it was mentioned that the guy told her that he does not want to misuse her pure love. He was so practical about age of a man and woman. I would say your mistake is your mother's.'

'Why should I empathize him? I am not his daughter but mom's daughter. What is there in age? An elder woman marrying younger guy was so common during those days. Actually homosexual marriages were so common in those days. Still former is far better than latter. The guy did not understand it. He might have achieved greater places in his life but I am sure he could have not found a loving soul like her.'

Dad smiled at her again. He set aside his laptop to involve in the argument with the girl

'Yes. He realized that he was hurting her and then he moved out of it. Don't you think it is right?'

'Dad, birds of same feather flock together' said the girl with irritation 'You, being a man wanted to support another man. You are not cared about mom's feelings and disappointment. On reading this book I lost the desire of falling in love with a man. I believe men are to mean. Had I fallen in love I would have too faced same fate.' said the girl angrily

Dad laughed at the girl.

'You are too young to understand this. You are getting too emotional after these many years passed by.'

'Why should I not? For others, it is just another romance novel of love failure. For me, this is a heart-breaking memory of my mother. If I even find the guy who broke my mom's heart, I will break his bones and jaws.' said the girl furiously

'You should not be disrespectful to elders. That guy is of same age as your father. Mom will feel so bad on hearing you scolding him like that.' said the dad with smile

The girl frowned.

'Your mother handled the things in her own way. She is fine. You don't have get your blood boiled for something which happened many years ago. She moved on in her life, got married and became the mother of you and your brother.'

'Perhaps she had moved but the pain still remains in her soul. This book is very close to her heart. I have seen the 'Love Paradise' in her shelf very recently. She is still having it as a part of her memory. It shows how deep her wound was. The guy who wounded her is living happily somewhere with his family. I am sure he would have forgotten mom in his life. If he meets mom by chance he won't be in a position to remind her and recognize her.'

Dad watched her keenly

'Why do you say like that?' asked dad

'I am saying this because he does not care about anyone. He is too selfish.'

'You are so judge mental and pre-prejudiced' said the dad and he again returned to his laptop

'Dad, this story ends with heartbreak. Mom did not mention what happened after she departed from the company. I have many times asked her to narrate her life post love failure. She does not want to answer it'

Dad was silent

'Dad, how did you enter mom's life? Did you know about her past when you married her? Have you met the guy who broke our mom's heart? Have you met him or seen his picture? Was he so handsome? Was he...'

'Stop' said the dad 'You are asking too many questions. Your mother did not answer them till now due to some reasons. I believe I don't have authority to answer. You better ask her'

'Dad' yelled the girl 'what is wrong with you?'

'I cannot forget how your mom reacted when I told you that this book is the story of her life. She was so furious. It took me ten days to console her. She felt very bad when you found the truth behind her book.'

'She is not understanding that her daughter respects her even more after knowing this story. What is there to feel bad about? I wanted to know what happened in her life post her heart-break.'

Dad remained silent

'Let me say. Mom would have been so sad in her life not willing to get married in her lifetime. One day you crossed her life like a storm. Your first meeting would have started in fight. You both hated each other. Whenever you met you fought with each other. Somehow one day you find that mom was broken inside due to love failure. It creates a sympathy in you for her. You become caring towards her. Eventually you fall in love with her and you propose her.'

Dad listened to her with smile

'Then?' asked Dad

'At first mom is not showing any interest in you. She hurts you a lot and she refuses to accept you because she is not able to forget her past love. Somehow you manage to win her heart. She accepts you but your love story faces twist with parents' acceptance.'

'Then?'

'Mom's dad was not ready to accept for your wedding as he has already seen his daughter broken by love. He is against you people getting married. After so much of ups and downs you finally end up in getting parents' consent and get married. I know your wedding would have been a fairy-tale kind. Is it not daddy?'

Dad grinned.

'I can see why you have scored low marks in your tests. You watch lot of movies and not focusing on studies. Though you don't excel in academics you are good at spinning stories for films.'

'Dad, please tell me. How did you marry my mother?'

Dad laughed

'So you are not going to say?'

'I need authority from your mom'

'Nonsense!' said the girl

Dad sat beside her.

'Leave the story aside. Now tell me what you will do if by chance you meet the guy who broke your mother's heart?'

The girl looked at her father with wonder.

'Dad, do you know that guy?' asked the girl surprisingly

'This is not the answer to my question. I need straight answer'

'I told you already that I will break his bones' said the girl angrily

'I need practical answer' said the dad

The girl got irritated

'Dad, if I meet him I will say only one thing.'

Dad listened to her

'I will say 'Thank you so much for rejecting my mother. It was because of his rejection, God brought you in my mother's life and a happy family was created. My mother deserved a guy who loved her truly and she got a one in her life. I will also say to him that I pity him for missing a woman like my mom in his life'

'You don't know what all the things he achieved in his life are. He would have completed his Master's degree in US, landed with a high paying job there, got married to the girl of his desire, got a daughter and a son and even more'

'But sure he would have not found a woman like my mom'

'You are surrounding the same statement.'

'I am doing because I know he would have not'

'You cannot be so sure.' said dad

'What I said is right.' said the girl

'I cannot accept'

'But dad...'

Both of them argued repeatedly until the calling bell rang loudly.

'Heroine arrived' said the girl.

Sumana entered inside the home and looked at both of them

'I can hear your voices near till our gate. You both have started your fight again?' she asked her entering inside the house.

'Mom, fault is not mine. Dad is too gender biased. He is not cared about his wife rather he supports some stranger just because he is man.'

Sumana frowned and glared at her husband.

'I got used to it.' said Sumana with an angry smile. 'The only women whom he supports in his life is his mother and his daughter.'

'My dear wife! You are mistaken. You don't know what our argument was and you cannot prejudice without knowing the entire conversation. You are blaming for being gender biased but I am blaming you for being so judge mental'

'All right! Then tell me what was your conversation all about?' asked Sumana

'About this' said the girl showing the book 'I wish I could hate you' in her hand

Sumana's face turned dark on seeing the book.

'Mom, I know you don't want to talk about this book and related incidents. I am sorry'

Sumana changed her expression to normal

'Not really. I don't want to talk about things which makes me sad.' replied Sumana 'what was the argument regarding this book?'

'Mom, dad blindly supports the villain of this book' yelled the girl

'Sumi, explain to her that he is not the villain' said dad

'Yes he is.' screamed the girl 'He broke the heart of a woman who truly loved him. He is a villain'

'I explained his perspective to you' said dad

'I won't accept' said the girl 'Mom, dad says that the guy would have found a girl who loves him more than you did. I am saying that he can never find a loving woman like you. Who is right?'

Sumana looked at both of them.

'Who is right?' asked Sumana to her husband

'That how do I know?' asked dad seriously but his eyes sparkled with mischief.

Both Sumana and her husband laughed.

'Mom, it cannot be right. I know how much you loved him. You would have been an angel in his life had he married you. He is a monster. He is …'

Shhhhh!' said Sumana with her finger on the lips. 'I don't want you to talk like this again.' she asked looking at the dad.

'You cannot deny the fact, mom and moreover that devil is not my dad. If he was my dad, I would have grabbed his shirt by this time for behaving so mean with a woman who loved him more than herself'

Sumana looked at her husband bewilderingly. She then warmly shake her daughter's head and said 'I don't want to talk about this anymore. It would be better if you wind up this topic.' said Sumana firmly.

'If you want me to wind up this topic then you have to tell me what happened in your life after the 'The End'?'

Sumana looked at her daughter with surprise. She looked at her husband helplessly. He shrugged his shoulder.

'Mom, you have to tell me this for sure. I wanted to know.'

'Know what?' asked Sumana

The girl asked in a firm voice

'What happened after your departure from that company? How did you marry my father?'

*****

Printed in the United States
By Bookmasters